Sunday's Child

Some Love for

Shock, suspicion and pain rendered Danny's heart asunder as he secretly watched Amee, the love of his very life, kiss and hug a dark, handsome Arabian man. Could the accumulated information about Amee and her family being in a secret mole cell for the terrorists be true? Danny, a secret agent, was ordered to investigate the family he had known and loved since high school. He had no choice. He had to do his job. He had to investigate Amee and her entire family.

Author Garvin Dykes writes a page-turning story of suspense, intrigue and tortured love with an underlining foundation that "God is too good to do wrong and too wise to make a mistake."

—Marjorie L Ellis, B.S.R.N.C.

Sunday's Child

Unpermitted Love

Garvin Dykes

Sunday's Child

Unpermitted Love

Tate Publishing & *Enterprises*

Published by Tate Publishing & Enterprises, LLC
127 E. Trade Center Terrace | Mustang, Oklahoma 73064 USA
1.888.361.9473 | www.tatepublishing.com

Tate Publishing is committed to excellence in the publishing industry. The company reflects the philosophy established by the founders, based on Psalm 68:11,
"The Lord gave the word and great was the company of those who published it."

Cover design by Lance Waldrop
Interior design by Stephanie Woloszyn

Published in the United States of America

ISBN: 978-1-61566-439-9
1. Fiction / Christian / Romance 2. Fiction / Christian / Suspense
09.11.17

This book is dedicated to Faye,

who is my wife, lover, friend, and completer.
Without her encouragement, I would have become "weary in well doing." She is also my sounding board and critic, for which I am most grateful. I have always felt safe when I have her counsel.

Acknowledgments

I am most grateful to Faye, my dear wife, for allowing me to spend hundreds of hours writing this novel without any complaint on her part. Because she is an avid reader, she provided kind but poignant criticism along the way that greatly improved the end result. She also spent many hours as a proofreader.

I also appreciate the contribution of my long-time friend Dr. Neal Beard, who undertook the challenging task of reading the finished product and giving me his honest appraisal. He has also consented to write the foreword.

Foreword

Don't read this book—unless you love romance, adventure, conflict, and Bible truths commingled into a unique blend of storytelling that offers an underlying shadow of the author's Celtic and Southern roots.

This intriguing story comes from the heart of a father, husband, friend, pastor, and missionary leader with over half a century's experience in the ministry. He knows and writes about people and their problems in a lucid, forceful manner that puts a practical face on the complex issues of life.

I have known, ministered with, trusted, and admired the author since we became best friends nearly forty years ago. We have shared sunshine and sorrows in family life, church life, and personal life. In these years one foundational element has become evident to me—his life is undergirded by character.

I take great pleasure in heartily endorsing *Sunday's Child: Unpermitted Love* by Garvin Dykes. It is a thoroughly contemporary, profoundly insightful, and troublingly challenging book.

—Neal Beard, Mdiv.
Hospice Chaplain
Assistant Pastor

Introduction

I had gone to answer the telephone and was standing on the landing of the stairs in the little apartment in Addis Ababa, Ethiopia, when I first heard of the events of September 11, 2001. The shock of such an atrocity, coupled with the uncertainty of our own situation, produced emotions I had never felt before. We were not certain what would happen to our country and when we might ever get back home. We were actually in the process of preparing to return to America the next day.

We were with our Ethiopian family (a group of Ethiopians we loved as deeply as our own kin) at the time, which gave us great comfort. We were allowed to leave Ethiopia on schedule for Kenya, where we spent the next week. As we waited for our flight, I sat next to a Muslim lady, every inch of whose body was covered except her eyes. She looked at me with tears and apologized for what had happened, assuring us that this was not the desire of all Muslims. By contrast, in the airport in Nairobi, we were taunted by a large group of Muslim men. We could not understand their language, but there was no mistaking their gestures, laughter, and looks.

It was during this time of conflicting emotions that the seed for *Sunday's Child* was born in my heart. All that governments, terrorists, and radical religions are doing culminates in the effects it has in individual lives. As the seed germinated, it sprouted into an idea for a romantic adventure that would explore these effects. It would be difficult to verbalize all that I have learned during my own adventure of writing this book. In my research I have learned many interesting cultural, religious, historical, and technological facts, but the most important thing I have learned is that beneath the different garb and skin color, people are the same. When we get away from the idealists, zealots, and tyrants, all people want the same things in life—liberty, peace, and love.

I have long believed that scriptural truth could be conveyed in many ways. Therefore, I have two great desires in writing, the first of which is to express the truth of God's love manifested in the life, death, and resurrection of his Son, Jesus Christ. The second is to show the victory in a life totally committed to him. The story is fiction, but every other fact has been thoroughly researched and is, to the best of my knowledge, true and accurate. This was necessary in order that the story have validity and therefore convey its primary message: love should find its own way and should not need the permission of anyone.

Chapter 1

Mid State College
Perryville, Georgia
August, 1983

Danny Brannigan was attending the reception for new students and teachers the first time he saw Ameenah Salim. At first glance two things were obvious about her. She was not an American, and she was drop-dead beautiful. Danny had never had an opportunity to test his inherent attitude toward other races, but one thing was immediately clear—it didn't matter so much if they were of the opposite sex and beautiful.

Danny was a compete contrast. The platinum locks that covered his head were thick and wavy almost to the point of being curly, and his large eyes were so blue they seemed to be transparent.

He was six feet four, bronze, muscular, and very athletic. However, he was also an enigma. His charming personality, boyish grin, and wry humor made him very likeable, but there was another side that was brooding and melancholy.

His first gesture was simply to be a Southern gentleman when he saw Ameenah sitting alone and obviously very bored. He saw a damsel in distress and decided to rescue her.

"Hi, my name's Danny Brannigan; are you a new student at Mid State this year?"

She giggled as she replied, "No, I'll be a senior at Braxton County High School. My name's Ameenah Salim, and my dad is the new physics professor. I'm just here with my parents."

"I couldn't help but notice that you were alone. So am I, and getting pretty bored. Mind some company?"

She smiled at him and nodded toward the chair beside her. "Are you gonna be a freshman this year?"

"Yes, and I suppose I'll have your dad for a teacher. I'll be pursuing a degree in some kind of physics."

"Good luck," she said as she giggled again.

"Are you saying he's tough?"

She smiled and answered, "No, he's a pretty nice guy for a father."

"What kind of name is Ameenah?"

"It is Arab and means *trustworthy* or *faithful.*"

Amee, as her parents called her, had raven black hair that hung in waves and ringlets almost down to her waist. Her olive complexion was without blemish, and she had what Southerners refer to as chinquapin eyes—eyes so black they seemed not to have any pupils. When she smiled, which was most of the time, her teeth looked like strands of perfectly matched pearls. That was the most beautiful smile Danny had ever seen. She was five feet two, petite, and her form was so perfect Danny was convinced that God had assembled her personally.

Danny found Amee easy to talk to and asked if she would like to go to the student lounge for a Coke. She agreed, and they went to ask permission from her mom and dad.

Dr. Ishmael Salim had quickly become popular with the other faculty members and was certain to be a hit with the students. He was handsome, soft-spoken, and extremely polite. He had an easy smile and an infectious laugh. No one seemed to have any problem accepting him on a personal level. He was really sort of interesting and exotic. He had a well-developed sense of humor but was still struggling with the southern brand of it, as well as the language.

Safa Salim was a charming lady as well as a gracious hostess. It was obvious where Amee got her beauty. Safa had large brown eyes with lashes so long they interlocked when she closed her eyes. She usually wore her long, dark hair up, which accentuated her high cheekbones. It gave her a look of elegance, and her movements were so graceful she glided across a room. Her name meant *"purity or serenity,"* and Danny was convinced she was appropriately named. She never seemed to be flustered by anything.

Amee had two younger brothers, Mohammed and Abraham, who were in middle school. The family called them Mo and Abb. She was a typical teenage sister, as she described how annoying they were, but she secretly admitted she loved them very much.

The two spent the next few hours talking, and a friendship quickly developed.

Gus Etheridge Baseball Field
A Few Days Later

"It's not just the speed of the ball, but the movement, especially at the end."

Danny was attempting to explain the art of throwing a fastball to Amee as he gripped a baseball in the proper fashion. He had taken her to the Amateur Athletic Association baseball game at the Gus Etheridge Park and Baseball Field, where she was seeing her first baseball game ever.

From early childhood Danny had shown unusual athletic ability, and he was especially good at pitching a baseball or passing a football. He had been an all-star quarterback and an all-American pitcher for Braxton County High School, but his passion was baseball. He vowed that someday he would pitch in the major leagues. The unanimous opinion in Perryville was that he had a good chance. The only other thing Danny showed interest in was aeronautics, which he wanted to study in college as he pursued his baseball career.

At that moment Amee started laughing uncontrollably, which was about to annoy Danny, when she said, "That's the funniest thing I've ever seen. Oh! He did it again. The ball jumped around all over the place."

Then Danny realized she was watching a knuckle ball. Now he had to show her how that was done. He could tell it was all going right over her head, but it gave him an opportunity to demonstrate his vast knowledge of pitching a baseball.

The Gus Etheridge Park and Baseball Field was the center of social gathering for young people around Perryville. It was made possible by a trust fund from the Etheridge estate. Gus had loved baseball and sponsored Amateur Athletic teams for many years before his death. The park was picturesque with its lush and immaculate field and giant, spreading live oak trees circling from one set of bleachers to the other. Their shade covered most of the stands in the afternoon. White picnic tables dotted the park here and there, complemented by two large pavilions. The peaceful and inviting atmosphere drew people for all sorts of events. Often in the late afternoon, young couples could be seen scattered through the bleachers.

Danny was about to get his first taste of things to come. He and Mitzi Moore had been almost inseparable since they started high school. She played basketball and was a cheerleader for all the other sports. She was stunningly beautiful with large hazel eyes and long, wavy blonde hair. She had the tall, graceful figure of a model. Everyone was sure they were soul mates as well as the perfect couple. However, it was never quite clear how serious they were romantically.

Danny thought it was perfectly acceptable to invite Amee to come to the ballgame. Mitzi was at cheerleading practice and would meet him later. He looked upon it purely as a friendly gesture to pick Amee up, because her family didn't have a car yet. But when she walked into the park with him, all heads turned and people began to whisper. He ignored them and soon was busy trying to impress Amee with his vast knowledge of baseball, especially pitching.

When Mitzi walked in, her unhappiness was written very legibly on her face. She had agreed for Danny to bring "a friend" but had never met Amee. Her beauty and charm were instantly obvious to Mitzi, and some of her friends had already whispered to her about Danny being with a person of another race. They didn't know what she *was,* but she was "*different.*"

The boys began to laugh and make gestures, and Danny could see that things were quickly getting out of hand. He whispered to Mitzi that it would be better if they took Amee home, even though she had not yet picked up on what was happening. Danny hoped she wouldn't.

"Amee, would you mind if we left now?" Danny said. "I have some chores to do at the farm and Mitzi needs to get home early."

"Of course, whatever you need to do," Amee replied.

It was already too late to prevent what Danny feared.

"Hey, Brannigan, you like chocolate *and* vanilla, huh? Wha'cha got there, a squaw woman or a mulatto or what?"

Buster Stovall was the loud mouth, and as usual Eddie Spinks and Sonny Faulk were his shadows. They loved to stir up trouble wherever they went, especially for Danny, because he was one person they could not intimidate as they did others.

What they were saying wasn't so different from what everyone else was thinking, but they were always obnoxious and were no doubt already well into their weekend drunk. Danny turned to move in their direction, but Amee and Mitzi pleaded with him to ignore them. Amee didn't want to see Danny get hurt, and Mitzi was embarrassed. The hooligans kept it up and got louder and cruder.

"You like 'em baked a little longer, huh, Brannigan?"

Danny might have stayed out of it if Amee hadn't been with him, but now his manliness had been insulted.

He walked over to them and quietly said, "Excuse me, what did you say?"

Buster Stovall, the leader of the pack, replied, "You heard me. Wha'cha got there, a half-breed of some kind? You get special privileges for escortin' her?"

"I think you should come apologize to the lady." Danny's voice was still calm, but his jaw was set and his blue eyes fixed and steely.

"Lady? I don't see no lady, and I ain't goin' to apologize. You wanna do something about it?"

That was all Danny could take. He had a black belt in Tae Kwon Do, and in a flash, he had the loudmouth on his knees with one hand behind his back. When the other two decided to help their friend, two swift kicks eliminated them.

He walked his captive over to Amee and said, "He has something to say to you."

Buster painfully grunted out, "I'm sorry. I apologize."

Danny released him and said, "Be more careful in the presence of a lady next time."

When he thought he was a safe distance away, Buster shouted back, "There'll be another time, Brannigan; we'll get you for this. Your time's coming."

"Just let me know when," Danny replied.

"I'm sorry about those three, Amee, but please don't judge Perryville by them. Every place seems to have at least a few idiots."

"Danny, I appreciate what you did, but I don't want you to get hurt because of me."

"You just happened to be the excuse today, but they'll always find some way to stir up trouble. I guess it gives 'em a reason for existing," Danny answered.

As they walked toward the car, Amee felt like hugging Danny but realized that would only set off more fireworks, especially with Mitzi, whose resentment was a poorly kept secret.

Mitzi didn't say a word as they drove Amee home. The atmosphere was extremely tense, so Amee just jumped out and said a quick goodbye. Mitzi moved over to her side and glared at Danny for a few minutes. He had seen that reaction before and didn't say anything.

"Danny, why in the world would you do something so dumb? You had to know how people would react. Were you just tryin' to embarrass me?"

"I was tryin' to help a displaced girl get settled into her new community. I don't see what the big deal is."

"The big deal is that she's not our kind of people, and you know how most people feel about that."

"Look, Mitzi, I'm not about to marry the girl. I was just trying to be kind."

"Yeah, it doesn't hurt that she's beautiful, does it?"

"I really hadn't noticed," Danny said with a wry smile, hoping that a little levity would ease the tension. His hopes were quickly dashed.

"Like a fish, you hadn't noticed," Mitzi shot back. "Well, if you expect us to be together, don't pull such a boneheaded stunt again."

"Wait a minute," Danny responded. "Are you saying our relationship depends upon me meeting your demands?"

"Danny, we're headed in a bad direction. I just want to forget all this. There are some things we can't do because we have to live in this community. Let's just pretend it never happened."

"Are you saying what I did was unacceptable?"

"Let me put it this way. What if you had showed up with a black girl?"

This changed the whole cultural context of the discussion. Instinctively, Danny himself would have frowned upon that, but now he had to think about it. How did he really feel about a simple friendship with a black person, boy or girl? He had worked in the fields with them and played with them when he was little. Some of his fondest memories were of happy times playing with his black friends. When the fields were freshly plowed in the springtime and the dirt clods would form on top of the ground, a war would break out. He and a few of his white friends would come from one direction and several black boys from the other, and a great "battle" would ensue with the clods for ammunition. Everyone had lots of fun as they ran and ducked behind the terraces and threw at each other. They considered themselves to be friends, and there was never any animosity. His morose side was developing quickly, so he said, "Perhaps we should leave this for a later time."

Chapter 2

None of Danny's core values or the norms of his culture had ever been challenged, because nearly everyone in his middle Georgia community held virtually the same views. Even those who didn't attend church or claim to be Christians shared most of the same values as those who did. They considered themselves to be a Christian community, and in most ways they were. Even those who were involved in wrong things agreed on the difference between right and wrong.

The rules of their society were the same for Christians and non-Christians. People of different race and social status simply were not involved with each other. Grace Bible Church, which Danny's family attended, attempted to follow all the teachings of the Bible. There were, however, some cultural and patriotic views that had always been accepted as normal without digging too deeply into what the Scriptures taught about them.

There was still an underlying resentment of the Japanese for their cruelty in World War II, and the hippies, who were the most recent subculture in America, were fair game for criticism and ostracism. Somewhere in the midst of all this was an inherent belief that it was acceptable to be separate from those who were different, and in some cases it was even required. While the civil rights movement had given Blacks a new status in society, it had created an undercurrent of resentment in the hearts of many people. As Arabs became wealthy from their oil, many of the young men came to America for an education, and several had now entered Mid State College in Perryville. They looked different, spoke differently, and ate different food, but worst of all, they weren't Christians. Because of their oil wealth, they had unlimited resources and beautiful cars and tried to date local girls, which touched off a powder keg of strife. Locals began to refer to them as "camel jockeys" and worse. This was the atmosphere Danny grew up in, and in most ways he was typical of his society.

Danny couldn't get the incident at the ball field off his mind. The rules of his society were well defined, and he didn't disagree with them. He certainly didn't want to be a lightning rod for conflict. He knew interracial dating and marriage was taboo, but that was the furthest thing from his mind. As he pondered these things, it became clear to him what had happened with Amee. Had he thought it out rationally, he might not have started such a relationship, but he was so captivated by her beauty, charm, and openness that he never once thought about her being of a different race. He was hooked before he had time to consider such things.

Danny's dark side was spawned by the many seething conflicts in his soul. He had lost his dad at an early age, and his mother had remarried. While they struggled to save the farm, Danny grew up without most of the things that even the common people enjoyed. He grew up resentful but tough and vowed that he would obtain for himself those things he had been denied. He could not imagine how severely his beliefs and ambitions would be tried on his journey toward his goals. He would have occasion to examine everything he had taken for granted in his life, even his faith in God and the Bible. He must decide if he were a true believer, and if so, was he really a Christian? He would learn that the two things can be very different, because a Christian is one who sincerely seeks to be like Jesus.

Danny had decided to attend Mid State College for two reasons. The foremost reason was financial. The local people knew his athletic ability and granted him a full scholarship, which suited him well because Mid State had one of the best baseball programs of any Junior College in the entire country. He could also stay at home and help with the farm work.

Danny knew the incident at the ballgame would be the main topic of discussion around Perryville for quite a while, but that didn't really bother him. He was concerned about Amee and Mitzi though, and didn't want to see either of them hurt. Though he tried hard not to be, he was more concerned about Amee than Mitzi. Perhaps it was because she was so tiny and alone. He also could not get away from the last question Mitzi had asked him. He had never thought about why he should not be a friend with anyone he chose to. Of course, he knew that social and romantic involvement would never be acceptable, and certainly not intermarriage—and he had no argument with that. He couldn't and wouldn't buck his culture over blacks, but why should the same beliefs apply to Amee? Try as he might, he couldn't get these things out of his mind.

Mitzi was trying to keep a stiff upper lip, but it was a bit too stiff and so was the relationship between her and Danny. He had not mentioned Amee again, nor had he been with her, but the damage was apparently already done. Mitzi just could not handle the embarrassment. Without any discussion about it, Danny and Mitzi began seeing less and less of each other, and finally broke it off completely. They never had any formal relationship and now did not see the need of a formal breakup. Neither of them was angry, and both were a bit sad, but Mitzi was relieved not to have to answer questions about him anymore. Danny was too deep into introspection for anything else to bother him much.

"Mr. Brannigan, I presume."

The words had to fight their way into Danny's conscious mind because he was so deep in thought. Even though school had not yet started, the college library was one place he could find some solitude to sit and think. When he heard that unmistakable giggle, it was as if his spirit suddenly moved back into his body. He started and looked around to see the smile that could break through the gloom in his soul like the morning sun through the deepest fog.

"Where have you been?" she asked.

"Nowhere. I've been here all afternoon."

"Maybe your body has, but you've been somewhere else. I hope it was a good trip."

Danny grinned sheepishly and admitted he had been absorbed by his own musings.

"I thought this time of day you would be with Mitzi," Amee said.

"We don't see each other anymore," Danny replied.

"Oh, I'm so sorry; I hope I didn't cause that."

"Absolutely not," Danny responded. "We just found some differences we didn't know existed before. We are still friends."

"Then perhaps it would be safe for me to sit down with you a few minutes," Amee said hesitantly.

"I would love for you to."

Chapter 3

Fort Benning, Georgia, August 1966

The South Georgia sun beat down mercilessly on the tarmac at Fort Benning as the heat did its dance on the runway, causing small mirages here and there. Katie Brannigan was standing there along with the other wives of soldiers who were shipping out to Vietnam. One-year-old Danny, who was in the stroller beside her, was able to bear the heat only because of the canopy over him and his mother's constant fanning. Katie and Danny had driven the hundred miles to Columbus the day before.

"Oh, David, I don't think I can bear to say good-bye knowing you're going to that awful place."

"Kate, I don't want to leave you and Danny to go to anyplace, but I have to do my duty, and you know the Lord will watch over me."

"I know all that, but it's still so hard to see you go. Danny won't understand and will miss you so much."

"I will miss the two of you more than I can possibly put into words, but I know you'll be able to take care of Danny and the farm until I'm back home."

The last call was given for everyone to board. David kissed Danny and said, "Daddy loves you, little soldier, and I'll see you soon." Then he gave Katie one last hug and kiss and walked up the steps to the plane. He gave her the I-love-you sign as he disappeared into the doorway. As Katie turned and pushed Danny slowly toward to the car, he pointed back to the plane and said, "Da-da."

Brannigan Farm, 1967

When Katie saw the plain black sedan pull up in the driveway, she felt as though her heart would burst and her feet had turned to lead. Two army officers got out and walked slowly to the door. She had already identified the chaplain's insignia. They didn't need to knock, because, even though her knees were weak and she was trembling all over, she had managed to get there ahead of them. Every soldier's wife knew what this meant. Her knees were so weak that she could barely stand, prompting the chaplain to escort her to the couch. No words needed to be said, but they quietly delivered their message. Her strong faith, coupled with her Irish pluck, caused her to regain her composure quickly. David had been in Vietnam just over a year when Katie received the news she had feared every day her husband was gone. A reconnaissance team had been surprised and cut off from their unit. The Viet Cong were closing in, and there was certain to be a massacre. Captain Brannigan, along with three other men, volunteered to take his Huey helicopter and attempt a rescue. Coordinates were set in the edge of a rice paddy near a grove of trees that could be used for cover. They flew low and hopped over the trees, plopping down as quickly as possible near the stranded soldiers. The men aboard the Huey gave rapid-fire cover while the recon team scrambled on board. Miraculously, everyone got aboard, including two men who were badly wounded, but on the climb out, they were hit by machine-gun fire. All vital parts were missed, and everyone escaped injury, all except Captain Brannigan, who was mortally wounded. He managed to maintain consciousness long enough to fly the chopper back to base and safely land it, but he was dead on arrival by the time they got him to the MASH unit. His fellow soldiers told the story of how he saved lives even after he was dead.

Braxton County, Georgia,
June 20, 1969

The moon landing was the subject of conversation by everyone at church that day, and four-year-old Danny was probably the most excited person there. It was Sunday, June 20, 1969, and the anticipation was great that the race between the United States and Russia to put a man on the moon was going to conclude that day in favor of America. President John F. Kennedy had stated that it ought to be the goal of the United States to put a man on the moon by the end of the sixties. As soon as Danny got home, he was glued to the television. The only way he would even eat was for his mother to place his lunch on a TV tray. When the actual landing came, he heard Neil Armstrong say, "Houston, Tranquility Base here; the *Eagle* has landed." He jumped up and down on the sofa for several minutes and cheered wildly. He never forgot those immortal words, "That's one small step for man, one giant leap for mankind."

It was only in later years that Danny learned about one of the most significant things that happened that day. When they'd landed, Buzz Aldrin had said, "This is the LM pilot. I'd like to take this opportunity to ask every person listening in, whoever and wherever they may be, to pause for a moment and contemplate the events of the past few hours and to give thanks in his or her own way." It was years later that he revealed he had privately taken communion. At that time, NASA was facing a lawsuit brought by the infamous atheist Madelyn Murray O'Hare because astronauts had read from the book of Genesis on a previous mission. Danny said to his mom that day, "Someday I'm going to fly to the moon."

Brannigan Farm, July 1971

"Danny, the plane is coming."

Six-year-old Danny came bounding out of the house and ran through the screen door, letting it swing wide and slam behind him. He never wanted to miss the plane when it came to dust the cotton for boll weevils. The pilots would swoop down to the tops of the cotton stalks as they let out the stream of dust, and when they got to the other end near the house, they would climb vertically up the huge sycamore tree in the edge of the yard. Then they would circle and do the same thing again. Some of them who were real daredevils would clip the tops of the plants. Danny didn't get as excited about anything else, except playing baseball.

Every time the Brannigans went to Perryville, they passed the little Union Grove Airport, from which the crop dusters flew, and every time Danny begged to stop and see the planes. They had stopped often enough that all the pilots knew him. Red Parker, who owned the airport and flew a crop duster himself, would let Danny sit in the cockpit and pretend to fly the plane.

"Katie, don't you think it's about time for me to take Danny for a ride?" Red asked.

"I don't think my heart could stand that," his mother responded.

"It's safer than riding in a car, and it won't cost you a thing. As much as Danny likes airplanes, it would be a shame if he didn't get to fly in one. It could be the only opportunity he'll ever get."

They all knew why Katie didn't want Danny to go up in a plane, so they wouldn't press her too hard. But she didn't want to punish Danny for her fears and finally gave in. He got the thrill of his life. He was never even nervous as Red took him up in the *Mosquito Hawk,* and he hit the ground wanting to know when he could do it again. He never noticed that his mother was ashen with fear.

Perryville was only about thirty miles from Robbins Air Force Base at Warner Robbins, Georgia; therefore, the jet fighters would often break the sound barrier as they came over the Brannigan farm. Danny would watch their smoke trails and dream of the day when he could fly one of the planes. His mother's only comfort was that most boyhood fantasies pass with time. She could not accept the thought that Danny would ever fly, especially in the military. His father's death while flying his helicopter in Vietnam was as fresh and as frightening in her mind as it was the day she got the news.

Danny did not remember his father, but his mother did a wonderful job of keeping his memory alive. Katie Brannigan was determined to stay on the family farm, and with help from her brother, who lived on the neighboring farm, and Jake Reese, a knowledgeable and dependable foreman, she succeeded. Katie loved the farm that David had inherited from his father. She grew up in the city, but this was the only home she had known in her adult life and could not imagine living anywhere else. Everyone knew everyone else around Perryville, and most of the time they knew each other's business. The party line telephones made sure of that. There were three or four houses on every line, and each one had a different ring. They all knew whose ring it was, but many times there were four clicks as four receivers were lifted, no matter who got the call. Children were obligated to obey every adult the same as they did their parents, and not to do so placed their backsides in serious jeopardy. Kids could have wandered for miles and still been in safe territory. If a dinner bell or car horn sounded loud and long, in a very short time everyone in earshot would show up because it meant there was some kind of emergency. There might be a fire or someone seriously hurt, and this was the 911 system.

Katie was a beautiful Irish woman, statuesque and strong. She could pitch hay, drive a tractor, or shoot a rifle or shotgun as well as any man; yet she could stun you with her feminine charm. Her auburn hair, which hung loose and wavy down to her shoulders, was always parted in the middle with full bangs. The sunlight made it look like it was going to catch fire. Her eyes were like clear emeralds that could be so soft and gentle they would melt your heart, but could instantly flash fire if she were challenged. As Danny grew up, he referred to her as a combination of steel and velvet, swearing that he experienced each side many times. He loved her dearly. One of his favorite things was listening to her play the harmonica and sing Irish ballads. The Irish had a ballad for every noteworthy event that had ever occurred and many that weren't of note. More than any other people on earth, they sing for the sheer joy of singing. Danny could still remember sitting on the porch late into the night as Katie played and sang. She blamed it on the heat, but he always knew the reason she couldn't sleep. Even at the age of four or five, Danny could sense how much she missed his dad.

Jake Reese, the farm foreman, could only be described as ruggedly handsome. His hair was as black as a lump of coal and as unruly as an incorrigible child. It was determined to go in its own direction and would never fully surrender its will to a comb. Danny never remembered seeing it all in place at the same time. His skin was like tanned leather, betraying his outdoor life, and if he had a flaw in his features, it was a slightly large nose. Ever since he came to Braxton County from Texas, there was a certain mystery about him that made him intriguing, but everyone liked him. They speculated that he could be of Mexican or even Indian descent. Jake could disarm you with his boyish grin and Texas drawl, but no one doubted his ability and willingness to back up his words with action if it was necessary. Jake, whose quiet strength always made Katie feel safe, was always the perfect gentleman. When Danny was six years old, Jake and Katie were married.

Danny didn't even understand the negative feelings he had in his heart against Jake. He didn't dislike him, and Jake always tried to be his friend, but it bothered Danny that he had married his mother. He felt she was disloyal to his father, and he resented not having his own father around. Maybe Katie had done too good a job of keeping the memory of his dad alive. The times Danny liked best were when Jake was away on one of his frequent business trips and he had his mother to himself. Katie didn't like it much, though, and had wondered out loud why he had to be gone so often. His explanation was that he had gotten involved in a business venture with some people back in Texas and would tell her all about it when he saw how it was going to work out. It was Jake who got Danny involved in playing baseball when he was coaching a peewee team. Danny was a natural and soon demonstrated what a great arm he had. As he grew up, Jake was tireless in his determination to help Danny develop his pitching, even to the point of hiring the best personal coach he could find. He never pushed him to do something he didn't want to but encouraged him in everything he did.

Chapter 4

Mid State College, October 1983

"Mr. Brannigan!"

Danny was jolted back from going over and over the football playbook in his mind by the voice of Mr. Jessup, his political science teacher.

"Mr. Brannigan, is your mind going to join your body for class today?"

"Yes, sir. I'm sorry," Danny replied.

"Were you daydreaming about galloping on the green with Mary Jane?"

This was vintage Charles Jessup, and everyone in the class had a good laugh at Danny's expense. Danny was a good student; Mr. Jessup simply needed a recipient for his weird humor.

The professor continued, "How many of you read or heard about the suicide bomber who, on April 18, this year, rammed a pickup truck loaded with explosives into the U.S. Embassy in Beirut, Lebanon?" Most of the students raised their hands. He continued, "Sixty-three people were killed, including seventeen Americans, eight of whom were employees of the Central Intelligence Agency, including chief Middle East analyst, Robert C. Ames, and station chief, Kenneth Haas. The Reagan administration officials said that Hezbollah operatives, a Lebanese militant Islamic group whose anti-U.S. sentiments were sparked in part by the revolution in Iran, carried out the attack. Hezbollah reportedly was receiving financial and logistical support from both Iran and Syria.

"Just last month, on October 23, another suicide bomber detonated a truck full of explosives at a U.S. Marine barracks located at Beirut International Airport. Two hundred and forty-one marines were killed, and more than one hundred others were wounded. They were part of a contingent of eighteen hundred marines that had been sent to Lebanon as part of a multinational force to help separate the warring Lebanese factions. It has become imperative that we face the fact that these are not isolated events, nor are they likely to subside anytime soon."

The class had a spirited discussion for two sessions about the cause of the attacks and whether there was any justification for them. The intense debate about how the United States should respond produced answers that varied all the way from complete pullout to full-scale war. It was a preview of things to come.

Danny was the starting quarterback that football season. The combination of his powerful and accurate passing arm and the blazing speed of wide receiver Dale Reichert gave the team tremendous offensive potential. They were supported by a strong offensive and defensive line, giving them a good chance of being number one in their division this year. Game by game, they were inching their way to a perfect season. Danny and Amee found every excuse to be together, though they were both quick to point out that they were just good friends. Amee was not allowed to date, but she could go to group functions like the ballgames and gatherings afterward. Besides, she and Danny weren't really dating anyway. Now that he was in college and she still in high school, he teased her about being a child and called her his *"Sunday's Child"* because her dad only allowed them to be together alone on Sunday afternoon. No two people ever enjoyed each other's company more; consequently, Danny no longer cared what anyone else thought about their relationship. For the most part it didn't appear to bother anyone much. He was so popular because of his athletic ability that no one paid much attention to other things. The last game was coming up, and they were playing the Camden College Bobcats, the only other unbeaten team in their division. This game would decide who was going to be number one, as well as who would get to play a post-season game at the University of Georgia. The Bobcats had an all-star running back, as well as a tremendous defensive backfield. Most of their opponents had trouble establishing a passing game against them, and passing accounted for most of the Mid State Cougars' offense.

Coach Mark McDaniel called the team together before the game and explained one more time what they were up against.

"We haven't played a team as strong as this all year, so it's crunch time. This will really determine what we're made of. If we are to score, we must establish a running game. You running backs haven't been called upon to play at this level before, but now it's going to be up to you to set the stage for our passing game. Can you do it?"

The running backs rose and answered in unison, "Yes, we can!"

Yes, they did! The Mid State Cougars were the junior college champs. Dale scored the winning touchdown in the final seconds of the game when Danny threw a forty-yard pass, which floated into his hands a half step in front of the cornerback. He turned on the afterburners, and the deal was sealed. He and Dale were everyone's heroes.

They had all gathered at Casey's, which was the local hangout for high school and college students. It was one of those retro places that still had curb service. The joke around Perryville was that Casey was just too lazy to change from the fifties look. Dating couples would sit in their cars while the general crowd gathered inside. The excitement level was so high inside Casey's tonight that no one could carry on a conversation. After a while, Danny yelled to Amee, "Let's get away from this crowd for a while, so we can hear ourselves think."

She nodded in agreement, and they wove their way through the crowd and out to Danny's car. He didn't know if Dr. Salim trusted him that much or just didn't fully understand the nature of American teen culture. However, he knew Danny and Amee considered themselves to only be buddies, and Danny thought that influenced him. The buddy idea suited Danny well because he didn't plan to have a serious relationship until he got his college behind him. He also wanted to be free to fully concentrate on baseball. Dr. Salim, for the most part, was just the average protective father of a beautiful teenage girl.

It had been raining all evening, and a light mist was still falling as they walked to the backside of the parking lot. Danny had not parked there on purpose, but he was glad to put some distance between them and the noisy crowd. For some unexplainable reason, he had always liked to ride or sit in a car while it was raining. He would laugh and say it was the dark side of his personality. He and Amee never tired of being together nor ran out of things to talk about. The overcast conditions made the car nearly dark inside, but while they were talking, the moon broke through the clouds and shined into the window. As it struck Amee's hair, every bead of mist glistened like a diamond. The moonlight also gave her face an angelic glow and caused her eyes to sparkle. Suddenly, Danny felt something he had never felt before. There was a tightening in his stomach and a lump in his throat. He could feel his heart speed up.

Danny spoke softly and his voice broke a bit. "I know we've always joked around, but I want you to know that I think you're the most beautiful girl I've ever seen, and sometimes it's hard to think of you as only a buddy."

Tension was building in Amee as she struggled to respond correctly. How much did she dare say? Honesty would compel her to admit to the same kind of feelings, but full disclosure would require her to tell him about the prohibitions. "Danny, I love you as my dearest friend, but sometimes my feelings for you scare me. Let's be careful not to let anything destroy our friendship."

By then Danny could feel her tension and realized he needed to resume this conversation another time—if at all. "We never will do that," he replied, and with that they turned the conversation to other things.

He sat facing Amee with his back against the door, his right leg curled in the seat and his left elbow on the steering wheel. She was in much the same position on the other side of the car, and when she leaned over to make a point, she briefly laid her hand on his knee. Their relationship had become so comfortable that normally neither of them would have thought twice about it. At that moment, however, it was like Danny was seeing her for the first time. She sat transfixed in that position, and as they looked into each other's eyes, they both gradually began to lean forward. Before either of them had time to think about what was happening, they were kissing.

Amee was suddenly startled and turned away with a frightened expression on her face, but not before Danny caught a glimpse of the tears already running down her cheeks. He felt like a horse had kicked him in the chest. He handed her a tissue and waited a few moments before he spoke. He didn't know the human brain was capable of handling the number of thoughts that were rapidly running through his at that moment. All of them crystallized into one horrible thought: he had just ruined a wonderful friendship. He had never thought about such a thing happening, but had he thought about it, he certainly would not have expected this kind of reaction from Amee.

He waited for what seemed like an eternity for Amee to get control of herself, but instead of getting better, things were getting worse. She was shaking and openly sobbing now. For the first time since he met her, he didn't know what to say or do. Finally, he could wait no longer, because anything was better than this. He mustered all his courage and laid his hand gently on her shoulder.

"Amee, I … I … I'm sorry. I would never purposely do anything to offend you. I didn't plan for this to happen, and I can't quite explain it. Please forgive me."

Nothing he had ever experienced as an athlete had made his heart race like it did as he awaited her response. What happened next confused him even more. Amee turned quickly, locked her arms around his neck, and cried on his shoulder until his shirt was wet with her tears.

Finally she looked at him and exclaimed, "I was not offended! I felt the same thing you did. That's not the problem."

"I don't understand. What's the matter then?"

"I know you don't understand, and that's part of the problem. I'm forbidden to have any physical contact with a man until I'm married, and then I must marry someone of my own religion. I'm not even supposed to hold your hand, and you're not allowed to touch me. That's why my father gave me permission to be with you; he felt our relationship wouldn't be a threat to our religious beliefs."

Danny sat there with a puzzled look as Amee continued.

"Danny, do you hear what I'm saying to you? Do you understand how serious this is?"

"No, I don't understand. What kind of religion are you talking about that makes one kiss so earthshaking? I would never compromise you in any way, but I don't understand the alarm over one kiss."

She blurted out, "We're Arabs! I am a Muslim! What we just did has already compromised me, according to my religion."

Other than a few theologians, politicians, and diplomats, not many people in the United States in 1983 could have told you what a Muslim was, even in the most general terms. To most people, Arabs were still nomadic tribes riding camels across the desert and living in tents. Their armies fought valiantly against superior weapons, and individuals were the comic relief in many movies. Part of Danny's Christian training was to be respectful of the beliefs of others, but he didn't even understand what Amee was talking about. He knew some people frowned upon Catholics, Jews, and Protestants intermarrying, but this was just plain ridiculous. Nobody was talking about marriage, and he certainly had no thought of compromising her sexually.

He got a further shock when Amee refused to talk about it. Her father had told her not to discuss religion with anyone, and if she were asked, to simply say it was a private matter. But Danny, whom she trusted implicitly, was more important than anyone else had ever been in her life.

"Please give me some time to sort things out and we'll talk again," she pleaded.

This wasn't the time to press her, so Danny didn't respond. There was the loudest silence he had ever experienced as he drove her home. He felt like someone had sucker punched him in the gut. He had been sacked several times as a quarterback, but nothing he had ever experienced on the football field hurt half that bad. It was hard to believe life could change so much in a matter of minutes. When they arrived at Amee's home, she whispered a quiet thank you, and suddenly she was gone. Danny feared his *Sunday's Child* was gone from his life forever.

The next week was Thanksgiving break from school, which was the last time Danny was with Amee. Her family didn't observe Thanksgiving, and they were so far from their relatives that they spent the time quietly at home. Evidently, she had not told her father what happened because he allowed them to be together on Sunday afternoon. Her eyes were swollen and red, and for the first time since Danny had known her, she didn't have a smile. Although the season was over, they were instinctively drawn to the baseball field. The trees looked as bereaved and lonely as Danny felt, with all their leaves gone and the dark clouds floating above them. There were no cheering crowds, laughter, or sunshine, which were all appropriate for his mood. He was sure he must feel the same way a man does who is on his way to the gallows.

"Please, just listen to me for a few minutes, and don't say anything until I'm finished," Amee began. "I know none of this will make sense to you because of your Western culture and religion, but in my world it's nonnegotiable. If a person violates the Sharia laws of Islam, he is subject to severe punishment and even death in some instances. You have choices, but I don't, and if you interfere, you could also be in danger."

Danny was listening and didn't break in, but other thoughts were also racing through his mind. Although they weren't written on paper or chiseled in stone, he also had some principles he lived by. At that moment, he would have taken on the entire Arab world for Amee. He couldn't believe anyone would be radical enough in their religious beliefs to kill others. Maybe that could happen in the Dark Ages, but not in the twentieth century. There was no way for him to imagine how dramatically he would be proven wrong.

Amee continued, "If it were in my power, I would give the world to stay with you, but it can't be. We both know we can't go back to just being friends, so we must not allow a relationship to develop that can only bring more hurt. That would be so cruel and painful that we have no choice but to end it now."

Although every fiber of his being was crying out against it, Danny knew she was right. Although he would never understand it, he had no choice but to accept the circumstances as they were.

They embraced, and he whispered to her, "I love you, Amee, and always will. I will never spend another Sunday afternoon or go to a baseball game that I don't think of you. This is not what I want, but for your sake, I will respect it."

When Danny drove away from her home, he felt an old bitterness creep into his soul again. Everything he loved was always taken away from him one way or another, and religion was a hindrance rather than a help.

Christmas was Danny's favorite time of the year. He loved everything about it, especially the gifts, food, and decorations. About a week before Christmas, his mother would make hot chocolate and popcorn one night, and the family would trim the tree. There were certain kinds of candy, cookies, pies, cakes, and nuts they only had at that season. Most local people also cooked a fresh ham in the oven instead of turkey, and it was Danny's very favorite food. After his mom trimmed all the fat off, except for a thin layer, she would put polka dots of black pepper all over it. They always held a Christmas Eve service at church, at which they would sing carols for a long time before the pastor would tell the Christmas story. Everyone would get a sack of treats, followed by a gift exchange for the children. For a week, family and friends would visit back and forth. He took no pleasure in any of it this year, however, because the one gift that meant the most to him had been snatched away.

Although the Salims didn't observe Christmas, Amee loved it. Her mom and dad, who were understanding and loving, knew that she and her brothers felt left out because everyone else around them was getting presents and having wonderful things to eat. Mrs. Salim would cook all their favorite dishes, and they would receive nice gifts from their parents. Amee also visited with her friends and enjoyed all the special treats they had. She was one of the few people they knew who actually liked the proverbial fruitcake. They would laugh at her as they told their favorite fruitcake joke, but it didn't matter to her. Her only explanation was that it was similar to some of the Arabic food she grew up with.

No one in the family could come up with a good explanation for her moodiness this year. She spent most of the time in her room and didn't seem to enjoy anything. Her mom tried to talk to her but got no answers. She just said she was not feeling particularly well. Of course, Mo and Abb, who thought they could annoy her out her moodiness, were quickly shot down. In the past no matter what the circumstances were, her genuine good nature would always come out, but not this time.

At least in the spring semester, Danny was able to absorb himself with baseball. As predicted, he was the number one pitcher in the rotation, with a record of ten and two and one shutout. He only saw Amee at a distance once or twice when she came by the college to visit her dad. He thought surely she would come to see him pitch, but she never did. He could only speculate that either she had gotten over him or that it was just too painful for her to be around him. He always wondered how she explained to her parents why they no longer spent time together, but whatever she told them didn't seem to affect Dr. Salim's attitude toward him. The professor even embarrassed him on more than one occasion by mentioning publicly what an exceptional student he was. He encouraged Danny to pursue his interest in aeronautical engineering, as well as baseball. He said, "I hope you have a long and happy future in baseball, but one injury can end your career, so you need to he prepared for whatever life brings."

Through some of the papers he had written, Dr. Salim was beginning to be recognized as one of the foremost physicists in America. He was offered and had accepted a position at the Massachusetts Institute of Technology. Even though the position was more lucrative and prestigious, Danny couldn't help but wonder if his and Amee's problems figured into his decision. The Salims moved as soon as school was out in June, and Danny spent much of the summer at baseball camp. One Sunday afternoon, he went to the baseball game to see some friends, but all he could think about was Amee. Sometimes Danny thought it must have all been a dream, that she was an angel who dropped out of heaven to bring joy into his life for a little while and then was snatched away. He wondered how well she was getting along up there with all those Yankees. They surely wouldn't be as kind to her as Southerners were. Did she have a boyfriend? It pleased him better to think that she had a good girlfriend.

Boston, Massachusetts, September 1984

As Amee was fighting a heroic battle to put Danny and Perryville behind her, she was also experiencing culture shock. Perryville was a small town in a rural setting with residents that were for the most part laid back and easygoing. Checkout ladies at the grocery store would stop for a lengthy conversation about Aunt Edna's lumbago or last night's ballgame while customers waited patiently in line, usually carrying on a conversation of their own. Everything and everyone in Boston moved at warp speed, and most people didn't seem to have time or inclination to be personable. She hadn't realized until now how much she loved Southern charm and hospitality with their "y'all come" and "yes, ma'am" and "no, ma'am." At least she was back where there were other Muslims and a mosque, so she began attending prayers regularly. Although she didn't want to admit it even to herself, it was hollow and left her feeling empty. The way she chose to deal with her unhappiness was to bury herself in her college work. Even if she had been inclined to have a relationship with someone, he would have had to pursue her.

Mid State College, Autumn 1984

When it was learned that the Salims were gone, the local girls began to hang around Danny again. Even Mitzi, who was also attending Mid State, came around often to flirt with him. While he enjoyed all of them collectively, he showed no interest in anyone individually. They all were either too blonde, too tall, or didn't know how to giggle right. Gradually, the attention waned.

That year, the Cougars' football team came one win short of playing a post-season game. Although he always gave his best on the field and wanted the team to do well, he was not personally unhappy about the season ending. He was always fine during the game but felt like a fifth wheel everywhere else. The baseball team was a different matter. They didn't lose a game. Danny's record was 12 and 0, with two no hitters and three shutouts. His name was already being buzzed about the majors, and scouts showed up at every game.

One day, when he was at home alone, two unfamiliar men in business suits showed up at the door. One of them said, "We are looking for Daniel Brannigan."

"I'm Danny Brannigan, but what does the FBI want with me?" he joked and invited them in.

After they introduced themselves and were seated in the den, Bob Folkes said, "We have been sent by the Atlanta Braves baseball organization to talk to you about joining our team."

Danny could hardly breathe, much less answer, but he finally sputtered out, "You mean now?"

"We mean now. We have been scouting your pitching and believe you are ready to take it to the next level. We are prepared to make you a good offer with a nice bonus if you would be willing to sign now."

Was this some kind of sick joke? Danny had dreamed of playing for the Braves as long as he could remember, and was it about to come true just like that? Because he didn't know what else to say, he stammered out, "You'll have to give me some time to talk to my parents about it, but I can tell you that this is what I have wanted to do all my life."

"We certainly expect you to discuss it with your parents, as well as enlist the services of a good attorney. We will give you a week or so and be back in touch with you."

When the men were gone, Danny sat down to try to absorb what had just happened. After he got over the initial shock, he began to think seriously. By the time Jake and Katie got home, he was ready to discuss it with them, but as usual, they didn't tell him what to do. Truthfully, Katie would have been delighted with either choice Danny made, as long as it kept him from pursuing his love for airplanes. Danny called Donnie Purser, his baseball coach, who had been a big league ballplayer, to ask him for his advice.

"Danny, I believe in getting a good education, but occasionally someone comes along with a gift so unusual that he must seriously consider taking an alternate route in life. I believe you are one of those people. I have no doubt you will make it because you are the best big league prospect I've ever coached. If something should happen while you're in college, it could hinder your career. I think you should seriously consider taking the Braves' offer. You could go to college in the off-season and work toward your degree. You would surely have time to finish it over the span of a normal big league career."

News travels fast in a small town, and everyone around Perryville was already congratulating him. They had visions of a hometown hero. The money would mean a new kind of life for him and his parents, as well as fulfilling his lifetime dream, but he had laid out a definite plan for his life, and in the end he could not bring himself to change it. Besides, with a good college career, he could demand even more money. He didn't understand himself all that was involved in his thinking, but he was sure of his decision, which was not to take the Braves' offer.

Nearly everyone was disappointed with his decision, but it was done, and Danny was satisfied with it. Although baseball was definitely his first love, he didn't want to give up aeronautics. A few days after turning down the Braves' offer, he received a letter at college. In his rush to get to class, he laid it aside until later. When he got into his car that afternoon, he noticed it on the seat beside him and decided to open it as he drove home. Without bothering to see whom it was from, he tore open the envelope. The weather was nice so the windows were down, causing the envelope to fly out. As he saw the handwriting, he nearly ran off the road. It was a letter from Amee, or, more accurately, a note. She said,

Dear Danny,

I was so happy for you when I heard about your baseball contract. Then, I learned that you had turned it down in order to finish your education, and I am proud of you. I know how you feel about baseball, so it must have taken all your resolve to turn the offer down. A friend from the college told me that everyone thinks you are making a big mistake. I want you to know that I don't think so. I wish you the greatest success at Southeastern Poly.

—*Sunday's Child*

Danny parked beside the road until his tears cleared enough for him to drive. Suddenly it dawned on him that he didn't have the return address. He went back to look for the envelope, but try as he might, he couldn't find it. He searched until dark to no avail. Every day that week he stopped on his way home and looked again but never found it. He attempted to get the Salims' forwarding address from the college, but none had been left. He thought that was strange.

Danny's summer was taken up with two baseball camps. He had been accepted at Southeastern Polytechnic Institute on a dual scholarship for baseball and academics, requiring him to go to their camp. He arranged the other camp through Coach Purser so he could work on developing his pitches. He had a full arsenal, among which was a blazing fastball. He could already throw ninety-three miles per hour, which was unusual for someone his age. He had a good curve ball and was rapidly developing a splitter. He also had a fourth pitch that he was almost afraid to use because of the urge to laugh every time he threw it. He was sure his expression would telegraph it to batters. He used the knuckle ball just often enough to keep batters honest. Every time he did, he thought of Amee's reaction and that caused him to want to laugh.

Chapter 5

Atlanta, Georgia, Autumn 1985

Once Danny started to South Poly in the fall, there was no time for anything but studying and baseball. He arrived in time to attend the fall baseball practice and even in the off-season worked on the mental aspect of his game. He studied the pitching greats and analyzed all the best hitters. He read and watched tapes and films of current major league batters because he could possibly be pitching against some of them in three years if his plans worked out. In two more years, his skills would be much better than they had been at the end of his sophomore year. If he could stay healthy, he might have a shot at going straight to the majors. He made no attempt to play football because the possibility of injury was too great.

Even though baseball was constantly on his mind, Danny thoroughly applied himself to his studies, maintaining a 4.0 grade point average. All the electives he took related one way or another to aeronautics. He'd never lost his love for planes or flying. He would have been doing more flying had it not been for his mother's fear. Even though Danny was born in 1965, two years after President John F. Kennedy was assassinated, JFK was his favorite modern president because of his influence on America's space program. President Kennedy insisted that the United States be first in space.

Winters were never terrible in Atlanta. There might be the occasional snow or ice storm that would last just long enough to provide a diversion from the monotony. A half-inch of snow would cause schools and businesses to close, and when the really bad snows came—three inches or more—everything stopped. There were a few days in January and February when no one could be outside, but every day he possibly could, Danny was out running five or six miles to stay in shape. On bad days, he worked out in the gym. He was anxious for the baseball season to start and wanted to be ready when spring training came.

Georgia was always an explosion of colors in the spring with the blooming of azaleas, camellias, rhododendrons, dogwoods, and cherry trees, along with a thousand varieties of annual flowers. This year, nature seemed intent on outdoing itself. Everything came early and all at once. Some students were obviously not interested in wasting their time by staying inside and studying. Couples in various displays of relaxation and romance dotted every lawn on campus. The love of Danny's life required a diamond before she would become involved with him but not one that was worn on her finger. She was flirting and teasing him more every day to get him to come out and play. At this stage of life, baseball was his mistress, and she had him completely under her control.

He always loved spring training with the personal discipline it brought, causing him to become stronger and faster each day. He especially liked developing his pitching arm until he could throw his now ninety-six-mile-per-hour fastball over and over without any strain. Another ingredient that made Danny such a hot prospect was that not only could he pitch, but he was also a good hitter. So far his college batting average was .323. Many sluggers didn't bat any better than that, and most pitchers were poor batters. He looked forward to this season as he had no other. If the major league scouts were snooping about in his sophomore year, they were sure to be at every game now. All of them would want him to know who they were, and he loved meeting and talking baseball with them. Although he would still rather play for the Atlanta Braves, he realized it was important to pick the team he had the best chance with. He didn't want a team that had more than two ace pitchers already, because that would make it more difficult to break into the pitching rotation the first year. It was also important to have a good batting lineup behind him, because the best of pitchers can't win games unless the team scores runs.

The season began as if Danny had written the script. South Poly had a good all-around team, and he won his first three games. In the sixth inning of the fourth game, Danny was leading 5 to 2. Both of the opposing team's runs were unearned, having come on fielding errors. Danny was in the groove, but the home half of the sixth was extremely long. There were several base runners and an unusual number of pitches, as well as a pitching change. As Danny took the mound in the top of the seventh, he felt a slight tightness in his shoulder but was confident he could pitch through it. The tightness turned into soreness by the time he had two outs. He would finish the next batter off and ask the coach to send in a relief pitcher for the last two innings. They had two good relievers, either of whom was capable of finishing the task.

The next batter stepped to the plate, and Danny threw a slow knuckle ball to keep some stress off his arm. It danced beautifully, but the umpire called it a ball. His curve ball was usually a sure strike, so he threw a slow one. Again, it was a ball. A second curve also missed. Now the count was 3 and 0, so it was crunch time. The game wasn't on the line, but Danny wanted this man out. He took his windup to throw a fastball down the middle. Everyone in the stadium knew what was coming, so it had to be a good one. He needed one that was at least ninety-five miles per hour and perfectly placed. He gave it everything he had, and just as he released it, there was a loud snap that echoed through the stadium. Instantly Danny was on the ground writhing in pain, and South Poly hearts nearly stopped beating.

The pain was so great that all Danny remembered about leaving the stadium was the coach saying, "Hang in there, Ace; everything will be all right." After all the X-rays and examinations were done, they gave him a painkiller, and he awoke the next morning to see Dr. Leslie Campbell, the doctor of sports medicine for the baseball team, somberly looking at his chart. Seeing that Danny was awake, he said, "How ya doin,' champ?"

The pain had returned but not as severe as last night, so he replied, "Fine, Doc. You?" Danny was encouraged that since his shoulder felt better it was only a matter of time, rest, and a little therapy before he would be pitching again. One look at the doctor's face dispelled his optimism.

"I wish I had better news for you, but I don't. We can repair the damage you did so that you can do anything with your arm you have ever done, except pitch a baseball. You did so much damage to your rotator cuff that it will never stand the strain of pitching again, especially your fastball." As the doctor talked, Danny felt like he was a spectator watching the horrible events of someone else's life. This could not be happening to him. The doctor ordered a sedative and said, "Rest for now, and I'll come by later to talk again." He drifted off to sleep, and three hours later when he awoke, his first thought was that he had suffered a bad dream. One movement of his right arm brought him abruptly back to reality.

As the seriousness of his situation began to sink in, Danny got angry. As much as he wanted to deny it, he knew his baseball career was over. Even if he recovered enough to pitch, the big leagues would never take a chance on him. Besides, he had known Dr. Campbell for two years and was well aware that he was one of the best orthopedic doctors in the southeast. He specialized in injuries to the bones and muscles and was seldom, if ever, wrong. Every thought that was going through Danny's mind was a negative one. *Why did this happen to me? Do I always have to lose everything I love? Am I such a horrible person that God must punish me?*

He drifted off to sleep and awoke screaming at God in his mind, "What horrible thing did I do to deserve this kind of life? Do you hate me?"

Dr. Campbell decided to keep him in the hospital for a few days until he could decide the best treatment plan and get a therapy program started. In reality, he was as much concerned about Danny's frame of mind as he was his physical condition. The next day, Danny felt better physically but was still in a state of near depression. He was sitting in the atrium in the sun to be alone. He just sat with a blank stare, paying no attention to anything that was happening around him. He saw the man coming down the hallway but was so deep in his own thoughts that he probably wouldn't have recognized his own mother. As the man approached, Danny gradually began to realize there was something familiar about him. Suddenly he was aware that it was Dr. Salim. *What could he possibly be doing here?* Danny thought.

This was the first thing that had stirred him out of his trance. Impervious to the pain in his shoulder, he jumped up and took Dr. Salim's right hand in his and gave him a hug with the other arm. He was not prepared for the Middle Eastern greeting he received in return; however, in a weird way it felt completely natural to him. Dr. Salim put both hands behind Danny's head and gave him a kiss on each cheek. Suddenly the consequences of his spontaneous action became apparent. His shoulder began to hurt as he and Dr. Salim sat down together.

"Doc, it's so good to see you. How's your family?" Danny asked, although he really had one particular family member in mind.

Was Dr. Salim teasing him as he answered? "Safa is entertaining more than ever now that we have relatives nearby. Mo and Abb are both good students and are also involved in sports, soccer mainly. The entire family is already tired of the Massachusetts winters and, oh yes, I almost forgot; Amee is a sophomore at Massachusetts Institute of Technology studying communications. She is more interested in a career than a husband and family."

Danny didn't say anything, but he found that very encouraging.

"I'm so glad to see you," Danny said. "How did you even know I was here?"

"I had a speaking engagement in Florida with a long layover at the Atlanta airport, so I called the school to see if I could speak to you. They told me what had happened, and I had enough time to have a taxi bring me here before my flight leaves. Danny, you were always one of my favorite students, and I can only imagine how you must feel about this injury. Remember, I urged you to pursue engineering as diligently as you did baseball. You have an unusual aptitude for the physical sciences, and while you and I might not call him by the same name, I believe there is a higher power that guides our lives. I believe he has something special for your life."

Danny didn't comment, but he didn't expect that from a Muslim.

"Is Amee doing well in school?" Danny asked as casually as he could.

"She is doing extremely well. So well, in fact, that she has no social life to speak of. We encourage her to get involved in other things, but she seems to have no interest in anything but studying."

Danny knew he had to be careful not to venture onto unholy ground but could not restrain himself from saying something. "Dr. Salim, I don't know if you are aware of this, but Amee is the best friend I ever had."

As Danny was talking, Dr. Salim was slowly nodding his head

in the affirmative. "I'm sure you must have wondered what happened those last few months you were in Perryville when Amee and I stopped seeing each other."

Before Danny could continue, Dr. Salim spoke, "Parents are not quite as dense as you young folks think we are. I know your friendship began to turn in a different direction. I know you fell in love with Amee, as she did with you. Her mother and I quite possibly knew it before either of you did. I am also aware that your Western mind can never understand our ways, but I was willing to give the two of you a chance to do the right thing before I became involved in it. I am very proud of you both. I am also sorry that circumstances are as they are, but all of us are helpless to change them. It is important to me for you to know how I feel and how much I respect you."

"Dr. Salim, I will always love Amee, and if I might speak freely, I don't understand why there is a barrier between us that cannot be removed. However, I have accepted the situation and would never do anything to hurt her or your family. I'm so glad you came by. I've wished many times that I could talk to you."

Dr. Salim replied, "Ours are ancient and unchangeable ways, and none of us have the power to alter them. If things were different, I could think of no finer companion for Amee than you."

That dashed any hopes Danny had ever entertained that things might possibly work out for Amee and him.

As Dr. Salim rose to leave he said, "Danny, you are always welcome in our home. If you are ever in our area, please come to see us. We would be offended if you didn't."

"I would count it an honor to visit your home, as long as my visit wouldn't hurt Amee in any way. By the way, could I please get your address? Amee sent me a note a while back, and I lost the address before I knew whom it was from. Please explain that to her. Her note and your visit have each encouraged me in two of my darkest hours."

Dr. Salim handed him a business card with all his contact information, shook his hand, and disappeared down the hallway.

As Danny sat there alone, he began to reflect on what Dr. Salim had said. Here was a man who didn't even believe in the same God Danny did, and yet his words made sense. Danny had a lot of unresolved spiritual issues, but he had never doubted the truth of the Bible or his personal faith in Jesus Christ as his savior. He made a profession of faith when he was nine years old and was baptized. He was painfully aware of the fact that he had not always practiced what the Bible teaches, but he did believe it. He believed he got what he deserved in life but didn't know exactly what he had done to deserve all the bad things that kept happening to him. He knew many others who did things worse than he did and yet didn't have the problems he had. Why was he different? He lost his dad to war, his mom to Jake, Amee to religion, and now his baseball career to a freak injury. He really didn't see that he had anything else to lose. Maybe he and everyone else would be better off if he were dead.

Chapter 6

Danny had never been a quitter, making it his goal to be the last man standing, but he just didn't have any fight left. He lay down and drifted off to a fitful sleep from sheer emotional exhaustion. When he awoke, Jake and Katie were sitting quietly in his room, and for the first time in a long time, he felt very comforted by their presence. Katie came over and kissed him and sat down on the side of the bed. Danny sat up and put his arm around her and wept uncontrollably. Jake just sat there with a sad look on his face, not knowing what to do. When it was over, Danny was embarrassed and started to apologize, but Katie placed her finger over his lips and said, "Shush." She kissed him gently on the forehead and sat rubbing her hand over his hair. Nobody said anything for a long time.

Finally, Danny said, "You will never guess who came to see me today; Dr. Salim."

"How in the world did he even know you were here?" Katie asked.

"He came through from a speaking engagement in Florida and called the college. They told him where I was, and he had time to come before his connection to Boston. The most surprising thing to me is that he would even want to see me."

"Why do you think he made the special effort to come?" Jake asked.

"He said I was one of his favorite students, but I think he really wanted to clear the air about Amee and me."

Katie said, "We never really knew what happened between you and Amee. We knew you became good friends and were inseparable for a time, but then you didn't see each other anymore. We always thought there was a bit more than friendship between you but didn't want to butt in."

"Mom, we both honestly considered it simply a good friendship until that night we won the championship game in football. We were just talking, and it happened to both of us at the same time. I kissed her, and you would have thought I had touched off World War III. The upshot of it is that they are Muslims, and Amee is not supposed to even touch a man until she's married. Then she must marry a Muslim. I don't even understand such things, but we both agreed that we couldn't back up in our relationship, and we couldn't allow things to progress toward something that can never be."

"Son, I'm sure it was painful, but you will thank God for it later. I don't believe he would be pleased for a Christian to marry a Muslim, and had your relationship continued, it would no doubt have led to that."

"Mom, I don't want to be disrespectful, but I'm not feeling too friendly toward God right now. It doesn't seem that my faith in him has benefited me very much so far. Even Dr. Salim has more faith in his god than I do mine. One by one, everything I love is taken away from me. I don't have the slightest idea what to do with life at this point. All my plans have blown up in my face."

"Sweetheart, I know you're bitter now, but God always has a plan. We just have to trust him and be still and listen. I felt much like you do when your father was taken from me, but gradually the Holy Spirit and the Word of the Lord showed me that he is too good to do wrong and too wise to make a mistake. We must believe in his unconditional love."

"You don't know how much I wish I could do that, but I don't have that assurance right now. I just don't know what God wants from me. I admit that I have never been a great Christian, but I'm not aware of any terrible things I've done to cause all this."

Finally, Jake spoke up. "Danny Boy, I've never had the illusion that I could take the place of your dad, but I have tried hard to be the best substitute I could be. I love your mother, and I love you, and I've never wanted to come between the two of you. I know there has been an underlying resentment toward me, and though I don't understand why, I've never let it be an issue. I'm quiet by nature, but I should've been more vocal about my faith.

"If you go to Castroville, Texas, and search the records, you will find that I was born Jacob Reiss, r-e-i-s-s. Our name was Anglicized to r-e-e-s-e somewhere along the way, and that just stuck. My parents, who were Jews that lived in Austria, were killed at Auschwitz. Just before boarding the train, they were able to get me into the hands of sympathetic Germans who ultimately sent me to my grandfather in Texas. I don't remember what my parents even looked like, but I grew up resentful and angry. I literally fought my way through life until I was a teenager.

"We didn't have a synagogue in that part of Texas, so just for something to do, I went to church with some of my friends. One summer, they had a crusade preached by a Jewish Christian named

Hyman Appelman. He told how he was on his way to becoming a rabbi when he heard the gospel of Jesus Christ in New York City and became a Christian. He explained the simple gospel, and I was saved that night. It changed my life and my attitude. I will be forever grateful that God in his infinite mercy brought me to that place."

Jake continued, "I understand bitterness, anger, and resentment as well as anyone in the world, and I want to tell you that it is the fast track to being a complete failure in life. According to my experience, there is no cure for it except absolute faith in God and submitting to his will in everything. Your mother is the best Christian I have ever known, and you would do well to listen to her and observe her life."

"But I'm already supposed to be a believer, and it hasn't changed my circumstances or my attitude," Danny retorted.

Katie took both his hands in hers, looked him straight in the eye, and with tears running down her cheeks said, "Danny, first make sure you are a true believer and then that you are fully committed to the Lord without conditions or reservations. He will take care of the rest."

Katie and Jake knew that they could do nothing more at this time, so they both hugged Danny's neck and went to their motel so they could come back to see him the next day. After they left, Danny just lay there looking at the ceiling and thinking. One thing was clear: he had to find some way to deal with life. Another thing was also certain: if he was to be successful or find any peace, he had to change his whole outlook on life.

He drifted off to sleep, and when he awoke, for some inexplicable reason, he felt more in control. He had much more resolve and determination to just make a decision and follow it through. He would turn to aeronautics now and give it the same dedication he had given baseball. It even flashed in his mind that he could follow in his father's footsteps. He also decided that although he still had some underlying feelings, it was time to square things with Jake.

Katie and Jake came over early the next morning, and the change in Danny was immediately obvious. He couldn't wait to tell them about his decision and that they didn't need to worry about him. Afterward, he said, "Mom, I'm sorry for the way I've acted all these years. I know you suffered a lot and always did your best for me. I was just too selfish to see it.

"Jake, no boy could have asked for a better father than you've been. I just resented you taking my dad's place and felt you came between my mother and me. I know you didn't, and you taught me all the things a boy should know. My love for baseball and my knowledge of the game came from you. Thank you for all you have done."

Jake never showed much emotion, but he shook Danny's hand and placed one arm around his shoulder. "Danny Boy, I never held any of it against you. I knew what you were going through but prayed that this day would come. I love you like you were my own son."

The three of them spent the rest of the morning together in the atrium and then had lunch in the cafeteria. Jake and Katie left soon after lunch so they could get back before night to take care of the animals. Danny had great resolve, but it began to settle in upon him that he didn't have a plan. He could finish his degree and see what developed, but that was not his way. He needed to know exactly where he was headed. Although he was now squared away in his resolve to face whatever life threw at him, he was far from being reconciled with God. A great deal of uncertainty and some degree of resentment still lingered in his heart. He was just pulling himself up by his own bootstraps.

He was released from the hospital after a few days of rehabilitation and immediately started to run several miles a day. He also worked out regularly in the gym and gradually built back the strength in his shoulder. Dr. Campbell was right; the only thing he couldn't do was throw hard overhanded with his right arm. The baseball coach invited him to rejoin the team as a pitching coach, but it was easier for Danny not to be around the game for a while. He buried himself in his studies.

Before Danny had time to assess his situation fully, he was summoned to the chancellor's office. It sounded very official and ominous, and he thought of all kinds of possibilities as he walked down the hall. Was his academic scholarship not sufficient to cover his school bill now that he couldn't play baseball? He was greeted by Chancellor Thomas Cooke himself and introduced to two men he had never seen before. They gave their names simply as Adams and Rubenstein. There was no small talk; they got straight to their purpose. Mr. Adams said, "Mr. Brannigan, first let me say that you have our sincere condolences concerning your injury and your lost hope of playing major league baseball, but since that's finished, we would like to talk to you about a different career. We've followed your scholastic progress for some time now and are aware of your interest in aeronautics, especially glider technology."

Danny didn't interrupt but wondered what they were doing snooping into his life.

Mr. Adams continued, "We need the best minds we can find with expertise in various areas to work with us on a special project, and we believe you could be one of those. The project is top secret, but we will explain as much as we're able. All we can tell you at this time is that it concerns the security of our country and, in your case, would involve aviation.

"We're also impressed by your physical skills, which could certainly be called for in certain circumstances. Should you agree to join us, you would need to transfer to the Air Force Academy in Colorado Springs for your senior year, where you would receive a degree in aeronautical engineering. You'll learn to fly, as well as take parachute and survival training. As far as anyone on campus will know, you'll be just another cadet. Upon graduation, you will be commissioned as a second lieutenant in the air force, and after a year of flight training, you will become a first lieutenant. We can't guarantee specifics, but I believe this will afford you opportunities you would not otherwise have in life. Honesty compels me to tell you that the next two years will probably be the most difficult of your life, and you will no doubt at times face some danger."

This was too much to absorb immediately. Danny's whole life had been turned upside down for two years, and now, as Uncle Cecil used to say, he was as confused as a monkey in a house of mirrors.

"I am honored and will admit that I'm interested in your proposal," Danny said. "But I must have a little time to consider it and talk with my family. Then I will give you an answer."

"That's certainly reasonable," Mr. Adams replied. "But don't take too long, because we must have everything settled in time to get you registered and squared away at the Air Force Academy for the fall semester. I must also ask you not to discuss the matter beyond attending the academy and receiving a commission in the air force."

Chapter 7

Danny really needed some guidance on this one, so he decided to go home for the weekend and talk to his mom and dad. Although he expected his mother to be upset because it involved flying, he was certain his parents could offer some advice that would make his decision clear. As soon as his last class was over on Friday, he headed south. As he drove through Perryville, he stopped here and there to chat with friends, who all expressed their regrets about his baseball career. He was glad they were concerned, but he had put that behind him now, never thinking about it unless someone else brought it up.

On his drive out to the farm, he passed the baseball field. It was late Friday afternoon, and a softball game was in progress. As he drove slowly past, watching the crowd laughing and cheering, he began to have flashbacks. His heart nearly stopped when he thought he actually saw Amee sitting in the stands. He knew it couldn't possibly be her, so his mind was soon occupied again with the decision that was before him. He didn't really know how he felt himself about becoming part of something he did not fully understand. Up to now, the only thought he had given to aeronautics was that he might get involved in aircraft design when his baseball career was over.

Katie had prepared Danny's favorite meal. The Southern fried chicken, butter beans, fresh corn, okra, and "cathead" biscuits caused him to eat more than he had in months, and if that were not enough, there was a seven-layer chocolate cake for dessert. Danny recalled how his mom used to make those cakes for him and his friends on Saturdays. She would bake thin layers and put chocolate icing between each layer. Then she would cover the entire cake with the chocolate icing. She would stick several holes from top to bottom, and the warm chocolate would run down through them. Nothing was better than a slice of that cake when it was still hot.

After a while, Katie said, "Oh, by the way, Sue Graham said your friend Amee came by the college yesterday."

Danny couldn't believe what he was hearing. "Why would she come back here?"

"Sue said she was on her way to Florida and came by the college to pick up some kind of paper for her dad."

Was it possible that he had actually seen Amee as he passed the baseball field? Did he drive right by her and not stop? Danny jumped up from the table so quickly that his chair went bouncing across the floor. As he ran to the phone, Jake and Katie laughed at him. The Grahams had been their neighbors since before Danny was born, and he still remembered their phone number. He dialed it as fast as his fingers would move.

"Hi, Sue. This is Danny Brannigan. How are you? I'm fine, just in from college for the weekend. Listen, Mom said you saw Amee Salim at the college yesterday. Is that right? You did? Did she say how long she was going to be around? Monday, huh? That's great. Do you happen to know where she's staying? Thank you very much."

Sue told Danny that Amee was staying with Jodie Morgan, a friend from high school, so he called the Morgan home. When Jodie answered, he breathed a sigh of relief.

"Hi, Jodie. This is Danny Brannigan. How are you? I'm doing fine now. I heard Amee was staying with you this weekend."

Jake and Katie could tell by the tone of his voice when he spoke again that his hopes had been dashed in some way. He trudged back into the den where they were having coffee and dropped onto the sofa. He looked like he had lost his last friend. As far as he was concerned, he had lost his *only* friend.

"What happened?" Katie asked tenderly.

"Amee was going to be here until she went to a meeting in Florida on Monday, but she got a call saying that her meeting had to be moved back to Saturday. It has to be then or not at all, so she left at five o'clock."

"I'm so sorry," Mom said. "I know how disappointed you must be."

"It's been a long day with classes and the drive home," Danny said. "Could we wait and talk about my situation tomorrow?"

"Of course; we know you're tired," Katie replied.

He kissed his mom good night, slapped Jake on the shoulder, and went to his bedroom. As tired as he was, he got very little sleep that night. He was tortured by how close he came to seeing Amee only to miss her. Who knows what would happen if they could actually see each other again? It was at times like this that Danny's mind didn't work rationally. In his saner moments, he knew circumstances had not changed.

As Amee was driving to Florida, she had plenty of time to think. Being back in Perryville stirred up old emotions that she had beaten back time and time again until, like whipped puppies, they only lurked in the shadows of her mind and poked their noses out occasionally. She let her guard down as she reminisced about the happiest time of her life, and all her feelings came running out at once, playing tag through her mind. The tears began to drop into her lap as she indulged herself in the bittersweet sadness of her thoughts. She was glad it was night and other drivers could not see her face. The headlights revealed deer grazing on the lush grass along the side of Interstate 16, and after a while, she began to count them. Finally, the ghost of happiness past began to release his grip on her mind.

Then her thoughts were occupied with the session she was facing tomorrow. It would be a pivotal point in her life. If things turned out well and she qualified for the offer that was made to her, she would be in a position to accomplish one of her major goals in life. If she wasn't successful in her bid, then she must go back to Boston and the life she didn't like. She was so keyed up, at least she was in no danger of going to sleep while she was driving.

The tantalizing smell of fresh-brewed coffee and bacon frying curled its way upstairs, slipped through the keyhole, and tickled Danny's nose until he sat up. He felt as though he had just gone to sleep, which wasn't far from the truth. The last time he looked, it was after four o'clock. Katie came to call him just as he started down the stairs. The sight of her in the morning always made him feel good. As long as he could remember, every morning she had worn the same old tattered blue robe and had her hair held in place on top of her head with a big plastic clip. Jake was already at the table, sipping his coffee. After tending to the animals, he always sat there as Katie finished making breakfast. They could talk for hours and would rather be with each other than anyone else on earth. For the first time in his life, Danny didn't resent that.

Though Danny had never even tasted alcohol, he was sure a hangover must feel a great deal like he felt this morning. One look at the table made him perk up. There was Mom's trademark: golden brown biscuits, eggs sunny side up, grits, bacon, sausage, and strawberry preserves she had made herself. When he was younger, Katie would place the eggs in the center of the plate like two large eyes, half one piece of bacon to make eyebrows, and curl another one for a mouth. Grits with redeye gravy served for hair. There they sat smiling at Danny this morning, and as bad as he felt, it made him laugh.

"Thanks, Mom. I needed something to cheer me up this morning, and you did it. I love you."

"I love you too, Danny, and I just wish I could do something to really make you happy."

It would be good to get his mind on something other than what had occupied it all night, so he explained to them everything Adams and Rubenstein had said. He admitted that it was exciting to think about the possibilities such a thing would offer. He needed some kind of challenge to replace what he had lost in baseball, and if he could contribute something to his country in the process, that intrigued him. He had not forgotten that his dad gave his life in service to the United States.

He apologized for rambling on, although Jake and Katie assured him they wanted to hear it all. By the time Danny finished, Katie was openly sobbing. "Mom, I'm sorry; I've been so messed up over losing my baseball career that I'm not thinking straight. I should have been sensitive to your feelings about my flying. I don't ever want to hurt you. If it still bothers you that much, I won't even consider it."

She blew her nose, wiped her eyes, and sat up straighter. "Danny, I don't want to hinder you in doing what you feel is right for you, but I don't think I can bear the thought of you flying fighter planes. I think my heart would fail if you ever had to go into battle. Can't you work with these men without having to fly?"

"I don't think so, Mom. The plan involves my going to the Air Force Academy and then to flight school. That seems to be my part on the team and the only reason I was chosen."

"We've never had a dilemma like this, and I don't know what the answer is. If you feel you must do it, and I can't handle it, what're we going to do? If God would only have let you play baseball, we wouldn't be facing this."

Jake's instincts told him he needed to sit this one out, because rational arguments wouldn't be effective. Katie already knew everything he could say. He did finally make the suggestion that they sleep on it, though he knew no one would sleep much that night.

Katie had breakfast ready the next morning just as she did any other day, but her red, swollen eyes and ashen face revealed the fact that she had not slept much. She smiled at Danny when he came down, and kissed him on the forehead.

"Did you sleep well last night?" she asked.

"I'm afraid not, Mom, and it's obvious you didn't either."

"I'm okay. We'll talk again after breakfast."

About that time Jake came in from taking care of the livestock, and they sat down to eat. It was apparent that he was making an attempt to carry on small talk during the meal. Katie was pleasant even though she was tired, and even smiled several times.

When they had finished eating, Katie poured another cup of coffee for everyone and sat back down. Danny spoke first.

"Mom, I've thought about this most of the night, and my decision is made. Nothing's important enough for me to hurt you like this, so the deal's off."

She laid her hand on his arm, looked at him, and said, "Shhhhh."

She took Jake by one hand and Danny by the other, smiled faintly, and said, "Jake knows what I'm about to say. I told him about four o'clock this morning. After praying most of the night, I realized that I've been wrong. God can protect you much better than I can, and he is not limited in where he can do it. I've lived in fear and not faith, and I'm sorry. You have my blessing upon this venture, and I really mean that. I want you to do it if it's what you want. The Lord has given me perfect peace."

Danny was always amazed at Katie's faith in the Lord. The fact that it took more courage for his mother to say what she had just said than anything she had ever done didn't escape Danny either. He was so proud of her, especially the strength to face life she had passed along to him. Now he was back to the decision-making process. He just sat there looking at them like a child expecting his parents to tell him what he must do. Initially, he was disappointed at their advice. Actually, it didn't seem like advice at all but just some platitude. They simply said, "Pray about it and look into your own heart. You will find the answer." He hadn't really prayed about it, and as for looking into his heart, he knew that was not where the answer was. So far, he had not had such good luck with his heart because every time he followed it, he got hurt. The answer lay in the facts of the matter, and he had even been very logical about it. He made a list of all the pros and cons and compared them, which served a real purpose: it confused him even more.

After breakfast, Danny decided to go for a drive and try to sort out his thoughts. He drove down by the old swimming hole where the boys used to go skinny-dipping on hot, humid, summer afternoons. If someone shouted, "Girls," they would scurry for cover if they had time, but occasionally some of them would have to stay in the water and swim around a bend in the creek until they were out of sight. Of course, the girls giggled with glee at causing such a commotion. That was the place he had learned to swim when the older boys threw him in and let him either swim or crawl out on the bottom. As he looked at the muddy creek now, he couldn't believe he ever swam in it with all the catfish, crawdads, and water moccasins. It was easy to become very sentimental about a place like that.

Sometimes, they would drive a truck onto one end of a long board and use a rock for a fulcrum in order to make a diving board. One Saturday, Willie Woodward, who was already pretty deep into his weekend drunk, decided to go swimming. He got out of his car and immediately made a run for the diving board. He was only about five feet tall, and he hit the board with all his force. He went about ten feet into the air, jackknifed, and started straight down headfirst. He had not taken off any of his clothing or his shoes or his wide-brimmed felt hat. He hit the water with a dull thud, and his hat stopped him cold. It looked for a moment like he had permanently stuck in the water, but then he fell like a dead tree. Everyone was sure he had broken his neck, but he started to swim as if nothing had happened. It was a miracle that he didn't kill himself.

By the time Danny finished reminiscing about the old swimming hole, he was at the crossroads where the remains of two general stores stood diagonally across from each other. They had long ago been abandoned, as had the gristmill and cotton gin, the remains of which stood as silent witnesses to a world now gone. Once, this was the busiest place in the whole area. Anything necessary to home or farm could be purchased at the stores, where any honest person could obtain credit, as well as a few dishonest ones. Farmers could trade eggs and butter for other goods. When Danny was a boy, their chickens ran loose, building their nests in various places. One morning, he got the bright idea that he could rob the nests and sell the eggs at the store before the school bus ran. It was only a mile to the store, and he could catch the bus there. He would say that his mother sent the eggs, which she had done many times before. His plan worked flawlessly, and Fred Barlow, who owned the smaller of the stores, was glad to buy them from him. He went to school loaded with all kind of goodies. He ate some and sold some to other students for much more than he paid for them. He had anything he wanted that day and still came home wealthy. The only problem in his well-laid plan was that the next time Fred saw Katie, he asked if she was satisfied with the price he paid for the eggs. Not only did Danny get punished for lying and taking what didn't belong to him, but he also had to go confess to Mr. Barlow. He had to give Katie the money he had left, and he spent nearly all summer paying the rest of the money back. It was such lessons that developed the right kind of character in him.

One of Danny's favorite things was to sit around the potbellied stove and listen to the spit and whittle club spin their yarns. He was certain that any boy's education was incomplete unless he had access to this institution of higher learning. Many skills were learned from those men, such as how to make the thinnest and longest shaving with a pocketknife or how to spit tobacco juice into a tin can without getting a drop on the floor. Because this was the heart of cotton country, during harvest season, the gin ran all night, so the stores stayed open all night. Trucks loaded with cotton were in line by the dozens, waiting their turn. Any boy thought the greatest accomplishment he ever made was to convince his mother to let him spend the night there with his dad. Danny had a good chance of getting Jake to take him along one or two nights a week. At night was when the best stories were told, and entertainment abounded. There were spectacular events, such as opening gun shells and feeding the shot to toads that had come to the lights to catch bugs. The trick was to bounce the shot just right so that the toad would snag it with his tongue, thinking it was a bug. Eventually they would become so heavy that when they attempted to jump, they couldn't get off the ground. Then you could pick them up by the back legs and all the shot would come pouring out. The toad, unhurt, was ready to catch bugs again.

The cotton gin itself afforded many hours of entertainment. The steady, rhythmic *bump, bump, bump* of the giant engine could be heard for miles. Children loved to play in the seed house and then cool off in the spray of the tower that cooled the water for the engine. In those days, anyone could walk through and see the entire operation of the gin from the giant tube that sucked the cotton out of the trucks all the way to the bales that rolled out the other end.

Danny also liked to go to the gristmill. The miller would be as white as a ghost from the meal dust, and it was fun to sneak a mouthful of warm meal when he wasn't looking. His favorite thing, though, was to watch the giant rocks grinding against each other. The farmers didn't need any money because they would bring their own corn, and the miller would take his toll, a certain amount for grinding it. He then bagged that and sold it in town.

He drove on past the crossroads where a drunk driver killed one of his best boyhood friends. As he thought about his friend, Mac Harper, he remembered all the Sunday afternoons they had spent together between the morning and evening church services. On most Sundays, they were at one house or the other and were always out inventing some kind of fun. He recalled the time when two good little Christian boys decided to make their own wine from blackberries. They had it working real good up under the Harper house until they got cold feet and decided to bury the evidence. They were better at winemaking than they were at physical science, so they buried the fruit jar with the cap closed tight. A few days later, it sounded like someone had discharged Mr. Harper's old twelve-gauge shotgun. The wine jar had blown a large hole in the ground, ending their careers as brewmasters. Another day, they had a wonderful ride on the axel and wheels of an old cultivator. They got aboard and started down the longest hill they could find. As it picked up speed, they realized they had forgotten two very important things: a steering wheel and brakes. It took several days to recover from the bruises inflicted by that ride.

He drove through the little town of Brewster, where he had attended elementary school. Long before Danny's time, when the W&T Railroad ran through it, Brewster had been a bustling town. They built a highway where the bed of the long-gone railroad had been. The road is still referred to as the Old Railroad Bed. Now, except for one store, a service station, and the post office, there were only old, dilapidated, deteriorating buildings. A thousand memories were clamoring for attention. Suddenly, Danny realized it was as though he were saying good-bye to all of this. Oddly enough, when he was not thinking about his decision, the answer became perfectly clear. That was no doubt what Jake and Katie had meant by looking into his heart.

Danny spent the rest of Saturday with his mom and dad, had breakfast with them on Sunday morning, and then was on his way back to Atlanta. He would come back as soon as school was out to spend a few days before heading for Colorado Springs and his new life. As usual, once he made a decision, he never questioned it again. On his drive back to school, he felt his first tinge of excitement about the adventures that lay ahead of him.

Chapter 8

Colorado Springs, June 1, 1986

The clouds that enshrouded the mountaintops diffused the golden rays of the sun into a spectrum of brilliant colors as Danny drove into Colorado Springs. The sun went before him like a scout as he drove the last of the three-day, 1,500-mile trip from Perryville. He had stopped by Southeastern Poly to say good-bye to friends before going on to Louisville, Kentucky, to spend the night with relatives. The next day was up to Indianapolis and then straight west on Interstate 70 for what seemed to be an interminable time. He wondered how the early settlers felt the first time they saw the Rocky Mountains. They must have thought the mountains moved away as they traveled toward them at a pace of fifteen to twenty miles per day. Even at five hundred miles per day, Danny thought surely they were teasing him by staying just out of reach. He felt a sense of relief as he finally came to Limon and turned southwest on Highway 24. He was now within an hour of his destination.

He planned to spend the night in Colorado Springs and make the twenty-minute drive to the United States Air Force Academy the next morning. Registration wasn't until August 15, followed by a week of orientation. Classes would begin one week later. Danny had learned that the Air Force Academy is among the most selective colleges in the United States, where candidates are judged on academic achievement, demonstrated leadership, athletics, and character. Every cadet participates in either intramural or intercollegiate sports, and in addition to academic requirements, there is a rigorous military training regimen. Along with all this, a letter of recommendation is required, usually from a senator or congressman. Danny more than qualified in all other ways, but he did not have a letter from anyone. He couldn't deny a little pride at being able to attend such an institution. He had been instructed to report to Dr. Rubenstein's office when he registered.

Dr. Rubenstein had made arrangements for Danny to stay in the dorms for the summer. Because of the unusual manner in which he was entering the academy, he had to take advantage of every opportunity possible to finish the requirements. Before classes started in the fall, he would do his three-week combat survival training and airborne parachute qualification. He actually enjoyed those, and it left time to do a lot of sightseeing, which was endless in Colorado. Danny was so busy that the summer passed quickly, and it was time for registration.

"Name?" the young cadet asked without looking up. Danny had arrived at the outdoor information desk.

"Daniel Brannigan."

Again, with barely a glance, the cadet handed him a folder. "Please wear the badge at all times until you receive different instructions. All other information specific to you is in the folder."

Danny was about to ask directions to Dr. Rubenstein's office. This time, the cadet looked directly at him. "All other information specific to you is in the folder. Please move along."

It was obvious he was in a very different environment. Later, Danny learned that from the moment a new cadet arrived, certain things were expected, one of which was to follow instructions explicitly.

Nature had placed the huge Hickory tree in just the right spot for first-timers like him. It was just beyond the information desk, standing tall and majestic, offering its shady comfort to many a beleaguered cadet. Someone had evidently discovered its strategic location and placed a circle of white, wrought iron benches around it. Danny sat down to look through his folder and found the cadet to be correct. The first page of the folder was a map prepared specifically for him. On it were directions to Dr. Rubenstein's office with the succeeding pages giving step-by-step instructions for the next week.

The building Dr. Rubenstein's office was located in surely must have been one of the first constructed back in 1954 when Congress passed legislation to create the United States Air Force Academy. On April 1, of that year, President Dwight D. Eisenhower signed the bill into law. The core values of the academy appealed to Danny: "Integrity first, service before self, and excellence in all we do." He would be proud to graduate from such an institution, where he would receive a Bachelor of Science degree in aeronautical engineering.

Because of his interest in aviation, Danny also researched the history of the United States Air Force and found that the United States Army Air Corps existed from 1926 until 1941 and was the predecessor of the United States Army Air Forces (1941–1947). That became the United States Air Force on September 8, 1947. He liked to read biographies of military men and was particularly enamored with the life of General Billy Mitchell. Mitchell was so convinced that future wars would be won or lost in the air that he pushed his case for a strong air force until it brought him a court martial for insubordination. He was a veteran of World War I and many years before 1941 had warned of a coming war with Japan, which was unilaterally ignored. Danny couldn't help thinking what a devastating mistake such a thing would be in the future with all the capability for destruction the world had developed. At Pearl Harbor, 2,333 lives were lost because a warning was not heeded. How many would be lost in such an incident now?

The creaky old mahogany stairs were still the only way to the third floor where Dr. Rubenstein's office was located. The six-panel doors with the transom windows above them reminded Danny of his first classroom at the old Brewster Elementary School. It even had the same musty smell, causing him to have a flashback to the second grade and his teacher, Mrs. Jackson. For a first offense in her class, she made you stand in the corner. In the winter it was always the one behind the old potbellied stove where you would slowly roast. A second violation earned you an indefinite sentence to stand in the hall just outside the classroom door. Danny learned by experience that your sentence lasted until the principal came by. Try as you might, it was impossible to hide from him in the doorjamb. He was a tall, fat, cigar-smoking man with a nose that stuck as far out as his stubby cigar. That way, he got to smoke his cigar twice. His actual name was I.M. Jolly, which was a serious misnomer because he was always gruff and cantankerous. Danny suspected that he had been hired as an enforcer more than anything else, probably from the mafia. When he found you in the hallway, he would take you to his office and grill you, more often than not, giving you two or three good swats with his paddle.

As Danny knocked on the door with the translucent glass, he had the sensation that he was entering the principal's office.

"Come in," answered a female voice so raspy that it betrayed a lifetime of smoking.

At his first sight of Mrs. Annabelle Lackey, Dr. Rubenstein's secretary, Danny was sure she must have come with the building.

After he got to know her, he was also certain she could just as easily have been the commandant of some military school.

"Good morning. My name's Danny Brannigan. I have an appointment with Dr. Rubenstein."

"In there," she said as she pointed without looking up.

As Danny hesitantly stuck his head through the doorway, he was surprised to see Mr. Adams. He still didn't know just what position either one of the men held in the government or what Mr. Adams's first name was.

Adams spoke first. "I hope you had an uneventful trip out here and a good and productive summer. Are you settled in well?"

"Yes, thank you," Danny replied.

"With all the applicants who are clamoring for an opportunity to become students here, I'm sure you must wonder why we would recruit someone. I can only speak in general terms at this time, but we must be extremely selective in securing the people we need for our purpose. Dr. Adolph Rubenstein is in charge of certain aspects of our project and will be your contact while you're here."

By now, Danny was suspicious that Adams was not the real name of his recruiter.

Now it was Dr. Rubenstein's turn. "This year we want you to concentrate on graduating from the academy. That in itself will be enough to keep you busy. As far as anyone else knows, you are a regular student, and in the future you will appear to be an ordinary United States Air Force pilot. By the way, please don't discuss this with anyone. You have the perfect cover in the truth. Just tell anyone who asks that when your baseball career ended, you decided to pursue your second goal. We'll get back to you soon with more details, but for the time being, just trust us."

Both men wished him a good year, and the meeting was over. Danny left with more questions than answers, but he was content to let things develop as they would for the present.

Scholastically, the academy was extremely demanding, but most of Danny's courses were fun because, one way or another, they were related to flying. Classes, homework, and sports took an average of sixty hours per week. There were a number of choices for intramural sports, but he chose soccer because he didn't have to use his right arm to any great degree. He was afraid he might injure it and wipe out another career.

When Danny went home for Christmas break after the fall semester was over, he was looking forward to the month he had off. He planned to spend time with his family and friends and consume large quantities of his mom's cooking. His major project, however, was to work on the thesis that was due by April 1. Other students were allowed to choose their topics, but his thesis on the design of heavy gliders was assigned to him. He learned that was what had gotten him the attention of Mr. Adams and Dr. Rubenstein in the first place. He had written about his concept of heavy gliders at Southeastern Polytechnic Institute. He believed aircraft of huge proportions and heavy weight could be made to glide just as easily as the light ones with long wings. As yet, however, he did not know what the application of his proposal would be.

Jake and Katie picked him up at the Atlanta airport and drove him the two hours to Perryville. Family and friends were around constantly until Christmas was over, so he didn't even try to get any work done. The day after Christmas, Jake and Katie drove down to Savannah to visit other relatives, leaving him alone to work. He had about three weeks now to get serious about his thesis, so he worked several hours a day, usually late into the night. One afternoon, as he dosed off while he was reading, he dreamed about Amee, and when he awoke, he had an undeniable urge to call her. The information Dr. Salim gave him was in his billfold. He got it out, went to the phone, and started to dial, but went back and sat down. He repeated the process several times before he actually got up the courage to make the call.

"Salim residence." Safa Salim's voice was unmistakable, although Danny hadn't spoken to her for over three years.

"Mrs. Salim, this is Danny Brannigan. How are you?"

"Danny! It has been such a long time. I'm so glad to hear your voice."

"It's good to talk to you also. I know you don't observe Christmas, but I hope you are all having a good time through the holidays and everyone is well."

"We are all doing well, Danny. How is your family?"

"They're fine; Mom and Dad are away for a few days. Could I possibly speak to Amee?"

"You certainly could if she were here, but she is gone just now. After the holidays, she is going to be relocating. She has been very secretive about it but has promised to tell us this week where she will be going. She has always been a good daughter, and we trust her, but we are anxious to know what she will be doing. All we know is that she has been talking to a young man quite a bit and went to meet him a while back."

Danny tried not to show the disappointment in his voice as he said, "Would you please tell her I just called to say hello and that I wish her the best in whatever she does?"

"I certainly will, Danny, and we wish all the best for you. Please come to see us if you are ever in the area."

"Thank you. I would love to do that. Good-bye."

He felt worse now than he did before. Was she finally interested in someone romantically? That could have been what the trip to Florida was all about. He still felt a need to know where she was and that she was safe. If she ever married, he might feel differently about it; however, that thought was not very pleasant to him.

When Jake and Katie returned, Danny told them about his phone call.

"I called today to wish the Salims happy holidays and talked with Mrs. Salim. Amee was not at home, but Mrs. Salim told me she's transferring to another school and hasn't even told them where she's going yet. I don't know what the secrecy is all about."

A mother's eyes miss very little, and her heart misses nothing. She knew how disappointed Danny was. She came over and kissed him and said, "I'm sorry; it looks like you and Amee have a star-crossed relationship. I wish things had gone better for you, but one day that perfect someone will come along and everything will be all right."

Danny loved his mother dearly and appreciated her concern, but his only thought just then was that the perfect person had already come and gone. Danny applied himself even more diligently to his assignment and finally finished the first draft of his thesis. Jake and Katie drove him back to Atlanta Hartsfield Airport, and on the way, they discussed plans for them to come to graduation.

"I'll meet you at the Denver airport and drive you down to Colorado Springs. After graduation, we will do some sightseeing.

"That'll be wonderful," Jake said. "As long as we see Pikes Peak."

"It'll be first on the list," Danny promised.

The airport was extremely busy, so they dropped him off at curbside. As he walked through the crowds of people, he observed that they were unusually happy.

George H.W. Bush had won a lopsided victory in the presidential election in November, pledging to continue the Reagan policies, but he also promised "a kinder and gentler nation" in order to win over some of the moderate voters. There were some people in the world, however, who had other things on their minds except kinder and gentler thoughts toward the United States.

After he finished his dinner, Danny settled back to get a little sleep. The flight was smooth, and he didn't arouse until he heard the thud of the landing gear locking into place. As he looked out of his window and saw that it was snowing quite heavily, he knew the hour and a half drive to the academy would be quite a bit longer that night. However, he had missed most of the crowd at the airport, so it didn't take him long to get to the parking lot and his beloved truck. He had bought the '65 Chevy at the end of his first year in college and rebuilt it himself from the frame up. He painted it candy apple red and installed a 350 engine and a Hurst shifter. He finished it off with rolled and pleated leather seats. It was his baby. It took him a few minutes to dig it out of the igloo nature had built around it in his absence, and he could already feel the thinness of the air as he shoveled, scraped, and brushed.

Colorado is a very seductive wench, however, and had soon cast her spell on him again. The beauty of the moonlit scene soon made him forget all the inconvenience of such a climate. The stars, which were beginning to break through the clouds, looked like sequins on a black mantle. The snow-covered trees sparkled brilliantly as they shivered in the wind, and the snow lay in symmetrical drifts like a ruffled white blanket. On the drive back to the academy, Danny began to focus once again on what lay ahead for him.

The next morning, he headed off to get a cup of coffee and look through the bundle of mail he had just picked up at the student post office. Most of it was junk, but he had a note from Dr. Rubenstein advising him of a meeting at 2100 hours that night. He was so absorbed in looking through the mail that he didn't see the form appearing from behind until suddenly his eyes were covered and he heard, "Guess who?"

He didn't have to guess but whirled around to come face to face with Amee. "Wh ... What? How?"

"Having trouble talking, old man?" she said as she giggled like crazy.

"I don't understand. What're you doing here?" They were just standing there holding hands.

"I apologize for doing things this way, Danny. I wanted to call you and even picked up the telephone a couple of times to dial, but I just couldn't get up the nerve. I didn't know what was going on in your life and was afraid if I talked to you by phone that I wouldn't get to see you in person."

Amee never stopped surprising him. Suddenly, she took his head in her hands and gave him a kiss on each cheek.

"Now I'll try to explain. A long time ago, I decided I wanted to become a United States citizen and spend my life here. I was stalled at every turn and realized it was going to be a difficult, drawn out matter, so I became pretty discouraged. Then one day a wonderful opportunity came my way. Recruiters came to MIT looking for people in certain fields to join the U.S. military. I made application, and they were interested in me. They promised if I would join the United States Air Force, they would mainstream my application for citizenship, so here I am! It's all a winning situation for me. I get my citizenship, a free education for a year and a half, a chance to prove my loyalty to this country, and I get to be with you, for a while at least."

"I understand your excitement about the citizenship, but I don't quite get how that makes any difference in our relationship," Danny said with a puzzled look.

"Right now, it doesn't really, but who knows what the future holds? I don't know how either of us will handle being together, but right now I am content to be where you are. My mom and dad want to live permanently in America also. They didn't object to me joining the air force but were concerned about us being together again. They both like you but warned me about allowing our relationship to take the wrong turn.

She blushed as she continued. "Oh, but have I assumed too much? I don't even know what's going on with you now. Maybe you have someone else in your life."

"I have to be honest and tell you that I have a mistress."

The astonished look on Amee's face almost made him ashamed of himself for what he was doing—but not quite.

"Yes and she's very demanding; her name is Miss Air Force Academy."

"Oh, you're a wicked man, Daniel Brannigan."

"Well, there have been many beautiful girls who threw themselves at my feet, but so far I've managed to escape them all. I still love you, but I've made some changes in my life and can handle things differently now. However, I don't know if I can be near you all the time without showing you my love."

"I totally understand," Amee replied. "I will have the same problem."

"I have decided that I could never marry you, though, so that's not a problem," Danny said rather sternly.

As hard as she tried, Amee could not keep the tears from welling up. "Why would you not want to marry me if you could?"

"I believe you will agree with me when I explain," Danny continued. "I'm concerned about us having children together." He tried to speak in solemn tones, but a grin was already beginning to form at the corners of his mouth. "I would be very worried about what they would look like," he went on. "They might look like skunks with black hair except for one blond streak down the middle. What's worse is that they might have one black eye and one blue one."

Danny thought he heard a rib crack when Amee punched him. As he bent over in both real and mock pain, she said, "What's the matter, old man? Can't you take a little punch from a girl? You know, I could make it so that you never have to worry about having children."

Danny pretended to put her in a headlock and whispered in her ear, "Oh, how I've missed my Sunday's Child."

It was as if they had never been separated. Danny explained that he had a meeting to attend, so they agreed to meet at 1000 hours the next morning and take a ride out into the country.

When Danny arrived at Dr. Rubenstein's office, Adams, as he always referred to himself, was also there. He was the most impersonal man Danny had ever met and had no sense of humor at all. His features fit his personality. He was about five feet ten inches tall, stocky, and athletic. He had closely cut hair, a receding hairline, and a chiseled face. His nose, which showed evidence of having been broken at least once, was accented by a crescent scar that circled under his left cheekbone. When he spoke, his eyes squinted slightly.

"We've been experiencing random acts of terrorism for several years. Now, hijackings, bombings, and assassinations are occurring at an alarming rate. A dangerous pattern is developing with respect to Islamic terrorists, which will be our primary objective. Some within our intelligence community believe these acts of terrorism will take on staggering proportions in the future. This view is not unanimous, but enough of the right people are convinced that we have been authorized to form a special intelligence force. There are others in our group whom you will get to know when the need arises, but we believe the less you know about each other, the safer you all will be."

Adolph Rubenstein was the exact opposite of Mr. Adams in every way. He was a short, pudgy man with wavy salt and pepper hair, bushy eyebrows, and a thick mustache. He was soft spoken and still had a fairly thick German accent. He could have been anyone's favorite uncle. Most of the time, when he spoke, he had a twinkle in his eyes, but when he was serious, his eyes became piercing and a bit intimidating. Dr. R, as Danny began to refer to him, was a special advisor because of what he had experienced in the past. He said, "Danny, I want to encourage you in what you're doing. I lived through some awful days in my old country, and nothing is more important than preserving democracy."

Danny later learned that Dr. R lived through much of World War II in a German concentration camp. He was the only member of his immediate family to survive. His mother and father, along with all his siblings, died either in the gas chambers or at the hands of some Nazi butcher.

Mr. Adams spoke again. "Danny, there's one more thing I must tell you. We have tried to become knowledgeable about every Muslim we can in the United States, and in so doing, we came across the family of Doctor Ishmael Salim. We know you had some contact with them in Georgia, which makes it imperative that we know what transpires with them. When it came to our attention that Ameenah Salim had applied for citizenship, I asked the air force recruiter to make contact with her to see if we could get her out here by offering her a fast track to citizenship. It's best all around to do so because she has a tremendous aptitude for computer science. If she proves loyal, she will be a great asset to us, and if not, we'll have her under better surveillance. She accepted our offer."

What he didn't reveal to Danny was that they were the ones who had delayed her citizenship in the first place. The thought of Amee doing anything treasonous was ludicrous to Danny.

"Sir, I have just seen her, and honesty compels me to tell you that if it weren't for the religious differences between us, our relationship would be much closer than it is. You are barking up the wrong tree if you think she or her family will be disloyal to our country in any way."

"I certainly hope you are right, but we're also keeping a close eye on the rest of the family, as we are all Muslims. We'll be in contact later."

With that, the meeting was over.

Danny had a major conflict in his soul. On the one hand, he was glad Amee was there, no matter what it took to bring her, but on the other, he was angry with Mr. Adams for the way he was treating the Salim family. However, there were other thoughts clamoring for attention that pushed this aside for the time being. He kept thinking about the millions who had died at the hands of Adolph Hitler simply because of his thirst for power and his hatred for the Jews. As Danny studied that period of history, he was impressed by the fact that people in many countries sat idly by and let it happen because it didn't directly affect them, while people in Germany did nothing until it was too late. He was affected deeply by Pastor Martin Niemoller's poem. Pastor Niemoller had been an early supporter of Hitler, but later opposed him.

> He said, "In Germany, they came first for the Communists, and I didn't speak up because I wasn't a Communist; And then they came for the trade unionists, and I didn't speak

> up because I wasn't a trade unionist; And then they came for the Jews, and I didn't speak up because I wasn't a Jew; And then they came for me, and by that time there was no one left to speak up."

There were a few voices crying in the wilderness, such as that of Sir Winston Churchill, trying to warn the world, but for the most part, they were ignored until the entire planet was threatened. Danny sincerely hoped history would not repeat itself with reference to the terrorists. If it did, he would not be numbered among those guilty of sitting idly by while it happened.

When Danny pulled up in front of Amee's dorm the next morning, she was already outside, sitting on the steps. Not to appear anxious, she was reading. When he reached over to open the door for her, he kissed her on the cheek. As he did he said, "You surely are beautiful today. I don't know if I want to take you out in public because I might have to beat the guys off."

She said, "Flattery will get you everywhere, so what're you setting me up for?"

"Oh, you stab me in the heart," Danny responded. "My absolutely sincere heart."

"All right. I humbly apologize."

"Do you want something to eat or drink?" Danny inquired.

"No, thank you. I'm fine right now."

She thought Danny's truck was the coolest thing she had ever seen. She especially liked the red color and the leather seats. He explained that he had chosen it because it was made the same year he was born.

"Wow! It's as old as you, and it's still running. As soon as we have time, you have to teach me to drive it."

Danny responded, "I'm sorry, but I only engage in safe activities like flying jets, jumping out of airplanes, and walking through snake-infested jungles."

His ribs, still sore from the day before, sustained another blow.

"Jodie told me I just missed you when I went to Florida, and I was so disappointed. It was probably for the best, though, because I never could keep a secret from you. I was scheduled to meet with some folks on Monday at Cape Canaveral to discuss computers and take some final tests, but I received a call on Friday and had to rush on down for a Saturday meeting. One of the key people wouldn't be available on Monday, and that meeting was a part of the approval process for me to come here. The final decision took longer than I anticipated, delaying my arrival until this semester."

They spent the rest of that week just hanging out together. It really didn't matter what they were doing; they were together again and that was all that was important. The closest they came to a problem was when Danny tried to teach Amee to drive his truck and she ground the gears.

She teasingly asked, "Which one of us do you love the most?"

"Well, you know girls are everywhere and easily replaced, but this truck is one of a kind," he said.

"You don't seem to have too many girls standing in line, so I think you have already realized that I'm irreplaceable. Besides, maybe you would prefer to hug and kiss your truck."

"All right, you are truly unique and would be impossible to replace, but could I still try to keep my truck in good shape?"

When school started back, the only time they had for each other was on the weekends and once in a while to study for the only two classes they had together.

Ever since Danny learned that on the return to earth, the space shuttle actually landed as a glider, he became interested in every flight. He was excited because it proved his theory about gliders. He was watching on January 28 as the *Columbia* disintegrated seventy-three seconds after lift off. He grieved along with the rest of America for the loss of the crewmembers, but it didn't dampen his enthusiasm for the space program at all.

Chapter 9

"Mom, do you have your bags all packed for a trip to Colorado?"

Graduation was only three weeks away now, and Danny had called to finalize plans with his parents.

"I don't think I've ever seen Jake so excited about anything." Katie laughed. "He has packed and repacked three times already."

"Activities actually begin on Sunday morning with an optional baccalaureate service and other religious services. It's up to you, but we have no obligation to attend those. I'll share the rest of the schedule when you get here, but I will be finished with everything by Wednesday afternoon."

Jake had been listening on the extension and said, "Don't forget about Pikes Peak."

"We'll go there first," Danny assured him. "It's less than two hours away, and there's a nice place to spend the night if you would like more than one day."

"I'll call back with the specifics as soon as our flight plans are certain," Katie assured him.

"By the way, I hope you don't mind if Amee comes along."

They assured him they would love to have her.

"Okay then. I'll wait to hear from you about your flight."

Danny had told Katie and Jake about Amee coming to the academy, explaining that it was a way to gain her citizenship more quickly. Although Danny still had some issues of his own to resolve with the Lord, he determined to learn about Islam so he could at least understand Amee's problem. With his college work finished, this would be as good a time as any to start. In the religious section of the bookstore downtown, he found a book entitled *Understanding Islam.* By the time he was finished reading it, he knew more about the subject than most people in America. He condensed what he learned down to a few pages for quick reference.

The religion originated with the teachings of Mohammed in the seventh century. *Islam,* which is the second largest religion in the world, means *submission* or *total surrender of oneself to God.* Adherents, which are called *Muslims,* believe God revealed the Koran, the basis of Islamic beliefs, to Mohammed. They do not regard Mohammed as the originator of a new religion, but as the final prophet who restored the original monotheistic religion of Abraham. They believe that Christianity and Judaism have distorted it. Muslims are required to observe the five pillars of Islam, which are: (1) *Shahadah,* a profession of faith, which says, "I testify there is no Ila but Allah and that Mohammed is the messenger of Allah;" (2) *Shalah,* ritual prayer every Muslim must observe five times a day; (3) *Zakah,* an alms tax to help the needy; (4) *Sawm,* fasting, of which there are three types: ritual (fasting during Ramadan), penitent, and ascetic; (5) *Hajj,* pilgrimage to Mecca.

In addition to the five pillars, there is Islamic Law (Sharia), which literally means *the path leading to the watering hole.* This is a tradition of rulings that have developed over the years, which touch on virtually every aspect of life and society. All Muslims must believe in God, his revelations, his angels, his messengers, and the day of judgment. Jews and Christians are referred to as "People of the Book." There are two groups of Muslims. Roughly eighty-five percent are Sunni and fifteen percent are Shi'a. The schism between them came in the late seventh century over differences concerning religious and political leadership of the Islamic community. Unique to the Shi'a is the doctrine of *Imamah,* political and religious leadership of the Imams, which, in effect, establishes an Islamic state.

Muslims believe there is one God and that the doctrine of the trinity is polytheism. They believe Jesus was a man. The Koran states, "Allah does not beget." They believe the Koran is the literal word of God, revealed to Mohammed by the angel Gabriel. Qur'an means *recitation.* Mohammed preached to the people of Mecca, but he and his followers were persecuted and migrated to Medina, where the first political and religious government was established. They believe in a day of resurrection (bodily) and a day of judgment, when certain sins will condemn one to hell. They also believe in paradise.

Muslims believe that everything is preordained of God but that man has a free will to choose between good and evil. *Jihad* means *to strive or struggle* and is normally used to refer to military combat against Muslim enemies. Jihad is the only kind of war permissible in Islamic law and may be declared against non-Muslims who refuse to convert to Islam. In effect, Jihad is perpetual until or unless there is world Muslim domination. Jihad is sometimes called the sixth pillar. *Ramadan,* the month in which the Koran was revealed, is the holiest of months. *Ramadan* comes from a root meaning *to burn.* It occurs sometime during our September, October, and November and begins at the first sighting of the full moon. Muslims observe a lunar calendar.

In order to gain a complete understanding of Islam, Danny would have to read the Koran and study Sharia law, which he resolved to do. He had no idea whether this would be important, but he was beginning to understand what an impregnable barrier existed between Amee and him. He knew Amee had been born into her religion, just as he was born into his, but even though he had many unresolved issues, he believed the Bible and that Jesus was the Son of God.

The mountains in the higher elevations still looked like craggy old men in their white nightcaps when Jake and Katie's plane landed in Denver, even though it was May. However, the sun was playing peek-a-boo behind them, and the weather in Colorado Springs was absolutely beautiful. Danny and Amee were waiting for them at the gate, and the four of them had a joyful reunion with alternating hugs, kisses, tears, and laughter. Jake and Katie had not seen Amee for four years and could not believe the mature woman who stood before them. They couldn't actually say she had grown up because she was still the same size as when last they saw her.

"Amee, it's so good to see you; we've missed you," Katie said as she hugged her.

She was a bit surprised when Amee gave her a kiss on each cheek. Jake just grinned shyly as she gave him the same greeting. He drawled his grin just as he did his words.

They had come on Thursday so they would have time to rest and prepare for all the festivities surrounding graduation. Danny rented a car, fearing the fellowship might be a bit too close in his little red pickup. As they drove to Colorado Springs, it was a wonder anyone knew what anyone else was saying, because they all talked excitedly at the same time. Finally, the talk split into two conversations. Jake and Danny were talking about the farm, the air force, and Pikes Peak, while Katie and Amee were talking about what they were going to wear and who was doing what back in Perryville. They stopped for a bite to eat at Danny and Amee's favorite place, and then it was off to the motel so Jake and Katie could get a good night's rest. They agreed to meet for breakfast at nine the next morning.

After they left the motel, Danny was very quiet, especially in light of the fact that he was about to graduate and his parents were there.

"Sweetheart, what's wrong?" Amee asked.

"Oh, nothing really. I guess I'm just tired."

"Danny, you know you can't fool me; I know you too well. This should be one of the happiest times of your life, and normally you'd be hyper. Please tell me what's bothering you, and maybe I can help."

For the first time in his life, Danny was afraid—not of any person or challenge—but he was afraid of what was going to happen to him and Amee. He could not imagine life without her, but he knew, even if she did not, that there were at least two forces trying to pry them apart forever. When she learned what his primary mission was, how could she help but be angry? It was also very unlikely that either of them would change religions. He was glad his parents were there, but neither that nor graduation nor anything else would mean much without Amee.

For four years he had shared everything with her, but how could he talk to her about this? Yet he knew they would soon be separated while she finished her final year at the academy and he went on to wherever he was assigned. He *must* talk to her, although he would rather have faced a firing squad. Again, he was on the precipice of the greatest disaster he could ever imagine—losing his beloved Amee. If it happened again, it would no doubt be forever. Finally, he resolved to do what must be done.

"There is something bothering me deeply, but I just don't know what to do about it."

"Danny, I love you. Please let me help if I can."

His voice was breaking now. "The problem is it concerns you, and I'm so afraid it will tear us apart again."

"Then we *must* talk about it," Amee said, the apprehension obvious in her voice. "What could possibly be so bad?"

Danny felt that he was about to fire the first shot in a hopeless war, yet he had no choice but to pull the trigger. It might not be the shot heard around the world, but it could very well be the shot that destroyed his world. The moment of truth had come.

"Sweetheart, since the day we met, religion has hung over our heads like a dark cloud. It has been the only barrier between us, but it seems to be one we can't cross. Our problem is that neither of us can accept the other's faith."

Danny paused for a moment, and Amee quickly seized the opportunity to propose a solution. She was afraid it was now or never. She said pleadingly, "It would obviously present many problems if either of us were to change, but why couldn't we just give up both ways, have a civil wedding, and be happy together?"

Danny could understand why that would seem like a perfectly good compromise to her because she did not know what it meant to be a born-again Christian. But how could he possibly explain that to her without seeming arrogant?

"I've been a very poor Christian, and even today I have some unresolved conflicts in my heart, but I do believe the Bible and that Jesus is God's Son. I know I could never give that up, and I'm sure it would be just as impossible for you to ever give up your beliefs. There is also another issue that doesn't involve us personally that I can't discuss at this time."

"Well, don't be so mysterious about it. Tell me what it is," Amee responded.

"I don't mean for it to be that way; I'm just under special orders that could be a problem. I think we will have to discuss it before everything will be clear between us, but I'm not at liberty to do that now."

"I can't imagine anything that would be that serious between us about your work since we are both in the air force, but I will trust you until you can talk about it," Amee assured him.

"Darling, I have the advantage over you in the matter of religion because I've been able to seriously study Islam, and you have not studied Christianity. All I ask is that you do what I've done in respect to Islam and read at least one book about Christianity. Will your love for me allow you to do that? I solemnly promise that I will never try to pressure you or talk you into anything."

"Danny, I love you so much. There is nothing I wouldn't do for you, so I will do this. I have to warn you, though, not to get your heart set on anything because it sounds like a fairy tale to me that God had a son whom he sent to earth by way of a virgin birth."

Danny had accomplished all he could hope to at this point.

After he left Amee that night, he made up his mind that he would get the best book ever written about Christianity for her to read. Could he dare hope that she might become a Christian? It would certainly take a miracle from the Lord, because to do so, an Arab Muslim would have to believe in a Jewish Savior!

Chapter 10

Danny didn't get much sleep that night, partly because of worry and partly because of thinking about just the right book for Amee to read. On Saturday, he would be the first customer in line at the little bookstore downtown. If he didn't find one there, he had already determined that, graduation or not, he would make a trip into Denver to a larger store. Even though the strain of all this was obvious, Amee's sweetness still prevailed. As she got in the car, she slid across the seat, leaned over, and kissed Danny on the cheek and held on to his arm like her life depended on it. They both knew they had to put all this aside for now and try not to let their feelings show as they met Jake and Katie.

Mothers are never fooled long, and the first time she had the opportunity, Katie whispered in Danny' ear, "What's wrong with the two of you this morning? Do you have some kind of problem?"

"No, Mom, the strain of this weekend and the fact that we'll soon have to be separated is just wearing on us."

All of this was true, but it certainly wasn't the whole truth. This was one time Danny felt he couldn't talk to his parents about his problem. All day, it was like a shadowy figure lurking around the edges of their minds, just waiting to sneak back into their consciousness, but they were able to keep it at bay most of the time and enjoy being with Jake and Katie.

Amee and Katie were going to get their hair and nails done, and Katie was going to get a facial. That was one thing Amee didn't need because her complexion was very nearly perfect. Katie told her how jealous she was. Danny asked Jake if he wanted to get a manicure, and Jake just gave him a dirty look and held up his gnarled hands with nails that looked like he had scratched his way through a concrete wall. They were going to visit the huge Rocky Mountain Outfitters store that was nearby. Later, they would pick up the girls for a late lunch.

That day, Katie and Amee fell in love with each other. They had more things in common than any two women from different worlds would ever be expected to have. The most important thing they had in common was that they both loved Danny immensely. They both were women of strength, character, and integrity, and if you could have taken away their cultural and religious differences, they could have been mother and daughter. Jake and Danny both loved the outdoors, and they enjoyed leisurely browsing through the gigantic store. After a while, Jake suggested that they sit down for a few minutes and have a cup of coffee.

For the first time, Jake asked Danny about his future. "After graduation, what will you be doing, and where will you go first?"

Danny wished he could tell him everything and talk with him about so many questions that were on his mind, but he dared not disobey orders. "I don't yet know where I'll be assigned, but I will find that out after my two-week furlough. All I know is that I will go for flight training somewhere." What Jake said next astounded Danny.

"Danny Boy, I believe we are entering a period of grave danger in the world and especially for our country. I don't believe communism ever posed as great a threat for the world as does the Islamic revolution that is underway."

Danny must have looked quizzical as he thought, *Is this really coming out of Jake's mouth, a cowboy from Texas?*

Jake continued, "According to the Koran, Muslims must pursue world domination, so jihad will never be over until the entire world is Islamic. They do not have armies that can compete with the superpowers, or many other developed nations of the world, and at present, they can't even stand up to Israel. They must resort to terrorism, of which we have already seen the beginnings."

By now, Danny's mouth was open. "How do you know all this, and why is this the first time you have mentioned it?"

Jake smiled at his astonishment as he responded, "You didn't think an old Texican farmhand like me thought about such weighty matters, huh? Well, all I know is what I read in the papers and see on the television, plus a few books I've read. If you study the life of Mohammed, you'll find that he employed such tactics in his battles with the people of Mecca, and most of the terrorism we have seen in the last several years has been done by Arabs."

"Why do you think this is happening now?" Danny asked.

"There's one paramount reason: their hatred for Israel. Mind you, not all individual Muslims are this radical, but more and more leaders are arising who are sworn to the destruction of Israel, as well as all nations who support them. Along with this is the renewed zeal to establish Islamic fundamentalist states."

Danny felt like he was listening to a stranger. Even the vocabulary was different from what he had ever heard from Jake before.

Jake continued, "The displacement of the Palestinians and the return of more and more Jews to Israel is only exacerbating the situation. There are also many Islamic purists who believe Western nations are raping their countries for oil and that infidels defile their land by their very presence. They want all Westerners off the Arabian Peninsula."

Danny would try to sort out his perplexity about the two Jakes later. Right now, as always, he was primarily interested in only one Muslim. Was Jake right? If he were, what did she think about all of this? Surely there must be some answers for sane people that would prevent these awful things from happening.

Danny asked pleadingly, "Can't something be worked out, starting with Israel? Can't there be a Palestinian state alongside Israel?

"Danny, they don't want a Palestinian state alongside Israel; they want a Palestinian state *instead* of Israel. They believe if they can alienate Israel's defenders, they can destroy her. They believe intimidation by terrorism is the best way to accomplish that. They have promised to leave those nations alone who do not support or defend Israel."

"There must be many more good Muslims than there are radicals," Danny protested. "Why don't they rise up against it?"

"No doubt there are, but fear and intimidation are also used against them. I'm sure you are aware of what happened to the shah in Iran, and I believe we will see more of the same."

"I've never heard you talk like this," Danny said. "And I have to ask why you're so interested and how you know so much about it. It's like you have an alternate persona."

Jake laughed. "There's no way to explain why people become interested in the things they do. Some folks get involved in sports, politics, or history, but I got interested in this, because I'm Jewish and because of what happened in Germany. I have read extensively and paid attention to all the news coverage, and it all just became clear. More people would understand the danger if only they were interested enough to listen and learn, but they are too busy playing games."

The explanation was believable enough, but Danny was still baffled about the change in Jake's personality and vocabulary. *Oh well,* he thought, *some things are just beyond logical understanding.* However, if Jake was right, all this certainly helped explain why Mr. Adams's project was authorized. What concerned Danny the most was what all this was going to do to Amee.

For a while at least, Danny's mind had not been on his and Amee's personal problem, but thinking about her brought it painfully back.

"Danny, Danny!"

Danny looked at Jake like someone coming out of a trance.

"Welcome back. Where have you been?" Jake asked with a great deal of amusement.

"Sorry, my mind just took a detour for a few minutes."

Jake laughed. "Down Amee Boulevard, I expect."

Jake was Danny's salvation that day because he kept him occupied one way or another. Jake took his last sip of coffee and asked, "Don't you suppose we ought to be heading back to pick up the girls? I think I've seen enough outdoor stuff today anyway."

Danny glanced at his watch and couldn't believe the time. "Yeah, I guess we'd better, or they'll think we got lost."

They had agreed to meet at the sidewalk café in the mall where they had dropped the girls off. As they drove up, Katie and Amee were just coming down the street, chattering away and laughing.

"Well, I see we're not late after all. I'm not sure we were even missed," Danny said.

He was impressed at how radiant his mother was after her facial and suggested she do more of that sort of thing. What the girls hadn't told them yet was that they had also gotten a massage.

Whether Jake and Katie were really that tired or just pretended to be in order to give the kids some time alone, they asked to go back to their room early so they could rest. There was an unspoken agreement between Amee and Danny that they shouldn't continue their discussion that night. They just chatted about the day until they got to Amee's barracks.

Danny walked her to the door and whispered, "I love you very much," as he gently kissed her ear.

Saturday morning found Danny at the bookstore when it opened at ten. There were several books of the sort he was interested in, and he was delighted to find one he was sure was just right. It was a simple, straightforward book entitled *Who is God?* It made a strong case for a God who is just but loving and merciful and sent his Son to redeem sinful man. He could hardly wait to meet Amee for brunch. Since they wouldn't meet Jake and Katie until dinner, they would have plenty of time to talk. She was very subdued but looked like she had at least gotten some rest.

"Sweetheart, I don't know what you've heard, seen, or read, but please keep in mind that there have been many perversions, distortions, and abuses of Christianity through the centuries. Many outright atrocities have been committed in the name of Jesus Christ that he would never have sanctioned. The only way to know what he really taught is to read the Bible, but the entire Bible is probably a bit overwhelming for you at this point. I have marked the *Gospel of John* and the book of *Romans,* and to help you understand a bit better, I also have a short book for you. Reading these things together will help you understand what I believe and why. Many Christians, including me, reject much of institutional Christianity as it has been practiced, but there has always been a group of true believers. I renew my promise to you not to pressure you in any way, but if there is something you don't understand, please ask me about it."

"I will keep my promise," Amee responded. "But I must also repeat my caution to you. At this point, I don't see how I could ever embrace Christianity. I could, and probably would, lie to you if I thought it would keep us together, but I know our relationship must be based on truth."

Her words kept ringing in his ears, and his heart felt like lead in his chest. He knew all too well what it meant if she did not become a Christian. The only hope he had left was God's divine intervention.

They attended the baccalaureate service the next morning and the reception for cadets and their families at one o'clock. Individual awards were presented on Monday afternoon, and at five o'clock the Muslim convocation was held. Although Amee wasn't a graduate, she wanted to attend, so Danny spent the time with Katie and Jake. He couldn't help but wonder if Amee was trying to make a statement. The graduation parade was Tuesday morning from 9:30 to 11:00, with the graduation reception at 6:00 p.m. and the swearing in ceremony at 7:30.

When he rejoined his family after he was sworn in, they all saluted and said, "Congratulations, Lieutenant Brannigan."

At that moment, it hit Danny that he was officially in the air force.

Wednesday at 10:00 was graduation and beginning at 12:45 was outprocessing. Danny was now totally finished with the academy and was free to begin his furlough.

Early Thursday morning, Lieutenant Brannigan and his party were on their way to Pikes Peak, and Jake was as excited as a ten-year-old child at his first circus. In order to make the trip more economical, the ladies planned to stay in one room and the men in another. That arrangement was good because of Amee and Katie's closeness, and Danny hoped to talk further with Jake about his views on the coming problems with Islam.

Even though it was summer, after their Pikes Peak visit, they went to Aspen and Vail, which were beautiful at any season. It was then on to Mesa Verde National Park and the mining and ranching town of Durango. There was also time for fishing in the Piedra River for Danny and Jake. The ladies passed the time wading in the shallow water, walking across the rocks, and talking.

One morning when Danny greeted his mother with a kiss and a hug, she whispered in his ear, "Amee is talking to me in confidence, so I can't discuss the details, but I want you to know she is asking lots of questions about the book you gave her."

Hope was again rekindled in Danny's heart. He was filled with excitement as he thought about the possibility of Amee becoming a Christian and the change that could make in their relationship. Even in the midst of his uncertainty, Danny couldn't help thinking how good God was to put Amee with his mother. Katie was one of the purest Christians he had ever known. She was kind and loving but unwavering in her faith. She knew what she believed and why, and Amee sincerely loved and respected her.

Danny was still intrigued by his conversation with Jake. "In what way do you think the terrorists will attack?" Danny asked Jake one night as they were preparing for bed.

"You're really into this, aren't you?" Jake said. Even though this was deadly serious, he couldn't help but chuckle. "I believe they will target the United States and Israel primarily and possibly the United Kingdom. They will try to kill large numbers of people, preferably on American soil, and they will certainly want to harm the economy of any nation they attack. Because of what I have read in some Islamic teachings, I believe we will see more and more Muslims willing to commit suicide in order to accomplish their purpose. If they die for Allah, they are promised immediate entrance into heaven with seventy-two black-eyed virgins awaiting them.

"One very important part of their strategy will be to make Israel look like the bad guys, and given the bias of the worldwide news media, that won't be difficult to do. The terrorists don't really care about the loss of life on either side as long as their objective is accomplished. They'll try to antagonize Israel until she retaliates and then show the world all the civilian casualties. It will also be important to them to try to draw Israel into conflict with any Arab country they possibly can. They will assassinate any leader and attack any nation who is willing to negotiate with the Jews.

The last thing they want is peace between Israel and either the Palestinians or Syria. To sum it up, they want to make Israel and anyone who defends or assists her look bad in the eyes of the world community."

Danny was puzzled. "As powerful as our country is, how can they hope to do this?"

Jake explained, "This will be a different kind of attack; it will be from the inside. Our immigration policies are very generous and our borders extremely porous. Since we are an open society, people move about freely. It is commonly believed that moles under deep cover are already in the United States, much like Russian spies were during the Cold War. Remember that Arabs are an ancient people and have learned to be very patient. They have already proven that they will try to use airplanes, either by planting bombs on them or commandeering them for their purposes."

Danny just shook his head. Had he not been recruited for the purpose he was and given special information, he would have concluded that Jake was crazy. "Most Americans would agree that they ought to come get you and take you away to some quiet sanitarium so you can rest and regain your senses."

"You're right, Danny, and that's precisely why their plan will work. I don't talk about this to other people. What others think about me doesn't matter, but what do you think?"

At that moment, Danny wished he could tell him everything, but he simply said, "You might think this strange, but I believe you're right. I've done a little studying of my own, although I certainly haven't taken it to the extent you have."

Danny wondered if Jake hadn't come into his life for this very time. Although he didn't have any idea what Danny was doing, everything he said reaffirmed Danny's decision. Long after Jake was snoring, he was pondering all that was going on in his life. He was amazed at how quickly his simple life had become so complicated. According to his original plans, he should be pitching major league baseball by now with no more serious decision to make than what the next pitch ought to be and no greater worry than how he could have blown his last outing so badly. He wanted to scream to the world, "Has anyone noticed that I'm only twenty-one years old?"

Friday, the day of Jake and Katie's departure, came quickly. When the hugs and kisses were over and all the tears were shed, they finally disappeared down the jet way. As Danny watched them go, he suddenly realized that he was entering an entirely new era of his life. He and Amee walked quietly back through the airport hand in hand. They were sad because Danny's parents were gone, but the thing that contributed the most to their somber mood was what lay ahead for them. Time and distance would separate them, but both of these could be overcome. What weighed heaviest upon them was whether they would also be separated by something that could not be overcome.

Chapter 11

The next day, Danny received his assignment to report to the Forty-seventh Flying Training Wing at Laughlin Air Force Base near Del Rio, Texas. He would be there for approximately fifty-four weeks, training to fly fighter jets. He was excited about everything that lay ahead for him, except that he would be almost nine hundred miles from Amee and would only get to see her on holidays. He didn't know if absence would make the heart grow fonder or allow love to grow cold. He knew the best thing for her would be to meet some Muslim man whom she could love and marry, but his heart just would not accept what his mind told it.

The only hope he had was that they could solve the only problem that existed between them.

Danny had picked a place for dinner where they could virtually be alone. "I received my orders today," he said after they finished eating.

Tears were already welling up as Amee took his hands in hers and just looked at him with those big sad black eyes.

"I'll be in Texas, and I only have three days before I have to report."

"I want to spend every minute of it with you," Amee said through her tears. She had one week left before summer school started. The only comfort either of them could find was that they would be extremely busy for the next year.

"Sweetheart, I don't want it to ruin our last few days, but I'm very concerned about the religious barrier between us," Danny said plaintively.

Amee's demeanor changed from sad to sober as she replied, "I'm really seeking an answer *and* praying for one, but I don't know what it could possibly be at this point. I read the Bible references you marked and the book you gave me, and while it is a beautiful story and would be wonderful if it were true, there are just some things I can't accept. I don't believe God has a son because the Koran teaches us that Allah does not beget."

"Let's just let it go for now, but don't give up on it," Danny replied wistfully.

Danny was able to catch a hop from Peterson Air Force Base to Laughlin on a C5A cargo plane, the largest plane ever built with a payload of 265,000 pounds. The only ray of sunshine in his otherwise dark world was the prospect of flying on that plane. Since they had a light load, a friend had even pulled some strings that allowed him to take his truck with him. It was raining lightly, so he and

Amee stood just inside the hangar until the plane was ready. All too soon, the staff sergeant waved to him that the bitter moment had come. On days like this, Amee's hair would curl on its own. She didn't like it, but Danny thought it made her even cuter, and he loved the feel of it on his face. He brushed it back and kissed her, holding her as tightly as a drowning man clings to a life buoy. The only words they spoke were a whispered "I love you" in each other's ear. Now it was absolutely necessary for him to board. At the top of the steps, he turned and they blew each other a kiss. Then he disappeared.

Laughlin Air Force Base, Texas, Summer 1987

"It's one hundred and six degrees down there today, boys. Welcome to southwest Texas." Danny was stirred from his sleep by the copilot's voice over the public address system. He rubbed his eyes and stood to stretch. If there had been a window, he could have seen the Rio Grande and Mexico as they were circling to land. It was obvious he would miss the Colorado weather, but he could handle that. What he missed most about Colorado was not the weather, and he wasn't handling that very well.

The military has a way of keeping people occupied though, and after he reported for duty, he didn't have nearly as much time to think about Amee. He missed her in the evenings, but his worst time was Sunday afternoons. They wrote to each other every week, called when they could, and made plans to be together at Thanksgiving. Danny had never faced anything more rigorous than the year of flight training. First, there was the classroom, then the simulators, and finally the planes themselves. He had a pilot's license for small aircraft but couldn't wait to get his hands on the fighter planes.

Danny had been challenged before, but never like this. The classroom, homework, and the training sessions had his head spinning. Another thing Uncle Cecil would say was, "I'm as dizzy as a boiled owl." That described how Danny felt pretty well. The technical data was enough to boggle his mind. The bright spot was that he was already working with his flight instructor on the T-6A Texas II, a two-seated, single-engine plane used for pilot training. From there he would move on to the T-38A Talon, which was a twin-engine, high-altitude supersonic trainer. The final plane in his course would be the T-1A Jay Hawk. It was a twin-engine, medium-range plane used in the advanced stages of training. Normally, pilots would be assigned to a squadron upon graduation, but Danny's case was unique, so he didn't know what to expect.

Danny had been saving his money since going to Texas and made plans to lease a small plane and fly to Colorado Springs for Thanksgiving.

Thanksgiving week arrived at last. He left early Wednesday morning after his final class on Tuesday. The weather was usually pretty good that time of year all along the corridor he would fly, so he was going to surprise Amee. She knew he was coming but did not expect him until Thursday.

Early Wednesday morning, Danny drove the twenty-four miles just across the Rio Grande to Ciudad Acuna International Airport. He filed his flight plan, and at 7:00 a.m. exactly he taxied out onto the runway. He had rented the same plane a couple of times before to take it up for short flights in order to get familiar with it. His flight was smooth all the way, allowing him to arrive just after 11:00 at Colorado Springs Municipal Airport. He knew Amee would be free at noon, so he rented a car to drive to the academy in order to be there when she got out of class. As he walked toward the building where her class was held, he saw her holding hands with an Arab-looking man and talking excitedly. Then she hugged and kissed him, and he walked away. Danny's heart fell at his feet as he stopped dead in his tracks. Had it finally happened? Had she met a Muslim and become interested in him? Danny was certain that all his fears had come true.

He knew he had to face her, but how could he do it without her knowing something was wrong? He would have run if he could, but he sucked it up and started toward her as he called her name. When she turned and saw him, she ran and leaped into his arms with her legs wrapped around his waist. She kissed him and then began to scold him for surprising her this way. Danny was certain she should be in the movies with all the acting ability she was demonstrating. For the time being, he decided to ignore what he had seen and just wait to see what happened. She would have to talk about it sometime; besides, it would be extremely difficult for him to enjoy any of the weekend under these circumstances. Now he wished he hadn't surprised her; at least that way he could have enjoyed part of his time with her.

"How did you manage to get here so soon? Did you skip class?" Amee asked.

"No, my last class was yesterday, and I had special transportation."

"Special transportation? Did you get another hop?

"No, I flew my own plane."

"Your own plane? What do you mean?"

"Well, it's mine today because I leased it. I wanted to surprise you, so I flew from Ciudad Acuna to Colorado Springs Municipal Airport. It only took about four hours."

"Didn't it cost you a lot of money? How could you afford it?"

"It's not as much as you think, and I've been saving for it."

As they got into the car, Amee said, "I have a surprise for you. There's someone I want you to meet."

Danny was thinking, *I've already been surprised; now all I have to do is meet him.*

He thought it would be best to go along with her and see how it played out. "Oh yeah? Who might that be?"

"I told you it was a surprise. You'll have to wait until tonight. I had already planned to have dinner with him, and I want the two of you to meet."

Danny couldn't believe how nonchalant she was about it; like he wanted to meet the man he saw her kissing, and he certainly didn't want to have dinner with him. He would love to meet him under other circumstances and teach him a little Tae Kwon Do, but at present, he was more upset at Amee. Besides, it would be hard to blame any man for being interested in her.

They had lunch and spent the afternoon together, and as best he could, Danny engaged in small talk about his experiences in Texas and how flight training was coming. Amee talked about her classes and how busy she was.

"Not busy enough," Danny muttered under his breath.

"What did you say?"

"Just that it must be tough," Danny replied.

He was staying at the academy guest quarters and went to get squared away and dressed for the evening while Amee did the same. Things were very quiet around town because many people were away for the holidays. He picked her up at six, and they were to meet her special guest at the restaurant.

Maybe he'll fall and break his neck before he gets there, Danny thought, but no such luck. As they walked into the lobby, there was a handsome young Arab man in all his glory. Danny didn't know him, but he already disliked him.

"Danny, I want you to meet someone that I love with all my heart. We were separated for a while, but he's come back to me." With that, she grabbed the man and kissed him on both cheeks and then on the lips. Danny felt himself getting sick and wanted to run.

"You've actually met him. You just don't remember, do you? Danny, meet Mohammed Salim; Mohammed, meet Danny."

Danny's relief must have all gushed out at once as he exclaimed, "Mo! Is that really you? Man, have you changed. You were just a kid the last time I saw you. Look at you."

Amee started laughing like crazy. "Had you going, didn't I, old man? I could see what you were thinking."

Danny had to confess he had seen them together that morning and was just waiting to see what happened.

"Did you really think I could become interested in someone else that quick?" Amee asked.

"I couldn't blame you if you did," Danny responded. "I'm sure you would be very happy with a Muslim husband."

"Only if I loved him, and I don't love anyone but you."

Danny put his arm around her neck and pulled it into a mock headlock. He pretended to punch her and said, "That's what you get for enjoying my misery."

Mo said, "Excuse me, but may I join this party?"

"Sorry, Mo," they both said at the same time.

"I didn't know Mo was coming until yesterday," Amee explained as they were being seated.

They caught Mo up on things in their lives and vice versa. He had earned a scholarship and was in premed at Boston College. Danny asked about the rest of the family.

"Abb is in the tenth grade, and he does all right in his schoolwork, but his one great passion is soccer. Mom and Dad are well, but Dad is far too busy with his teaching and speaking schedule. He is away quite a lot. As usual, Mom is enjoying her family and entertaining."

The events of the day proved one thing: Danny was not going to be able to give Amee up easily. However, that didn't bring them any closer to a solution for their problem. He had decided not to even bring it up unless she did. Mo was leaving the next day to avoid the crowds at the airport, so they would have two nights alone before Danny had to leave on Sunday.

They drove Mo to the airport early the next day and stayed

with him until his plane left. Very few restaurants were open on Thanksgiving Day, so they had lunch in the academy dining hall, where a special meal was prepared for all those who stayed during the holidays. They had turkey and all the trimmings with special desserts just for the occasion. There wasn't much to do, so they just drove around a bit and then watched the football game on television and talked. Nothing was mentioned on the subject of religion.

They spent most of the day Friday flying. Colorado is a beautiful state to fly over at any season, but it was particularly so at this time. The snow had already started to blanket the upper elevations, and with the leaves gone from the trees, they could see elk, deer, and other animals moving about. Here and there, the smoke was rising from a hunting camp, and occasionally they would see hunters on horseback. It was fun to be able to see both them and their prey at the same time. Amee had never been up in a small plane and was mesmerized by it all. Later in the day, they drove into Denver to the mall to shop a bit and see a movie.

At lunch on Saturday, Amee just picked at her food. It was obvious she was concerned about something. Danny drove to a secluded overlook they had discovered and parked. They walked along a wilderness trail for a few minutes to a place that provided a breathtaking view of the valley below. Danny sat down on a rock and leaned against a tree. Amee sat in his lap with her arms around his neck and her head on his shoulder. For a long time they just sat quietly as Danny waited until she was ready to talk. Suddenly she raised her head and kissed him and spoke as seriously as he had ever heard her speak.

"Danny, I love you, and I'm tired of all the frustration. Let's just go somewhere and be together in the manner we both want to. Let's know complete joy for at least one day."

"I want that more than I can possibly tell you, but because I love you with all my heart, I can't do it. Eventually, you would hate me for it because it would destroy your self- respect, and you would realize that I took it from you. If we can't have each other in the right way, we can't have each other at all."

"I know you're right, but that's what my selfish nature wants. I love you because you're the kind of man you are. You're so strong in every way."

"I'm not nearly as strong as you think I am," Danny confessed.

"I think you have something I don't have," Amee said with a far away look in her eye.

It thrilled Danny that she saw a difference. Could it be that she was seriously thinking about the difference in his faith and hers? He wanted to dive right into a conversation about that, but realized he had better let her decide when it was time to talk about it again.

Again they sat for a long time until the air began to get cool. The only thing that broke the silence was a bird that stopped long enough to serenade them. As they were driving back to the academy, Amee said, "I think the answer will come soon because I can't keep living like this. One way or another, I have to have some relief, and I know you must feel the same way."

Danny didn't say anything, but he was willing to put off the wrong answer as long as he could. Even a little hope was better than none at all.

The sun was just breaking the eastern horizon when Danny picked Amee up on Sunday morning. At that time of day, the mountains to the west were breathtaking because there were no shadows on the eastern slopes. On such a crystal clear day, the snow-covered peaks sparkled like silver in a setting of jade as they jutted out of the evergreens. A doughnut and a cup of coffee would have to do this morning because time was short. Other than being sad at Danny's leaving, Amee was in better spirits. As they sat at breakfast, he looked across the table at her and said, "Well, it's Sunday, and here I am with my Sunday's Child." Amee even giggled a little and replied, "And me with my old man."

She dropped him off at the gate so he could check out the plane and file his flight plan. As soon as that was done, he would be on his way. They only had time for a short and painful good-bye. Neither wanted to break away, but finally Amee pushed him a little and said, "Go on now; it takes old men longer to do things, and I don't want you to be late."

"And little girls shouldn't be smart alecks," Danny said over his shoulder as he walked away.

"Please be safe, my love!" Amee shouted as he disappeared around the side of the hangar.

She drove to a vantage point from which she could see the runway and waited until she saw him take off. As he disappeared from sight, she had a sinking feeling in her heart.

Chapter 12

"Amee, you have a call in the day room," the duty officer said as she woke her from a deep sleep. She wobbled down the hall, rubbing her eyes, and glanced at the clock as she passed by. She was surprised to see that it was only 10:00 p.m.

"Hello?"

"Is this Ameenah Salim?"

"Yes."

"Miss Salim, I'm Colonel Skip Johnson, Daniel Brannigan's flight instructor. He left your name and number as a contact during his visit there."

"Yes, sir. How can I help you?"

"We expected Dan back into Ciudad Acuna by midafternoon, and he still hasn't shown. Can you give us any information about his status?"

Amee's voice was already breaking as she replied, "Sir, he left Colorado Springs this morning around eight. I watched him take off."

"That's really why I'm calling. You see, there is a freak winter storm in the vicinity of Amarillo, and small aircraft warnings have been issued since around 0900 this morning. We have checked with all the airports near his flight pattern, and no one has seen him."

By this time, Amee was sobbing, and Colonel Johnson realized he had been too abrupt in his conversation. He didn't know the intimacy of their relationship.

"I'm so sorry, Ameenah, I didn't mean to upset you. We haven't had any reports of downed planes, and I'm sure he's all right. He might have had to fly around the storm and hasn't been able to get in contact. If we learn anything, we'll let you know."

When Amee got back to her room, her roommate was still up, "What's the matter Amee? Why are you crying?" Sarah asked.

Amee just fell on the bed, sobbing uncontrollably. Finally, she was able to stammer out, "It's Danny; his plane is lost in a storm."

"Oh, honey, I'm so sorry. What can I do? Can I get you a cup of coffee?"

Amee managed to nod, and Sarah went for the coffee. Amee started to pray, without really thinking about Christian or Muslim fashion. She prayed, "Oh, God, please help Danny to be safe; please don't take him from me. If you will reveal yourself to me, I will do whatever you want me to do. I'm so confused; I don't know what to think, but if you will show me the truth, I will believe."

Sarah was back with the coffee, and while Amee sipped it, she sat beside her on the bed with her arm around her. As Amee told her all about the conversation with Colonel Johnson, she was shaking so badly that she nearly spilled her coffee. Sarah Lassiter was one of those people who was genuinely sweet and kind and mothered everyone around her, but she had a tough side that came out when an injustice was done or someone was mistreated. That no doubt explained the fact that she was working toward a career as a judge advocate. Sarah had a button nose and mousy brown hair that clung to her head in tight curls. Her cheeks were freckled and always a bit red. As soon as she was through for the day, she would put on an old pink duster and oversized bunny rabbit bedroom shoes. If anyone ever looked out of place in a military barracks, it was she. Looks were deceiving, however, because she was a model cadet and loved everything about military life. The discipline suited her temperament perfectly.

Amee was certainly not going to sleep that night, but what could she do? She had never felt so helpless in her entire life. Suddenly she thought about Danny's parents. Should she call them and let them know what was happening? Sarah advised her to wait until morning; there was no need to alarm them during the night unless there was some specific news. That sounded reasonable to Amee. She was so thankful to have someone like Sarah with her at a time like this. Amee insisted that she ought to go to the day room and wait by the phone even though the duty officer was there. Sarah went with her and was attentive to her every need throughout the long night. She would doze now and then when Amee was quiet, but she would awaken at the slightest movement.

Sometime in the wee hours of the morning, Amee said, "Sarah, may I ask you a very personal question?"

"Certainly you may. What is it?"

"What is your religious persuasion?"

Sarah laughed and said, "I'm not really persuaded by any religion."

Amee couldn't hide her shock. "You mean you're an atheist?"

Sarah laughed again at Amee's expression. "That's not what I said. I didn't say I didn't believe in God; I said I wasn't persuaded by any religion."

"I don't think I understand."

Now Sarah was serious. "I'm not much for institutionalized religion, but I have a profound faith in God. I believe the Bible is the infallible Word of God, and I believe Jesus is the Son of God, who died on the cross for my sins. I have placed my complete faith in him as my Lord and Savior. I also believe in church, if it follows the Bible."

Amee couldn't believe it, but she had found Danny's spiritual twin sister. Sarah said exactly what he said.

"Why did you ask me that?"

"I'm just trying to sort some things out right now. Thank you for talking to me."

Sarah didn't say anything else, but she had seen Amee's registration form and knew she was a Muslim. She blamed it on the lawyer in her, but she wanted to know whom she was sharing a room with. After learning that, she had been praying for an opening to witness to her.

"Sarah, would you do me one more favor?"

"Anything I can."

"I love Danny with all my heart, and I'm really scared. Would you please pray for him that he will be safe?"

Much to Amee's surprise, Sarah bowed her head and began to pray out loud right there. She said, "Father, we don't know what has happened to Danny, but you know exactly where he is. Would you please take care of him and bring him back safely? Please bless Amee too, Father, because she's frightened. Give her peace and assure her that you are in control of all things and that you will take care of Danny. I ask this in Jesus' name. Amen."

Amee didn't know how to explain it, but she felt a calm come over her. She had never heard anything quite like that. Sarah talked to God like she knew him personally, and her prayer was so simple and to the point.

"Thank you," Amee said. "I hope I'm not worrying you to death, but may I ask you about your prayer?"

"You aren't worrying me at all, and you can ask me anything."

"You called God 'Father' and ended by asking in Jesus' name. Why did you do that?"

"When we trust in Jesus Christ, we are spiritually reborn and are called the children of God. We are taught then to call him Father. I ask in Jesus' name because it's through him that we have access to God. The Bible says, 'There is one God, and one mediator between God and men, the man Christ Jesus.'"

"Wow! I never thought of Allah as a father. Do you know that Danny believes exactly like you do?"

"That's wonderful. Evidently, he's a very smart man."

"No, it's not wonderful for Danny and me because I'm a Muslim. I don't know what's going to happen to us. I just know he's the only person I've ever loved, and I believe he's the only one I ever can love."

Sarah patted her hand and said, "Don't give up too quick; God loves you and wants to help you both."

Amee was beginning to think that God did want to help them, but it didn't matter much right then because she didn't know what had become of her beloved Danny.

"Amee, wake up. You have a phone call."

Amee shook herself and rubbed her eyes. She couldn't believe she had fallen asleep, and she felt guilty for having done it while Danny was lost.

"Who is it, Sarah?" she asked.

"It's the Civil Air Patrol from Texas."

Amee's first thought was that they had found the wreckage of Danny's plane. "Dear God, please don't let him be hurt," she whispered.

She was not even aware that in her anxiety she was saying "God" and not "Allah." Although it was really just semantics, it was significant for a Muslim.

"Hello? This is Ameenah."

"Good morning, ma'am. This is Buck Wheeler with the Texas Civil Air Patrol. How are you?"

"Frightened to death."

"I'm sure you are, but don't panic yet. We haven't found any evidence of a downed plane, and the storm is over. Flying conditions are great, and I just wanted to let you know what's happening. I also want to ask you a couple of questions if you feel up to it."

"If it will help Danny, I'll do anything."

"Did Lieutenant Brannigan say anything about stopping anywhere along the way?"

"No, in fact he needed to be back as soon as possible."

"Do you know exactly what time he left?"

"Yes, when he disappeared from my vision I looked at my watch, and it was exactly 8:15."

"Thank you; that helps a lot. We can chart his progress from his normal cruising speed and cross-reference his flight plan in order to tell fairly accurately where and when he would have encountered the storm. We'll be back in touch."

After they hung up, Amee wept for a while on Sarah's shoulder and then said, "Sarah, you've got to get some sleep."

"No time for that now. I've got to be in class in a few minutes. I've already talked to the duty officer, and she has had you excused from classes today."

"Sarah, you've been my special angel through all this, and I will never forget it."

"It's been my pleasure; I just wish I could do more to help you."

When Sarah went to get dressed, Amee's first thought was of Katie and Jake. Now they had to be told.

Her heart was in her throat as she dialed the number. How could she possibly break such news to them? They would be devastated. Again, as a reflex, she whispered a prayer for God to help her.

"Hello? This is Katie."

Katie sounded so cheerful; it made it even harder to give her bad news, but it must be done.

"Hi, Katie. This is Amee."

The moment she heard her voice, Katie knew something was wrong. "Amee, what's the matter; are you okay?"

"I'm fine, but I have some bad news about Danny. I'm so sorry to have to tell you in this way, but he rented a small plane and came to see me for Thanksgiving, and on the way back, there was a snowstorm somewhere in the vicinity of Amarillo, Texas. His plane has disappeared."

She could already hear Katie snubbing her tears back, so she continued as fast as she could to mitigate her fear as much as possible.

"I had a call a few moments ago from the Civil Air Patrol in Texas, and they haven't had a mayday call from any aircraft, nor have they found any wreckage. The weather's good there now, and they have been searching for some time. The reason they called me is that Danny had left my name and number at the base for a contact while he was gone."

Jake had been listening on the other phone and said, "Listen, both of you, everything they have told you is good news, so don't panic."

By that time, Katie had gotten control of herself and said, "Amee, I know what you must be going through because I've been through it myself, but we will pray and trust the Lord to take care of everything. We love you like you were our very own daughter, and we will be praying for you as well as Danny."

"I love you both also, and I'll call the minute I know something," Amee promised.

Amee thought she understood a mother's heart very well, so she was mystified at Katie's response. How could she be so calm and think of her at a time like this? Did Americans handle their grief differently? Then it struck her that it wasn't Americans but Christians who handled grief differently. Amee had never seen such a demonstration of faith and strength, and she was still trying to figure it out when the phone rang again.

"It's for you, Amee."

When Amee said hello, she heard a strange voice on the other end. He sounded fairly old and had a Scandinavian accent. "Ya, iss yore name Amee?"

"Yes it is."

"Vell, ve haf a yong man who vants to talk to you."

The next voice said, "Hello, my love."

"Danny! Is it really you?" Everyone at the academy surely heard Amee's scream.

"It's me in the flesh and all in one piece."

"What happened? We have all been worried sick."

"When I saw the storm, I realized I could not fly above it nor around it, so I determined the best thing to do was to try to land. While I was trying to locate a nearby airport, I saw a windsock and went down to investigate. There before me was a beautiful grass runway, so I landed. The Johannsens saw me and, believe it or not, waved me into a hangar big enough for my plane. It was like I had intended to land there. It turned out that their son, Sven, was a pilot who was killed some time ago. They took me in, fed me, and gave me a place to stay until the storm was over. Phone service was out until a few moments ago. Mr. Johannsen has already scraped the snow off the runway with his tractor, and I am about ready to take off again."

"Oh, Danny. Thank God that he has answered prayers and taken care of you."

What she said didn't get by Danny because he had never heard her use the English in reference to God before or mention specific answered prayer. However, now wasn't the time to talk about that. Amee told him about calling his parents, and he asked her to please call them back. He didn't want to place any more calls on the Johannsens' phone, though they wouldn't have minded. They were ranchers, and alone much of the time, so they were delighted to have someone to talk to. Danny's problem was that he only had two ears, which were not nearly enough to do all the listening that was required.

"Danny, I love you so much and was so afraid I would lose you. I wish you could come back here so I could hold you and love you."

"I love you too, with all my heart, but I gotta run now before I am officially AWOL."

"I know you do, but please, no more adventures, at least on this trip."

The next thing Amee did was to call Danny's parents.

"Katie, I have the best news possible! Danny's fine and so is his plane. He's already on his way to Laughlin."

"As I prayed last night, the Lord gave me peace that he would be okay, but it is so good to have it confirmed," Katie replied.

Amee heard what Katie said, but she surely didn't understand it. This was what she had referred to as the spooky side of Christianity. The closest a Muslim could come to that kind of assurance was that whatever happened, Allah willed it. She thought to herself that they would have to talk about it more when the time was right. She told them all about Danny's experience with the Johannsens, and right away Katie wanted to call and thank them for taking care of her son. Then she inexplicably broke out into a laugh.

"That's just like Danny," Katie said. "Who else could make a forced landing in a snowstorm only to be waved into a waiting hangar and spoiled by a couple who treated him like a son?"

That was the first time Amee had been able to laugh for several hours.

Finally, she could rest, so she lay down across her bed and hugged her pillow. Her body was worn out, but her mind wouldn't quit. She was trying to unwind from her tension over Danny's disappearance and also sort out all the things she had heard about God during her ordeal. As she eventually drifted off to sleep, her last thoughts were of thankfulness to God for keeping Danny safe. She left a note for Sarah that simply said, "Danny and plane safe. Will explain later." When Sarah came in, Amee was sleeping so soundly she did not dare wake her. As she read the note, she looked up to heaven and softly whispered, "Dear Lord, thank you. Please help Amee to understand who you are."

Chapter 13

"Eleven hundred miles," Danny said. "Our families are separated by eleven hundred miles. How are we going to handle Christmas break?"

Amee and he had already agreed that they wanted to spend the holidays together while they visited both families. They were on the phone trying to work things out. Not only were the families far apart, but also the two of them were nine hundred miles from each other. Since Dr. and Mrs. Salim observed New Years but not Christmas, Danny suggested that they go to Georgia first and then to Boston because he wanted very badly to have Amee at their home for Christmas. He proposed a plan. "We'll be out of school from December 20 until January 7. I believe I can catch a hop to Colorado, and we could travel together from there. Every little girl ought to have a big, strong man to protect her anyway."

"It's more like every old man needs a strong young woman to travel with him so he won't forget where he is going or fall and hurt himself. I'll talk to my parents, but I don't believe they will have a problem with that. I know they would love to see you."

When they talked again, Amee confirmed that the proposal was fine with her folks, so they made their plans to leave Denver on December 21, for Atlanta. They would go from Atlanta to Boston on December 28, and back to Colorado January 5. The next two weeks were like an eternity for both of them. Danny was successful in catching a hop and arrived in time for dinner on the twentieth. They had reservations to leave at 6:10 the next morning on a direct Delta flight to Atlanta.

They arrived in Perryville in time for supper. Although Amee had gotten to know Katie and Jake well, she had never spent much time in their home. She was fascinated with the farm, especially the animals.

"I'm really sorry we don't have any camels and goats to make you feel at home," Danny teased.

"Well, you sort of favor a camel and sometimes you smell like a goat, so that will have to do for now."

He was never going to win a battle of wits with her.

There was one thing Danny had purposely avoided in all their plans. The family always went to church on Christmas Eve for a service completely dedicated to the birth of Christ. He desperately wanted her to go but didn't want her to feel bad if she didn't.

"Sweetheart, I need to explain our family's Christmas schedule to you, and I want you to know that you are under no obligation to participate in anything you don't want to. Mostly, we just eat for two weeks, but there are a few other things we do. One is that we go to church on Christmas Eve. I want to be totally honest with you; it is all about the birth of Jesus, which they will probably dramatize.

Nothing would make me happier than for you to come with us, but I'll understand if you don't."

By now, Danny ought to have been prepared for Amee to shock him, but he still hadn't totally learned.

"Of course I'm coming with you. I wouldn't miss it."

He tried not to show how surprised he was, but there was no fooling her.

She laughed and tousled his hair. "You didn't think I'd come, did you?"

He held her so tightly that she could hardly breathe and whispered in her ear, "I love you more than life itself."

One of the most enjoyable things about the week for both of them was not to have a schedule. They had been so busy for so long that it was wonderful to just relax. After sleeping in military bunks for months, Amee loved the queen-size bed in the guest room. Danny had told her, "As little as you are, we might have to organize a search party to find you in that bed in the morning." Katie let them sleep until they were ready to get up, and then she prepared her trademark farm breakfast. As always, Jake was sitting at his place chatting with her and reading the paper when they came down. Sometimes they would catch him just looking at them and grinning. There was no doubt that this was the best week in Danny's entire life.

After breakfast they borrowed the car and visited the old ball field and Casey's Restaurant. They both wanted to go by the college, although nearly everyone was gone for the holidays. They had not discussed it, but they just naturally drifted in the direction of the reception hall where they first met, and when Danny was sure no one was looking, he kissed her and said, "The day I met you here was the greatest day of my life."

"That feeling is quite mutual, Lieutenant," Amee whispered.

Later, they drove to Macon for some shopping and to see the Christmas decorations. Amee had always loved the parts of the season that didn't seem religious. The lights and beautifully wrapped presents brought back great memories, even of her own home. Danny promised to take her to see the fancy homes at night if she was a good girl.

"I'll be as good as my escort," she promised.

"Oh, I don't know if I can be seen with a girl like that."

That night, she was so excited about helping Katie trim the Christmas tree that she was like a little girl. It was the first time she had ever had the opportunity to do that. Jake had been called to Atlanta to take care of some year-end business, and Danny sat on the sofa, criticizing their work, so she threw a handful of icicles at him. He chased her around the tree and covered her hair with them, finishing it off by pushing some down the back of her blouse.

"Oh, I've got to get out of this. These things scratch," she said as she began to unbutton her blouse.

"Ameenah Salim, don't you dare do that in here," Danny yelled.

"Why? Would it embarrass my little Danny?"

"No, it would embarrass my mother."

Katie just observed the show and said nothing.

Amee started up the stairs, laughing hysterically. "I'm sorry; the way you were acting, I forgot you were old enough for it to matter."

Of course, she had no intention of taking off her blouse; it was a good way to annoy him.

It was Christmas Eve, and Amee was genuinely looking forward to the service at church. She had not told Danny yet about her conversation with Sarah, but she could not put it out of her mind and was eager to learn more. Danny was pleased to learn that this year they were going to do an old-fashioned Christmas pageant, complete with the nativity story. It might be old hat to some, but Amee had never seen it. At the very worst, he knew she would love the kids.

The service started with caroling. Anyone could request his

favorite Christmas song, so they sung nearly every one in the book before they were done. Amee had never heard the Christmas songs before and found them to be beautiful. Next, the platform was turned into a stage, complete with the cattle stall and manger. As the pastor read the corresponding Scriptures, the various characters marched in. As usual, the children had on their fathers' bathrobes or a bed sheet with their heads covered by a towel tied on with a rope. There were also the two or three kids wandering about with no idea what was going on. Mary and Joseph came first to talk with the innkeeper. Later, the shepherds followed with the angels in attendance, and finally the wise men came with their gifts. Danny whispered to Amee that the magi came from her part of the world, maybe from Iraq or Iran. The angels, some with broken wings and others with falling halos, were belting out their glad tidings, albeit slightly off key. He glanced at Amee, and she was totally immersed in the drama. She was like a child who was seeing the inside of a candy store for the first time. Danny didn't know what she thought about it, but it was obvious she was impressed.

The pastor made a clear presentation of the gospel at the end and closed with prayer. Then it was time for fellowship. The deacons and their wives always prepared bags of treats for everyone and passed them out. There were presents for all the children, and they tore into them with paper and ribbons flying every which way, which was funny to Amee. Finally, there was hot chocolate, apple cider, and cookies, while people talked and wished each other Merry Christmas. Everyone was very nice to Amee and made her feel welcome.

"Why are presents given to everyone else when it is Jesus' birthday?" she asked Danny on the way home.

"It's in the spirit of God giving his Son as his greatest gift to us. The Bible says, 'For God so loved the world that he gave his only begotten Son, that whosoever believeth in him should not perish, but have everlasting life.' Because of that gift, there is another gift possible. 'For the wages of sin is death; but the gift of God is eternal life through Jesus Christ our Lord.'"

"I'm sure for many who have been Christians all their lives, tonight was just routine, but for me, it was amazing and made the whole thing real," Amee said.

Danny wasn't sure what she meant by "real," but the way she said it excited him. He wondered if it were real in the sense of comprehending the facts, or if there were stirrings of belief in her heart.

"It ought not to be commonplace to anyone," Danny responded.

For the first time in a long time, Danny felt some old stirrings in his own soul.

Danny felt he would explode if he didn't talk to Amee about the service. He was excited and afraid at the same time. He didn't want to do anything to interrupt what might be going on in her heart, but he couldn't contain himself any longer.

"Amee, I know you've been taught that Jesus was a true prophet, but what do you really think of him?"

"Can we have a long talk about that later tonight?" Amee said.

He didn't know what to expect but replied, "We'll talk as long as you wish."

Jake built a fire in the den, and after he and Katie went to bed, Danny and Amee sat on the floor in front of the fireplace to talk.

"Danny, I've never been so frightened in my life as I was when your plane was lost. I realized I never again wanted to be without you. In that moment, I found myself praying to God in a way I have never prayed before. I pleaded with him to keep you safe, and then I asked him to show me the truth and said I would believe. I sincerely meant what I said. I don't think I can live without God or you, so I must know the truth."

Danny spoke softly, "Jesus said, 'Ye shall know the truth, and the truth shall make you free.'"

She shifted nervously in her seat and looked down for a couple of minutes. Then she peered straight into Danny's eyes, and with the plaintiveness of a person in pain seeking relief, she said, "My roommate, Sarah, was a lifesaver for me during that awful night. I've never known anyone besides you and Katie who are that unselfish and loving. When I was trying to reach out to God on your behalf, I asked about her religion, and I swear, she is a carbon copy of you. I made up my mind that night that I was going to settle this matter once and for all, no holds barred. Whatever the truth is, I want to know it. That's why I didn't hesitate to go to church with you tonight. There are only two things I fear anymore: offending God and losing you. I must settle once and for all whether I can both honor God and have you. What shook me the most was that I prayed a very simple prayer, and I *know* God answered me. I have never had that happen before.

Danny didn't say it, but he was thinking, *The goodness of God leads to repentance.*

"Darling, I don't know exactly where you are in your search, but I want to ask you a question. There is no pressure, and I want you to be totally honest. Would you be willing to pray a simple prayer? It goes like this, 'Dear Lord, if Jesus is your Son and if he died on the cross for my sins, please show me and I will believe.'"

"I will do that, Danny. I'm no longer afraid of the truth. I'm only afraid of *not* knowing it."

Danny bowed his head and prayed, "Dear Lord, I know you will hear Amee. I ask you to answer her in such a way that she will absolutely know what the truth is. Now, Amee, just pray as your heart leads."

She was sobbing, and Danny could feel her tears falling on his hands. She began haltingly, "Dear God, I must know the truth. Is Jesus Christ your Son and did he die on the cross for my sins? If you will show me the truth, I will believe."

Suddenly, Amee opened her eyes and grabbed Danny's arm. She looked at him with a startled expression and exclaimed, "Oh, Danny, it *is* true! I have no doubt about it. How can this be? How can I be sure so quickly?"

Danny was laughing and crying at the same time as he said, "I will explain it all to you in due time, but it's just one of those spooky things about Christianity. Are you ready to do what you told the Lord you would do?"

"Yes, I meant what I said, and I do believe."

"That in itself is all that is required because the Bible says, 'Believe on the Lord Jesus Christ and thou shalt be saved.' However, there are some other things that are important in reinforcing your decision. The Bible says, 'If thou shalt confess with thy mouth the Lord Jesus, and believe in thine heart that God hath raised him from the dead, thou shalt be saved.'"

"I believe Jesus Christ is the Son of God and that he died on the cross for my sin and rose again. I believe! I believe!" Amee exclaimed.

"There is just one thing more. The Bible also says, 'Whosoever shall call upon the name of the Lord shall be saved.' Will you pray one more simple prayer with me?"

"Yes, if I ought to, I will."

"I will help you with the words, but you must pray them as your own and mean them."

"I'm ready."

They bowed their heads, and Danny said, "If you truly mean what you are saying, just repeat after me." Then he began speaking slowly, "Dear Lord, I confess that I'm a sinner. I believe Jesus died on the cross for me. I confess that He is the Lord. I trust him right now as my Savior." Amee repeated each sentence behind him, and then Danny thanked the Lord. He asked Amee, "Did you mean everything you said?"

"Oh yes. I've never meant anything more in all my life."

"Then do you believe the Lord has just given to you eternal life?"

"Yes, I do believe it. I don't understand it, but I can feel his presence in my soul. I guess I'm spooky now also, huh?"

"You were always spooky, but now you're indwelt by the Holy Spirit."

Danny happened to look at his watch and noticed it was past midnight. It was not only Christmas day, but it was Sunday. He showed his watch to Amee and said, "Now you truly are Sunday's Child.

"You are also a personal gift *to* the Lord Jesus Christ on the day we celebrate his birth. You have been born again on Christmas Day. It's also the Lord's Day. The Bible calls it that because Jesus arose from the dead on Sunday, and we are spiritually raised from the dead and will literally be raised someday. So you are really Sunday's Child."

They sat up far into the night for two reasons. Neither of them could sleep, and there were so many things to talk about.

Finally, Danny said to her, "You must know by now that I want you in my life forever. Where does this leave us in regards to marriage?"

Suddenly reality settled in upon her, and Amee's mood turned very somber. "Oh, Danny, in all the excitement I forgot about my family. First, they would be devastated if they knew I became a Christian, and it wouldn't change anything in respect to marriage. We have to pray for another miracle regarding that." Then she kissed him with a passion she had never shown before. They sat and held each other until the fire died out and finally went to bed. When Danny lay down, he truly thanked the Lord for Amee's salvation, but at that moment he was more aware of his own spiritual problems than he had ever been. He could face life with great determination and resolve that nothing was going to stand in his way, but he wasn't able to put aside his disappointments and truly get his heart right with God.

Danny and Amee came wobbling down the stairs about nine the next morning. Katie said, "Good morning. The two of you probably scared Santa Claus away last night; you must not have gone to bed until daylight."

Danny yawned. "You're very nearly correct."

"I apologize if we disturbed you," Amee offered. "But I don't believe you'll be too upset when you hear what we were doing."

"What were you doing? Wrapping gifts?" Jake asked.

"No, I was receiving one," Amee replied.

As Jake and Katie glanced at each other, they tried not to let their concern show. The first thought on each of their minds was an engagement ring. They loved Amee, but knew the kids would be asking for trouble if they married while one was a Christian and the other a Muslim.

Neither Danny nor Amee missed what was happening.

"Oh, no. It's not what you're thinking," they said at the same time.

Amee went over and put her arm around Katie and took Jake's hand and said, "Believe it or not, the gift I received was much greater than an engagement ring. I've been in turmoil for a long time, trying to know the truth about God, and last night I got it settled once and for all. I put my faith in the Lord Jesus Christ and received him as my Savior. I was born again last night and became a Christian."

When she finished, tears were running down the cheeks of all four of them. Katie hugged her and sobbed for joy. Jake never knew quite what to do at a time like that, so he just sat with his tears dropping into his lap and his lips trembling. Finally, Katie wiped her eyes and said, "Well, we can discuss this just as well over breakfast." She had everything ready except for putting it on the table. They ate, drank coffee, and talked for nearly two hours. Everyone was so excited about Amee's salvation that they forgot about exchanging gifts.

Danny had never lost the excitement of opening the presents, though, and he soon reminded them that it was time. It was a good thing they had planned for a late dinner because it was past noon when they finished with the gifts. This was another first for Amee, and she thoroughly enjoyed it. Later in the day, Katie's brother,

Kent, and his family joined them for dinner. He was funny, and she liked him instantly. He thought Amee was beautiful and dubbed her "The Arabian Princess." He couldn't believe she was an air force cadet and asked her, "What do you want to be when you grow up?" He called Danny "Lieutenant."

Joy, Kent's wife, was appropriately named. She was always chattering away or laughing about something. She possessed endless energy, and nothing was much of a challenge for her. Her blonde hair was straight and silky and hung nearly to her waist. When she sat down, which was not often, she would lay it over her shoulder and let it hang down in the front. She wasn't much bigger than Amee, and her perfectly proportioned body always moved gracefully. All of this was finished off with a perfect complexion, which was naturally tanned by all the time she spent helping her husband on the farm. Amee was not surprised to learn that she had been a cheerleader when she was in high school.

Amee had never seen a more handsome couple than this one in their early thirties. Their two children, Ian and Shana, were nine and six, and thought their Uncle Danny was the world's greatest superhero. Shana especially always wanted to be in his lap, by his side, or playing a game with him. Amee was sure she would be jealous of her. Danny was Ian's sports idol, and he wanted to be just like him. He was already starting to pitch baseball and play football. Danny spent many hours with him, showing him how to do things.

That evening after supper, Amee sat quietly with a faraway look. When Danny called her name, she didn't acknowledge it. He snapped his fingers and said, "Amee, please come home."

"Oh, sorry. I was just thinking."

"Obviously. It must have been a very deep thought."

Amee looked worried. "I've just been thinking about my family, and I guess reality has begun to set in. I honestly don't know what to expect when they find out I have become a Christian."

"We'll pray about that," Danny assured her. "And the Lord will help."

"What if they disown me? I think I would die if I lose my family."

"We don't even have to get into that on this visit."

"But I've already learned that I am supposed to love the Lord even more than my own mother and father and not be ashamed to confess him before men. I do love the Lord, but I also love my family, and I'm scared I will lose them."

Danny sat down beside her on the sofa and put his arms around her. "You are right about everything you've just said, but the Lord will give you time to grow in grace and strength. David said in the psalms that God pities us like a father pities his children and remembers our frame that we are dust. Any panic we feel doesn't come from God." Danny was saying the right words, but they were sticking in his throat because he knew he wasn't living them.

Amee whispered, "You're always my rock and my strength. It's no wonder I love you like I do."

The flight on Wednesday was so early that they were going to Atlanta on Tuesday afternoon to spend the night in a motel. Tuesday morning at breakfast was their last relaxed time with Jake and Katie. Amee asked them to please pray for her and her family for the next week. Before they left the table, they all prayed together. On the drive to the airport, Danny said to Jake, "I still want to talk to you again about the things we discussed when you were in Colorado. You surely got my curiosity up."

"Of course, we can talk all you want when we have the time," Jake responded, obviously pleased that Danny wanted to know what he thought.

Katie and Jake dropped them at the Mark Inn, which was only about a mile from the airport, and after a tearful good-bye, they started for home. Danny and Amee had to be up at 4:00 a.m. to catch the motel limo to the airport, so they went straight to their rooms.

Chapter 14

Boston
January 1988

On Wednesday morning, they grabbed a quick cup of coffee and a doughnut just in time to catch the shuttle to the airport. They checked their luggage at curbside and literally ran through the main terminal. After rushing through security, they walked down the escalator to catch the subway to terminal C. When they arrived at the gate, they handed their tickets to the agent and went directly into the jet way. Just as they settled into their seats, the announcement came to fasten their seatbelts, and the plane began to push back from the gate. They had barely spoken to each other until they were seated.

Danny turned to Amee, stuck out his hand, and said, "Hi, my

name is Daniel Brannigan. Wow! I sure got seated by a pretty girl. What's your name?"

"I'm sorry, but I don't give my name to strange men, and you are about the strangest man I've have ever met."

"Did you sleep well, darling?" Danny inquired.

"After I finally got to sleep." Amee said. "I couldn't stop thinking about my family."

"Let's just ask the Lord to guide us each step of the way and then follow his lead," Danny suggested. Every time he said something like that he felt like a big hypocrite because he certainly hadn't lived his life in the light of God's guidance. He knew all the right things to say and even believed them in the abstract, but had given up a long time ago on the Lord helping him personally. What he felt toward God wasn't bitterness, but ambivalence. He couldn't understand why the Lord had allowed him to help others but hadn't answered his prayers for himself. He was convinced he had eternity taken care of but wasn't doing so well with the present.

What he had said calmed Amee, and she snuggled up to him, put her head on his shoulder, and dozed off to sleep. She slept for most of the two-and-a-half hour flight and didn't even wake up for breakfast. Danny realized she must not have gotten much sleep at all during the night and wished he could have been with her.

Amee knew her way around Logan Airport pretty well, so she had asked her father to meet them at the Delta luggage carousel. They arrived a little early, but Dr. and Mrs. Salim's smiling faces greeted them as they rounded the corner. As he was receiving kisses and kisses and more kisses, Danny faced the reality that he had entered an entirely different culture. He had not seen Safa Salim for four years, but she was as beautiful and charming as ever. The Salims wanted to know everything about their lives, so there was endless talk all the way to their home. They actually lived in Cambridge, Massachusetts, just across the river from Boston.

The boys met them at the door and helped bring the luggage in. They were more Americanized than their parents and weren't into so much of the kissing as the rest of the family, much to Danny's relief. For the first time in his life, he was the outsider, and it was an uneasy feeling that he didn't like. He didn't know all that was expected of him and how to respond to everything. Amee teased him, "Don't be such a wimp, my big, strong lieutenant. I'll take care of you." He felt like really hitting her. She had seriously promised to prompt him on anything that really mattered, and that was some relief. Knowing that the Salims had not changed their minds about his and Amee's relationship, he wasn't sure why they had so readily agreed for him to come home with her. Perhaps they wanted to observe the situation and he might have a lecture coming before they left. One thing that was comforting was that he was pretty sure they really did like him.

Mrs. Salim made coffee to go with all the wonderful Arabic food she had prepared. She had made baklava, falafel, halva, hummus, labenah, and ma'amul. Danny's favorite was hummus with pita bread. They sat around the dining table and ate and talked until nearly noon. Mo was interested in Danny's flight and parachute training, and Dr. Salim wanted to hear more about the Air Force Academy.

Since school was out for the holidays, there was no schedule to keep. Both Dr. Salim and Mo wanted to show Danny their schools, and Danny was hoping to visit the Old North Church and the Plymouth Colony if there was time. The entire area was rich with history of all kinds, but that must be left for the future. This was Amee's time, and he wanted her to do whatever made her happy.

Early Thursday morning, they were off to Massachusetts Institute of Technology and Boston College. Safa and Amee decided to stay at home and spend some mother-daughter time together. Abb was unusually quiet and went his own way for the day.

The men came back in time for lunch.

"MIT and Boston College are impressive," Danny said. "I enjoyed seeing them. One day we can get free medical care from Dr. Mohammed Salim."

"Don't count on that," Mo said. "Doctors have lots of expenses, like Mercedes automobiles, yachts, and country club memberships."

Everybody laughed.

"Well, who's going to be my guide today?" Danny inquired at breakfast the next morning. "This would be a good day to go sightseeing if it won't interfere with anyone's plans."

Amee raised her hand, and Danny said, "Yes, you may be excused."

"Knucklehead, I'm applying for the job."

"Evidently you didn't hear what I said. I need a guide; I can get lost all by myself without any help."

Amee wadded up her napkin and threw it at him. "Well, just go get lost then; no one cares anyway."

"Okay, you can be my guide."

"I'm not available; I'm otherwise occupied," Amee responded with pouting lips.

Danny walked around the table and got down on his knees. He folded his hands in a penitent position and pleaded, "Oh, great all-knowing and all-seeing one, will you please condescend to help a poor, unworthy mortal in his quest for knowledge?"

Amee laid her knife on his head in a regal fashion and replied, "Arise, mortal; I will have mercy on you lest you ride forever 'neath the streets of Boston like the man who never returned."

Everyone had a good laugh at their antics. They invited everyone to go along, but all politely declined. Abb was still in bed when they left.

Danny loved history of any kind, but he especially liked that which had to do with patriotism. However, he was just as excited today to be alone with Amee. He begrudged every moment they were apart, and even when they were in her home, he wasn't quite able to be himself. He didn't want to do anything to offend her parents, so there was no physical contact. The first order of the day when they were out of sight was to give her a big kiss. Then they walked off arm in arm. When they were together like this, the rest of the world didn't matter.

Amee delighted in showing Danny things because now he was on her turf for the first time. She sort of liked being in control for just a little while, but then she would be glad to turn the helm back over to him. She was very self-confident and capable, but she truly liked her role as a woman whose man was in charge. After all, no one forced it on her; it was her decision. This was one thing she liked so much about the United States.

They went first to see the Old North Church, from which Paul Revere had gotten his signal as he made his famous ride in 1775. Danny learned that it was still an active church under the authority of the Episcopal diocese and was now called Christ Church. It had been operating continuously since 1723.

Plymouth Plantation would not be open and operating, as it did much of the year, but Danny didn't know if he would ever again have the opportunity to see it, so they hopped a bus and went down. The *Mayflower II,* an exact replica of the original, was also there.

"Do you realize 102 pilgrims sailed for more than two months on a ship like this just to flee religious persecution and find a place where they could worship God as they saw fit?" He told Amee about the voyage and the Mayflower Compact and how they sighted land there November 9, 1620. She was wide-eyed through it all. Danny was thrilled to tell her how America was founded upon the principle of religious freedom and how that principle had lasted for over two hundred years.

"Danny, I believe I have an answer from the Lord about when to tell my parents about my salvation, or at least when *not to,*" Amee said as they were riding home. "It really is not from any fear or hesitation on my part, but I don't believe now is the right time. I have some reasons in my own heart that I really am not ready to talk about yet. Will you trust me in this?"

"Of course. I trust you in everything. We'll wait until you are convinced the time is right."

"Oh, you make me love you more all the time."

"I feel the same way; I love me more all the time too."

"You pea brain, you really know how to spoil a romantic moment," Amee said, pretending to pout.

"I'm the most romantic person you will ever know, and I'll prove it." With that, he started kissing her all over the face. She was laughing and fighting back at the same time.

"You're about as romantic as a porcupine," Amee said.

"I'll bet I know something about love you don't," Danny said.

"Oh yeah? What's that?

"I know how a porcupine makes love."

"How does a porcupine make love?"

"Very carefully."

With that, Amee just turned and looked out the window in mock disdain.

At dinner, Dr. Salim asked, "Danny, may we have some time alone with our daughter tonight?"

It was only to be polite that he asked, so there was only one answer. "Certainly, Dr. Salim. I probably need to get to bed early tonight anyway."

Abb had not had one meal with the family, and Danny was beginning to be a little concerned about it.

Shortly after dinner, Danny excused himself and read for a while before going to sleep early for a change.

Mo also had gone out, and Amee and her parents took their coffee and sat in the den to talk.

Danny kept slapping at his face and finally was awake enough to realize that drops of water were hitting him. He looked up at the ceiling and all around with a puzzled look. The sunlight coming in through the window made him squint. He muttered something under his breath and laid his head back on the pillow and closed his eyes. It was time to get up, but surely a few more minutes wouldn't hurt. In a moment, he felt it again and jumped up to examine things. This time he even looked at the wall behind the bed. He lay down again but kept his eyes open to see if he could identify the source of the water. In a moment, he saw the problem. Some kind of horrible, indefinable creature slithering like a serpent was creeping up from behind him. He waited until the strategic moment and captured it with both hands. It struggled and writhed, trying to get loose and made the most awful giggling sound. He turned and abruptly came face to face with the dreaded *Ameenah monster.*

He wrestled her to the floor while growling ferociously. She was laughing so hard she could barely breathe. "You ought to have seen yourself; you were so funny."

He put on the angriest look he could and said, "I didn't think it was funny. I was trying to sleep."

He was above her with her arms pinned to the floor. "I'll show you how funny it really is." He pursed his lips and pretended he was going to spit on her. She was flipping her head from side to side so fast that she got dizzy. Suddenly he stopped, like he was paralyzed. "What're are you doing in my bedroom? Do you want to get me thrown out of this family before I even get in?

Again, Amee started laughing. "Mom and Dad know I'm in here, and if you care to look, you will notice that the door is wide open."

He let her arms go and looked at the door. Then he moved over beside her and did a pushup and kissed her. He quickly repeated the process three times, and said, "You know I can do a hundred pushups without stopping, don't you?"

"Go ahead and prove it."

He did a couple more and said, "If you insist on coming into a man's bedroom, you will be taken advantage of. Now, will you please go away and let me get dressed?"

"Go ahead. I'll just sit here and talk to you while you dress."

"Ameenah Salim, I think the devil got into you during the night. Now, go away before I call your dad."

Amee frowned, stuck out her lips, and started toward the door. "All right, but I'll bet someday you won't throw me out of your bedroom."

Danny threw a pillow at her as she went through the doorway and yelled, "You're a bad girl."

She yelled back from the stairs, "By the way, I woke you to tell you that we're having company for dinner this evening."

Two sets of aunts and uncles were coming over for dinner. It was Safa's brother and sister and their families.

"You'll really get the Arab treatment tonight," Amee told him. "We will probably even have goat meat and camel milk."

"I think you've already been taking mischief pills," Danny retorted. "Your parents need to do something about you."

Uncle Hasim, Safa's brother, and his wife, Noor, were a delightful couple in their fifties. They had a son and a daughter who were both grown and had their own plans for New Year's Eve. Aunt Raphia, Safa's sister, and Uncle Ahmed had two little girls who were three and five. They were both beautiful with chubby cheeks, curly black hair, and big dark eyes. Danny could just imagine seeing Amee when she was that age. They immediately took to him, as most children did. Amee said it was because he was on their mental level. The rest of the day, they wanted to be in his lap or sitting beside him when he wasn't on the floor playing with them. Safa's family was pretty well Americanized, and if they had any problem at all with Danny, they hid it well.

Amee had spotted a small church whose service was at eleven on Sunday morning. She asked Danny if they could go, and he didn't have the heart to refuse. They asked to be excused to go out for a while without mentioning where they were going. It was only the second church Amee had ever been in, and she had never experienced a regular service. God had directed them to the right place. It was a small group of believers who held a simple service. Amee had never seen a group of people show so much joy. She wept when the choir sang "How Great Thou Art," and she drank in every word the preacher said. As he preached about the Good Samaritan, she realized how Jesus had received her even though she would have classified herself an enemy of the Jews before. At the conclusion of his sermon, the pastor made an appeal for anyone who wanted to be saved to come forward, and two people responded. Amee was amazed that they would do that in front of everybody. Someone came and took each of them through a door behind the pulpit. There were some announcements about coming events, and they sang a fellowship song called "The Family of God."

Amee felt like her heart would burst as she tried to sing along with them, realizing that she was indeed now a part of the family of God. When they were finished, the four came back out and stood together in front of the congregation. The two counselors gave the pastor a nod, and he said, "These folks have something they would like to share with the church." Again, Amee was amazed that they would speak before the whole group. The pastor simply asked, "James, would you like to tell the folks what happened to you today?"

The young man replied, "I trusted Jesus Christ as my personal Savior."

"Sandra, what about you?"

"I also received Jesus as my Savior today."

The congregation began to clap spontaneously. Then the pastor continued, "We will counsel them about baptism and the Christian life. After our closing prayer, please come by and shake their hands and tell them how glad you are that they have been saved. Don't forget to get acquainted with our visitors."

Amee looked up at Danny, and he could see the questions in her eyes. He knew a long Bible lesson was coming.

The people were very friendly, and after the service, all of them came by to speak to Danny and Amee and shake their hands. "They were genuinely interested in us," Danny said as they left.

"And the girls thought you and your Southern accent were so cute, y'all," Amee said. As soon as they cleared the building, Amee's questions began in staccato fashion.

"Where did those people take the two who came forward?"

"They took them to a counseling room where they could talk without being disturbed."

"What did they do there?"

"They talked just like you and I did that night at my house when you trusted in Jesus."

"I can't believe they actually spoke in front of the whole congregation. Why did they do that?"

Danny couldn't help but laugh at Amee's quizzical face as she asked all these questions. "The Bible says we should confess Christ before men."

"Am I supposed to do it in the same way?"

"Yes, when you are ready."

"Oh boy. That's when the grace of God will really have to work in my life. Now for the big one. What's this business about baptism?"

"The Bible teaches that those who trust Jesus as their savior should be baptized, which I believe means to be immersed in water. The Scripture says, 'We are buried in the likeness of (Christ's) death.' It's one of the symbols of our redemption, picturing the death, burial, and resurrection of Jesus. You stand in the water as he hung on the cross, the preacher lays you back under the water as he was buried, and brings you up as he was resurrected. It's the first act of obedience and a testimony of your faith in Jesus' death, burial, and resurrection."

The look of incredulity on her face was hilarious to Danny, but he tried not to laugh. These were serious learning moments for Amee.

"I want to do everything the Lord commands, but this scares me."

"Again, like everything else, just wait for him to show you when and where. It will be a wonderful experience when that time comes."

When they got back home, Amee had an overwhelming urge to tell her family all that had happened to her, but she was afraid it would ruin everything. She was no longer primarily concerned about her relationship with Danny, but she longed to see them become Christians too. She knew that was something only God could do, and she didn't want to make it more difficult.

"Did you kids have a good time?" Safa asked.

Amee didn't hesitate to answer that. "We had a wonderful time."

She was delighted her mother didn't ask any more questions, because she wouldn't lie, and she didn't want to be evasive. Abb was there for Sunday dinner but was obviously irritated. He didn't speak to anyone and didn't even look toward Amee or Danny. He ate rapidly and excused himself to go to his room. When Danny went up to change, he heard Abb on the phone.

"The Great Satan has invaded my home and was brought in by my own sister. I'm embarrassed and concerned that the Imam will think I had something to do with it. Can you help me with that? Okay. Thank you very much. I will see you later this evening. Praise Allah!"

What Danny heard alarmed him, because he had read of the barbaric things radical Muslims had done to their own family members in the name of Allah. It also broke his heart to see Amee hurt.

He knew it would devastate her, so he wouldn't say anything until he could find out more. After all, he was supposed to be some kind of spy sooner or later. Just after Abb left, Danny asked to be excused so he could go out for a short run. He had glanced out the window to see which way Abb went, which allowed him to catch up quickly. Because of the cold weather, it was natural for Danny to have his hood over his head, providing him with some cover. It didn't take Abb long to get where he was going. There was a pickup game of basketball at the local mosque. As Abb walked up, three other guys pulled aside and huddled with him. Shortly, the Imam came up, and they all talked with him for several minutes until the cleric slapped Abb on the back and smiled as he said something. Abb then joined the game, and Danny went for a short run before returning home. It was obvious where the indoctrination was coming from.

They spent the next three days visiting with the family and just relaxing. Danny enjoyed hearing about Dr. Salim's work and telling him about his. He wanted to know all about Danny's flying and the fighter planes, and Danny was more than glad to share all his experiences about anything that wasn't classified. He recounted the entire adventure about his flight to see Amee at Thanksgiving. Dr. Salim was sure the Johannsens must have been very amusing people. Thursday morning, Dr. and Mrs. Salim drove them to the airport and dropped them off. It was snowing, so they didn't try to park and wait with them. Danny was sort of glad because the kissing was abbreviated in the car. He was relieved that he was leaving without Amee's parents confronting him. He did wonder if he had been the subject of conversation in their private meeting with Amee. He felt sure she would share anything important with him.

"If you have any difficulty with the weather or anything, call us," Safa said. "We are going straight home."

They waved good-bye and watched them drive away. Danny wiped away the tears that were forming in Amee's eyes and said, "Better not cry out here or you will have icicles on your nose."

C ✝ ★

When the plane started to descend, the Denver airport looked like someone had shaken up a huge snow globe. Big, soft snowflakes were floating gently down. At times like these, the world was always so quiet and clean. It was one of Danny's favorite times. However, as soon as they stepped inside the airport, the scene changed rapidly. The noise level was off the chart, and there were wall-to-wall and hall-to-hall people. Some flights had been canceled because of the weather. When they heard the announcement that Logan Airport was completely closed, they laughed, realizing they must have gotten one of the last flights out.

Danny had to fly back to Ciudad Acuna commercially, and Amee had made plans to ride the shuttle to the academy. She insisted on waiting until Danny's flight left because if something happened to delay him, she was determined to stay with him.

"You aren't secretly praying for a delay, are you?" Danny asked.

Amee looked a little sheepish and replied, "I might be."

Danny hugged her and kissed her on the forehead. "You know there are some rules to prayer."

"I know that, but God loves me, and he might just give me whatever I ask for."

"Oh, Ameena, what a Christian you're going to make. With your approach to God, he just might give you *everything* you ask for. You are truly an Arab in which there is no guile."

Danny's flight was called on time, but he was the last person to walk through the jet way door. They clung to each other until the last minute and shared the last kiss possible.

The stewardess smiled and said, "Last call for flight 207 to Acuna, Lieutenant Brannigan."

"How'd you know my name?" Danny asked as he gave her his ticket.

"You're the only one left," she said as she gave him a wink.

One more kiss blown to each other and one more "I love you," and Danny was gone.

Chapter 15

Danny was now alone with his own thoughts and was pondering everything that had happened since they left just over two weeks ago. It was hard to believe how his life had changed so much so quickly. It suddenly came back to him poignantly that Amee had no idea about his involvement with special intelligence. Since her people were the focus of it, he felt as though he was being dishonest with her, but there was nothing he could do about it. When he could finally tell her, surely she would understand; after all, she knew how the military worked.

When classes resumed, he moved up to the T-38A Talon, which

he was excited about flying because it was a supersonic plane. First there was the classroom work and the technical data to learn and then flying second stick for a while. The first time he broke the sound barrier was a rush like he had never felt, and he was in love all over again. It was more exhilarating than pitching a no hitter. He had never thought much about becoming a military pilot, but now he couldn't think of anything that was more exciting to him.

"Okay, Brannigan, it's solo time," Colonel Skip Johnson said. "I fly second stick today."

The first time out was strictly basics, which Danny managed flawlessly. For the next several times, there was a routine to follow, and then one day Colonel Johnson said, "All right, just take off and I'll give you instructions after we are airborne." Danny was excited and nervous at the same time. The butterflies were all fluttering. The colonel put him through rolls, dives, loops, and every other kind of maneuver he could think of. Danny had never felt the force of 5 Gs before, but his body handled it well.

In a short time, he went through the same process again on the T-1A Jay Hawk. Now he was qualified for regular missions. There were still many hours of classroom work left and more tests than he wanted to think about, but he and Amee talked at least once a week. Her studies were going well, and she was already thinking about graduation. She wanted Danny to be a part of everything in her life, so she called him just to be reassured.

"You are going to be able to come for graduation, aren't you?" she asked.

"Why should I do that? I've already been through one, and if you've seen one, you've seen 'em all."

"You haven't seen the most important one yet, and if you don't see that one, you won't live to see any others.

"In that case, I can probably steal a jet and fly up there for a few minutes."

"Don't even joke about this; it's too important."

"I'm sure I can work out something if you can just make it a few more days without me. Everybody in my unit knows about us, and the skipper seems to be a good guy," Danny replied.

"I don't know if I can manage to hang on that long or not," Amee teased. "There are several men after me, and I'm not sure how long I can resist."

"Yeah, you just tell 'em I know very painful ways to kill a man and a few things that are worse than death. Seriously, I have some good news. The colonel has arranged for me to fly a training mission to Petersen Air Force Base for three days, so I will at least get to be there for your graduation and swearing in."

Early on May 25, Danny took off from Laughlin bound for Peterson. This time the entire flight was just over an hour, and when he deplaned, the first thing he saw was Amee waving to him from the waiting area.

When he got within range, she shouted, "Hey, flyboy, if your wife's not around, how about coming home with me?"

"I don't know about that; I was sort of hoping for a blonde; I hear they have more fun."

"Well, blondes might have more fun, but what about the men who're with them? I think you'll have more fun with me."

"You talked me into it, so I'll give it a try then."

It felt so good to hold her in his arms again and feel her soft hair against his face. There was a special smell that he recalled any time he was thinking about her.

"This time, I'm the pilot," she said.

Danny made the sign of the cross in mock prayer, and Amee punched him. Everything was normal.

As much as they regretted it, her parents weren't able to come. Dr. Salim was in the midst of final exams, and Safa was so nervous about flying that she didn't want to come by herself. Amee was very disappointed, but as long as her Danny was there, she could handle anything. There were no must-attend activities until the graduation the next morning at ten, so they had all day together except for a few minutes. Amee was graduating with honors, and she had to attend a short ceremony to receive her award. She wanted Danny to get to know Sarah better, so Amee invited her to go to lunch with them. It didn't take Danny long to realize that Sarah was a mature Christian. Amee was sure she was a gift from God to help her come to Christ and also to help her grow in grace. The first thing Amee had done when she returned was to tell Sarah about her conversion. Sarah danced around and praised the Lord until she kicked off her bunny rabbit shoes.

"I'll finish my flight training in one month, and I don't know where I will be assigned when I finish," Danny said when they were alone again. Now more than ever, he wished he could tell her about his special duty because he knew that could complicate things.

"Call me as soon as you receive your orders, and I'll call you the moment I get mine."

Danny felt so proud and blessed as he watched Amee walk across the stage to receive her diploma. The most beautiful and intelligent cadet there belonged to him! The swearing in ceremony was held that afternoon, and after it was over, the commanding officer came to the podium and said, "Will Lieutenant Ameenah Salim please return to the platform?"

Amee walked resolutely toward the stage as a good officer should, but she was about to faint from the uncertainty and anticipation. This time, Danny didn't even know what was going on.

"We have one more presentation to make," the commanding officer announced.

Amee arrived at his side with a great deal of apprehension and feeling quite conspicuous.

"We asked if this special presentation could be made before her graduating class and friends and were granted the privilege. On behalf of the United States of America and President Ronald Reagan, I am happy to present to Lieutenant Ameenah Salim her certificate of citizenship, subject to her taking the oath of allegiance."

The entire auditorium erupted in applause, and as it died down, she was given the oath. They had arranged to have a federal judge present for that.

> I hereby declare, on oath, that I absolutely and entirely renounce and abjure all allegiance and fidelity to any foreign prince, potentate, state, or sovereignty of whom or which I have heretofore been a subject or citizen; that I will support and defend the Constitution and laws of the United States of America against all enemies, foreign and domestic; that I will bear true faith and allegiance to the same; that I will bear arms on behalf of the United States when required by law; that I will perform noncombatant service in the Armed Forces of the United States when required by the law; that I will perform work of national importance under civilian direction when required by the law; and that I take this obligation freely without any mental reservation or purpose of evasion; so help me God. In acknowledgement whereof I have hereunto affixed my signature.

When she was dismissed, Amee bounded up to Danny, saluted, and said, "You no longer outrank me, Lieutenant Brannigan."

"No, you're just as rank as I am now, but you won't be in a few days. The worst thing about it is that now I can't have you deported if you act up."

Upon the completion of flight training, Danny would receive the rank of First Lieutenant.

The next morning, Amee drove him back to Peterson Air Force Base. There were far too many partings in their lives to suit them, and they longed for the day when there wouldn't be any more.

"You remember what happened last time you flew back to Texas? We'll have no more of that," Amee warned him.

"If I run into a snowstorm in May, I will fly right through it," Danny said.

After he put his flight gear on, he kissed her and said, "I'm sorry, my love, but I must go."

Amee watched until she saw his plane disappear into the clouds. Less than two hours later, her phone rang.

"I wish to report that no snow was sighted," Danny said. "I'm here safe and sound."

After they hung up, it dawned on Amee that for the first time in over four years she didn't have one single thing she had to do. She knew that wouldn't last for long, and began to think about her orders. Where would she be sent, and how far would it be from Danny? Of course, they wouldn't know the answer to that until he received his new orders. She didn't have to wait long, and the first thing she did was to call him.

"Danny, my orders came today, and I know what I'll be doing and where I'll be stationed."

"Well, break it to me gently."

"I've been assigned to the Air Force Communications Command's Tactical Communications Division at Langley Air Force Base in Virginia for computer training. It seems that personal computers are going to be used extensively for communications and guidance programs in the future."

"I've been reading about them," Danny replied. "Apple Computers has been selling them for personal use since 1977. They say personal computers will revolutionize communications in the world, and in just a few years most people will have one. It seems like a wonderful opportunity for you."

"I'm very excited about it, but I'm not excited about being farther from you."

"You don't really know if you'll be farther from me or not. I certainly won't stay here. Who knows? Maybe I will be assigned to Langley also."

"Now, that *would* be a miracle," Amee exclaimed.

"Well, we will soon know."

Langley Air Force Base, Virginia, June 21, 1988

Amee had barely gotten settled in at Langley when her phone rang.

"Hello?"

"This is First Lieutenant Daniel Brannigan speaking."

"Second Lieutenant Ameenah Salim here, sir. Danny, you're finished!" she shouted.

"The United States Air Force claims I'm a qualified fighter pilot and ready for action. I guess we'll find out if they are right in due time."

"I have my orders, and I think you should sit down for this one."

"Is it that bad?"

"It depends on your perspective; for me, it's a disaster."

"Oh, Danny, why is it a disaster?"

"Well, it seems I am going to have to put up with you for some time to come."

The excitement grew in Amee's voice. "What do you mean?"

"God is in the miracle business, and I have been assigned to the Sixth Airborne Command and Control Squadron based where? Langley Air Force Base!"

"Danny, please don't joke about something this important."

"It is absolutely a fact, my dear. I'm coming to Langley," he said, imitating Rhett Butler.

He didn't need a phone to hear Amee squeal.

Chapter 16

Afghanistan, 1988

On December 25, 1979, Russia deployed the Fortieth Army to Afghanistan to support the Marxist People's Democratic Party in their struggle against the rebel forces. The Russians had become distrustful of President Hafizulla Amin and even accused him of being a CIA operative. He had made friendly overtures toward China but never was anything but loyal to Russian interest. On December 27, they stormed the Tajbeg Palace, to which Amin had moved the government offices with the clear purpose of deposing and killing President Amin. They announced that he had been executed for his crimes. Within two weeks, five Russian divisions were in Afghanistan, which included 1,800 tanks, 2,000 armored fighting vehicles, and 80,000 soldiers. In those first two weeks, 4,000 flights had been made from Russia to Afghanistan.

The opposition against the Russian invaders was the loosely organized mujahideen fighters. These were significantly financed, armed, and trained by the United States Central Intelligence Agency, Saudi Arabia, China, several European nations, Iran, and Pakistan. Ronald Reagan praised them as freedom fighters. A wealthy Saudi Arabian was a prominent organizer and financier of an all-Arab Islamic group of foreign fighters.

His name was Osama Bin Laden, and when the Russians left in 1988, he formed an organization from the groups he had led in Afghanistan. He called the organization "Al Qaeda," which means "the base." Al Qaeda was formed with the avowed purpose of driving all foreigners from the Arabian Peninsula, driving Israel out of Palestine, and establishing Islamic fundamentalist governments in every Arab nation. They succeeded as no other group in recruiting suicide bombers and corrupting the minds of Muslim youth. He was incensed about the presence of United States military forces in Saudi Arabia, which was considered the cradle of Islam, and started writing treatises against the Saudi royal family. The Saudi government revoked his citizenship, and he went to Libya, from which he was later expelled, and ultimately he moved back to Afghanistan. He would become known as the world's number one terrorist. His group was made up of Sunni Muslims who were strong proponents of Islamic jihad.

Langley Air Force Base Virginia, July, 1988

Amee had been at Langley for two weeks and was beginning her new work with computers. Danny believed God could work miracles, such as placing him there, and that he had answered their prayers. As to the human means God used, Mr. Adams wanted Danny in proximity to the CIA headquarters, so Langley was the only choice. On July 1, he arrived at the airport in Richmond, Virginia. He and Amee were both off work the whole week of Independence Day, and since she had never been to Washington, they decided this was the appropriate time for her to see some of the sights. They went by Mount Vernon and Arlington Cemetery and then saw the various monuments, as well as the capitol and the White House. Of course, Danny had to demonstrate his vast knowledge of history for her. Amee was duly impressed with all she saw and learned. On the way back, they took a slight detour to see Monticello, home of Thomas Jefferson, as well as Montpelier, James Madison's home.

He took her by Appomattox, where General Robert E. Lee surrendered to General Ulysses Grant to signal the end of the Civil War. As best he could, Danny tried to explain what that war was all about. Amee wanted to know why she still heard so much about it, to which Danny replied that Southerners weren't ready to give up on it just yet. He told her the story of the little boy who was studying the American Civil War for the first time at school. When he got off the school bus, his grandfather was rocking on the front porch. The boy told him what he was studying and said, "Grandpa, the teacher told us the South lost the war. Is that true?"

His grandfather spit his tobacco juice into the yard and said, "It's too soon to tell, son."

As Amee returned to her job, Danny began to get familiar with his new surroundings. He was going about his business like any other pilot and waiting to hear from Mr. Adams or Dr. Rubenstein. He was about to conclude that they had forgotten him when his phone rang. "Lieutenant Danny Brannigan here," he said as he answered.

"Lieutenant Brannigan, this is Adams. Would you please meet Dr. Rubenstein and me in the reading room of the base library tonight?"

It was nice to see that he still had his same charming personality. Danny arrived first, and soon Mr. Adams and Dr. Rubenstein appeared. As usual, Mr. Adams spoke first.

"The purpose of this meeting is to update you about what's happening with respect to global terrorism. Islamic jihad groups and the Palestine Liberation Organization are responsible for numerous acts of terrorism. We're hearing more and more hate talk from the Islamic clergy. They're calling America 'The Great Satan' and encouraging Muslim youth to join in the jihad against all who are considered enemies of Islam. Of course, they hate anyone who helps Israel, but what alarms us most is the incitement of Islamic youth to terrorism. The leaders are teaching them that they can't compete with the powerful armies of other nations, but they can intimidate the people of these countries by creating fear through terrorism. The youth is full of zeal, and many are buying into it. The one truth they *are* telling them is that terrorism is a powerful weapon.

"There have already been a few incidents of suicide bombers, and we're hearing increasing talk about it. Those who are willing to blow themselves up are promised direct entrance into heaven and a reward of seventy-two virgins. The dangerous thing is that people really believe this kind of nonsense because it's coming from the Imams. Some Muslim leaders are trying to counter this twisted teaching and even say there is a mistranslation of the Koran. They say the word ought to be translated *grapes* instead of *virgins,* and still others say it should be *angels.* Our work is not to try to prevent these random acts of violence—there are other agencies for that—but to try to predict and prevent a major catastrophe. There are many ways we will approach this."

Danny thoroughly grasped the gravity of the situation, yet, try as he might, he could not help but find what Mr. Adams said to be extremely funny. He had a vivid imagination and could picture some poor Muslim man arriving at the gates of heaven, having just blown himself to bits, expecting to be met by seventy-two beautiful virgins. Then Mohammed himself greets him and says, "Well done. Because you died for Islam, you have earned a great reward. Not only will you be ushered into heaven, but here are your seventy-two grapes."

He was quickly sobered by the fact that all such misguided people would wind up in hell.

Mr. Adam's voice brought him back to reality.

"We believe in the future they will want to hit targets that will demoralize Americans as well as cripple the economy. Suggested targets by our brain trust are places like the World Trade Center, the Pentagon, the Capitol Building, the White House, a World Series game, the Super Bowl, or the center of any large city. Various scenarios have been suggested as to how they could accomplish their mission. A commandeered jetliner with full fuel tanks could bring down any building. It would virtually be a huge bomb. Even a small nuclear warhead would be devastating in any large city, and bridges and tunnels would be desirable targets, easily hit with conventional or homemade explosives. Surface-to-air missiles could do great damage in many ways. This is not an exhaustive list, but I think you get the picture.

"Our job will be to stay one step ahead, to predict and prevent. We believe most Muslims would be content to coexist peacefully with the rest of the world if the radicals would leave them alone, but for those involved in jihad, the battle will never be over until the entire world is under Muslim domination. Now, as for your role in this, you will function as any other pilot until you are contacted. Though only a few people know what you are doing, you will always have clearance for your clandestine assignments."

Finally, it was Dr. Rubenstein's turn. "My job is scientific and technical advisor, so if there's a question about electronics, chemicals, detonators, and the like, I will always be available to you. In the meantime, I'm working on possibilities for destroying these buildings we have speculated about, commandeering planes, sabotaging tunnels, and other scenarios. If we know how the terrorists are going to do something, we will know how to stop it. If you should have a suggestion that we might follow up on, don't hesitate to let us know."

Mr. Adams said, "If you have questions, now's the time for them."

Danny said, "I have just two questions. First, if something were to happen to both you and Dr. R, what do I do?"

"There will always be a next in command, although you probably won't ever know who it is until the circumstances require it. Should anything ever happen to both Dr. Rubenstein and me and someone else contacts you, he will identify himself as 'Guardian Angel,' and he will address you as 'Thunderbird.' Danny, you must know by now that this is a very serious endeavor and that we are leaving nothing to chance."

Danny nodded thoughtfully.

"My second question is, what's your first name?"

"That's on a need-to-know basis, and you don't need to know."

Danny laughed, and Mr. Adams continued. "There's one other touchy subject I need to bring up. We have investigated Ameenah Salim and her family thoroughly, but you certainly know more about all of them than we do. I have one question for you. Is your relationship with her a security risk?"

"I assure you that it is not. She wanted nothing more than to become a United States citizen, and she even joined the air force in order to streamline that process. She has also recently become a Christian. I don't know what your belief is or if you understand what that means, but her entire life has been changed. Her conversion actually places her life in jeopardy with some Muslims."

Mr. Adams responded quietly but firmly. "I'm sorry, but her conversion doesn't impress me much. I don't mean to hurt your feelings, but I've never had much use for religion of any kind. Some of my worst experiences have been with Christian as well as Muslims."

He didn't think that they would understand the one thing in Amee's life that gave him the most assurance, but he knew that if she were truly saved, she could not possibly be involved in such things because the Bible says, "Therefore if any man be in Christ, he is a new creature: old things are passed away, behold, all things are become new."

Danny was about to answer him when Dr. Rubenstein spoke up, and what he said shook Danny. "There is evidence of long-term

Muslim moles that have been here for years already. They are given special permission to live like others around them, not to openly practice their religion, and to form intimate relationships with Americans. We believe they will even marry, have children, and pretend to become Christians. What better way could they bide their time and learn things to help them in their cause?" It felt like an arrow went through Danny's heart just to admit to himself that Amee and her family were perfect examples of what Dr. Rubenstein was describing.

Mr. Adam's spoke again. "I have only one more question. Have you told her anything about your special service?"

"Absolutely not," Danny answered.

"Good. We must keep it that way. Now, I will be honest with you. We arranged for both of you to be stationed at Langley for several reasons. We realize you have no doubts about Ameenah's loyalty, but we must be a bit more objective. Second, she's in a field we can monitor closely without it being obvious, and finally, we need you here near our headquarters. From time to time, you will be asked to fly special recon missions, and it will not raise red flags in the squadron to which you are assigned.

Danny walked out of the meeting more perplexed than he had ever been in his life. He felt like he was suffering from a split personality. One side of him was hopelessly in love with Amee and respected her entire family, but the other side was already locked into his intelligence work. To do that job well meant he had to be skeptical of anyone and everyone. Amee was already a part of him, and surely he would know if there was any deceit in her. The rational side of him, however, knew Dr. R was right, and as much as he loved the Salims, they easily fit the description of the moles he mentioned. He certainly couldn't deny that Abb had some problems. He had heard that for himself.

Chapter 17

Danny kept the same schedule as any other pilot assigned to his squadron, with the exception of flying special reconnaissance missions that only Mr. Adams, Dr. Rubenstein, and General Burton Travis, the base commander, knew about. When Amee asked about his trips, he just said they were classified. She was busy studying computers and was fascinated by them, so she never pressed the point.

Danny was soon summoned to another meeting in the base library where Mr. Adams wanted to speak with him on a personal level.

"Thank you for coming, Danny. I hope things are going well."

"Things are going very well, thank you."

"We have been monitoring all suspicious Islamic groups, and information has come to my attention about Abdullah Salim, Ameenah's brother. We know that he's involved with an anti-American group centered in a mosque in Boston. I'm sorry, but that places his entire family under suspicion. I'm not accusing them of anything, but we must keep an eye on them."

Danny wasn't at all sure that he had acted wisely in withholding what he knew about Abb, but he couldn't say anything about it now without exposing Abb, as well as putting himself in a bad position. He just changed the subject. "Although Mr. Salim is a committed Muslim, he agreed for Amee to join the air force, and Abb's only a kid. I recently spent a week in their home and was never treated better by anyone. They have virtually become Americans in every way and..." Danny's voice trailed off as he began to realize he was giving the perfect description of deep-cover moles. *No, It can't be, no matter how it looks,* he thought.

"Danny, my years in this business have not made me a warm and fuzzy fellow, but I want to talk to you as a friend. Keep your eyes open for your own sake. I'm not saying throw it all away without evidence, but be careful."

"All I ask, sir, is that you be cautious with the Salims and don't hurt really good people. If it were ever proven that they are involved in anything damaging to America's security, I will do my duty to my country."

"If I had any doubt about that we wouldn't be having this conversation right now," Adams responded.

Danny sat trying to absorb what had just transpired after Mr. Adams left. He felt like his and Amee's relationship had been cursed from the beginning. He couldn't help but think once again that he was always dealt a bad hand, and no matter how he played it, he lost the game. If God really loved him, why didn't he help him sometime? By the time he got back to his station, he had decided to talk openly with Amee about Abb. He had something to go on because of Abb's behavior and what he had heard at the mosque.

After dinner that evening, he drove to a secluded spot and parked his truck. "Sweetheart, there's something that has been bothering me, and I need to talk to you about it."

"You know we can talk about anything."

"I was concerned about Abb's attitude toward me when we were with your family. He and I got along so well before, but it was apparent that he resented me. He avoided me and wouldn't even speak when he saw me." He purposely didn't tell her yet about the phone conversation, until he heard what she had to say.

"Oh, he's just a typical teenager and has been going through some difficult changes in his life. It's really nothing for you to be concerned about. My parents and I discussed it, and my dad has been talking to him. They believe over time he will be able to deal with it and get everything straightened out."

This was just too important for Danny to let it go this time. "I'm sorry to have to talk about this, but I believe I do need to be concerned about it. I feel it has something to do with me, and I don't want to be the source of problems for your family." He was trying to take the route of least offense.

"Danny, I've never hidden anything from you, and I won't do it now. I have only tried to spare your feelings. Abb's going to school at the mosque and is getting some anti-American influence. Because of that, he resents our relationship, but he's the only one in our family who does. My mom and dad are very concerned about him, and Dad's trying to reason with him. He even suggested that Abb go to another school, but he threatened to leave home. They think it's best to leave him there for the time being and keep talking to him. My parents and Mo love you and were embarrassed by Abb's behavior. He is just confused right now."

At that moment, Danny felt like he was caught in a vise and someone was slowly turning the screw. Once, Amee had chosen her religion over him; must he now choose between her and his loyalty to his country?"

"You are obviously still troubled, so let's talk it all out now. I don't ever want anything between us again." Amee said.

"I pray I'm doing the right thing. I have never kept anything from you either except what I have been commanded not to tell anyone because it's classified. There are some things I can't even tell my mom and dad, but I'm going to tell you some of it because I believe our relationship depends on it.

"Amee, you know there are different levels of security clearance. I'm not just a pilot, but I can't tell you everything, at least not yet. You simply have to trust me for a while. I was recruited for a special assignment that is top secret, and only a few people in the government even know about it."

Her eyes were wide now and her brow furrowed. She had the most incredulous and puzzled look on her face. "This sounds serious. What're you involved in?"

"I'm walking a very thin line to even bring this up and would no doubt be court martialed if I cross that line."

"Why do you bring it up now if you can't tell me about it?"

"Because I need to give you some explanation of what my problem is."

"But why is your cloak-and-dagger work somehow linked to a discussion about Abb?"

Now Danny really needed wisdom to phrase what he was about to say very carefully. "That's what makes this so difficult; it all does tie together in a certain way. I must speak in the broadest terms possible, but what I'm involved in has to do with the security of the United States. Anyone who might pose a threat could possibly be under surveillance. In the process of monitoring groups with anti-American sentiments, the mosque Abb attends came up on the intelligence radar screen, and of course they eventually came up with specific names. I have nothing to do with that, but I work with someone who does, and he could tell me because of my security clearance."

He told her what he had heard Abb say when he was talking on the phone. "He might be misguided, but I don't think he is confused. He knows exactly what he believes."

"Have they made the connection between Abb and me?"

"Yes, they know he's your brother; that's why my friend told me."

"And are they concerned about me?"

"They will no doubt keep an eye on your whole family."

"I can't believe it. My mom and dad love America and want to make it their home. I even chose to fight for it if necessary and took an oath of loyalty to defend it, and now my family is under suspicion for some sort of subversion?"

"You have to realize that they don't know you; they're just doing their jobs. Everything will be fine because there is nothing for them to discover. Even if Abb follows his present thinking, the rest of you can't be held accountable for his views."

Suddenly a light came on for Amee. "This makes your job more difficult, doesn't it?"

"That doesn't matter. Time will prove your allegiance and mine."

Amee had a look of horror on her face.

"I see exactly what's happening; I'm guilty until proven innocent, and I'm being put on probation, even by you."

"Oh, sweetheart, that's not true. I absolutely have no doubts about you or your family."

"Danny, I love you. I love America, and I am loyal to it, and I love the Lord Jesus Christ with all my heart, but evidently that's not enough for anyone. The rest I can let time deal with, but I can't handle a relationship with you under these circumstances. One thing that never changed even when we thought we were separated forever was our love and trust. I think you're confused, and I know I am. I think it's best if we stop seeing each other."

"Amee, please don't do this. That's the last thing I would ever want."

"I'm not sure you know what you want right now, and until you do, it must be this way."

As he drove her home, Danny had the same feeling of hopelessness he had when he drove her home from Casey's that night so long ago. "Danny, it's not that I don't *want* to see you. I *can't* see you under these circumstances."

"We at least have to continue to work on things," Danny pleaded.

"I just can't do that, not right now. You're going to have to give me some time."

"How much time?"

"I don't know. I think you need to take stock of your heart and see where you really stand. I can't be involved in a relationship that's conditional upon an intelligence report on me and my family."

"Please, sweetheart, it's not like that."

"It sure feels like it is."

He walked her to the door, and she gave him a quick hug and went inside.

If they had still been in Colorado, he might have driven his truck off a cliff. Oh well, the ocean would do just as well.

When the sun arose the next morning, Danny was still awake. By then all he felt was anger toward everyone and everything, including Amee this time. He felt that she should have been more understanding about his dilemma. He wondered how she could break up with him so easily after all they had gone through to be together. Was it possible that her family was involved with the terrorists in some way, or, God forbid, that she wasn't what she appeared to be? He would never have entertained such a thought before, but now he wasn't sure of anything.

He was angry toward the government, Mr. Adams, Abb, and even God. "Lord, why can't I just have this one thing? Is that so selfish? I would be willing to give up everything else." Danny had no desire to live without her, yet he had to go through the motions, so he dressed and reported for duty. He didn't have much time to brood over the situation before he received orders that he was to leave immediately for a covert operation, location unspecified, danger level high. He tried to call Amee but got no answer, so all he could do was to leave a message. "This is Danny. I'm so sorry I didn't get to talk to you. I must leave immediately for a mission, and I don't know where or how long. I just know it is dangerous. I love you, and I promise you we will work everything out as soon as I get back. Pray for me."

While Danny was away, Amee had time to think things through. She felt that no matter what she did, her family would always be under suspicion. She was beginning to second-guess her decision to become a citizen of the United States and a member of the armed services. What difference would it all make if she would never be accepted at face value? It wasn't supposed to matter in America about your race, creed, or color, but in her case it did. She also felt that she had always brought pain and confusion to Danny, so the best thing she could do for him was to get out of his life forever. The most difficult thing to understand, though, was why her problems intensified when she became a Christian. With all of these things going on in her mind, she still wished she had been there to talk to Danny before he left. There was no telling where he was and what danger he might be facing.

The eight-year war between Iran and Iraq was nearly over, but it had permanently sealed the fate of the United States with the Islamic militants. Along with the Soviet Union, Britain, France, and others, the United States had supported the Iraqis to counterbalance Iran's military advantage. There were already longstanding border disputes between Iran and Iraq, and when Tehran called for the overthrow of Saddam Hussein's regime, Iraq invaded on

September 22, 1980. They were beaten back across the border by superior Iranian forces, but the Ayatollah Khomeini had no intention of leaving it there. He believed the oppressed Shiites in Saudi Arabia, Iraq, and Kuwait could follow the example of Iran, turn against their governments, and join a united Islamic republic. The world began to understand the brutality of Saddam Hussein during the war. He used weapons of mass destruction not only against the Iranians but also against the Kurds and others in his own country.

It was rumored that in order to expedite the ceasefire, two United States Air Force F-16 Fighting Falcons had taken out some strategic Iranian targets. It rippled throughout the air force that there was an ensuing dogfight in which three Iranian planes were shot down, and in the process, one of the F-16s went down also. Of course, neither the White House nor the Pentagon had any comments.

When the news reached Amee, her first thought was about Danny. *Could this possibly have been his mission?* He had been gone two weeks, and she had heard nothing from him. She knew he could just be honoring her request for him to give her some time, but she needed to know whether he was all right.

She called one of the pilots in Danny's group. "Hi, George. This is Ameenah Salim. How are you?"

"Doin' good. How 'bout you?"

"I would be doing a lot better if I knew where Danny was. Do you happen to know?"

"Not officially, but the scuttlebutt is that a couple of our guys are in the Middle East."

"That's what I'm concerned about; I'm afraid Danny's there."

"I don't know for sure, but that's quite possible."

Now Amee was really concerned because if Danny was there, he was in harm's way.

"George, be honest with me. Do you think Danny is involved in the situation in Iran?"

"Of course I don't know for sure, but my gut instinct is that he's one of the two pilots who bombed targets there."

Try as she might, Amee was not able to get any official information about Danny, and it was driving her crazy. The only comfort she had was that if he had been killed or captured, it would have been reported. Her phone rang, and when she answered, a strange voice said, "Lieutenant Salim?"

"Yes."

"You don't know me, but my name is Adams. I have some information that you might be interested in."

"What kind of information?"

"We have a pilot down in Iran, and I believe you are acquainted with him."

Amee's heart nearly stopped as she asked in a quivering voice, "Who is it?"

"His name is Daniel Brannigan."

"Oh no! Danny! Do you know anything about his condition?"

"We know he ejected before the crash, but we haven't heard anything since."

It felt like someone had driven a stake into her heart. She knew even the best case scenario was not good. She could not, and would not, believe he was dead, although she was aware that death would probably be preferable to what would happen to him if he were captured.

"Sir, will you please let me know as soon as you find out anything?"

Adams promised her that he would. Because she was so concerned for Danny, she hadn't even asked who he was. She felt some relief just to know that Danny had ejected.

Adams had two purposes in telling Amee frankly that it was Danny. In the first place, she would have to know soon anyway, and second, he wanted to know what her reaction would be. What he could not have known was Amee's ability to conceal her feelings when necessary. He elicited no telling reaction at all from her. However, as soon as she got to her room, she fell across the bed and had the cry she had needed for several days.

Chapter 18

Early the next morning, a special plane was on its way to Kuwait International Airport. On the flight was a team made up to rescue Danny, consisting of Mr. Adams, Richard Slocum from the state department, and a Special Forces team. Danny's plane went down near the city of Ahvaz after he had successfully completed his bombing mission and had taken out two Iranian fighter planes on the way back.

The Kuwaiti-Iraqi-Iranian Border Region

Permission had been granted by Iraq to move along inside its border in order to avoid the Iranian army. That was not guaranteed, however, because the Iranians were crossing into Iraq regularly. The plan was for the team, along with an Iraqi named Ahmed, to move to the last known coordinates and endeavor to find Danny. An attempt would be made to avoid all contact, but if locals were encountered, Ahmed would do the talking. Danny was in perfect physical condition, armed, and a master of Tae Kwon Do, so if he wasn't badly hurt, he had a good chance. The Iraqis had already done reconnaissance and identified the best point of entry into Iran.

Ahmed had an easy smile and a good sense of humor, and everyone liked him. They also would like to have him on their side in a fight. Although Ahmed was fluent in English, he and Mr. Adams conversed most of the time in Farsi, so Adams could brush up on it. The team crossed into Iran without incident and was winding its way toward the crash sight when they came upon a small band of Bedouins. Ahmed chatted with them for a few minutes, during which time they laughed a lot. Finally, they gave him something to drink and then plodded on their way. The soldiers were getting agitated and impatient at this waste of time.

"Did you have a good time with your buddies?" Lieutenant Davis asked. "We do have a mission, you know."

"And now I have a great deal more information to aid us in our mission," Ahmed said in perfect English.

"What kind of information?" Lieutenant Davis asked impatiently.

"The Iranians have found the wreckage but did not find the pilot. They are desperately searching for him, which will make our job much more difficult.

"Or it might make *their* lives more difficult," one of the soldiers said.

"Don't ever underestimate a Persian in the desert," Ahmed replied.

Lieutenant Davis called a team meeting to discuss strategy.

The lieutenant began, "We must examine our possibilities and determine our best option. If he is alive and uninjured, he will try to make it back to friendly territory. If he is holed up, he stands a better chance, but it would take longer to locate him. Our best plan is to assume he is physically sound and will be on the move. We can work other possibilities from there. What is our best guess as to which way he would go?"

"My guess is that he would first seek food and shelter if he can find a place where there are no Iranian soldiers," Brad Curtis offered. "He would probably travel at night."

Mr. Adams spoke up. "Danny is extremely intelligent and a logical thinker. He grew up in a hot climate, and the conditions here would not pose an insurmountable obstacle for him. If he is able, he will move in the straightest line possible to get to safety. In my opinion, we should lay out a course to intersect that line at a point that would reasonably guarantee he hasn't gotten ahead of us."

Lieutenant Davis was studying the map intently. "If that's our plan, we should move back into Iraq and proceed along the border. It looks like its only four or five hours by foot to the border from the crash site. We can make a good guess about where he would cross. If in a reasonable time we don't make contact, we can spread out and move toward the crash site. The quieter our presence here is, the better it is for everyone. If Captain Brannigan makes it to the border, we won't even have to fight." Everyone agreed they had devised the best strategy.

Twenty-five miles inside the İranian Border, A Bit Earlier

Danny at least found one thing to thank the Lord for: soft sand to land in. He and Jeff VanderMeer had been deployed to Saudi Arabia to fly special missions. They were given orders to take out two rocket installations inside Iran that were decimating the Iraqi forces. They accomplished their mission without a hitch, but on the way home, they encountered three Iranian MiGs. Danny took care of one of them in short order while Captain VanderMeer was battling another. The third MiG came after Danny, and he shot it down, but not before his plane sustained a hit. He could no longer maintain control and was forced to eject. He saw his plane go up in flames. When he landed, he buried his parachute, secured his survival kit, checked out his sidearm, and started off toward the west. He knew he was fairly close to the Iraqi border but had no idea what lay between him and there. He knew Captain VandeMeer would report all the particulars. He thought his best chance was to travel at night and try to find a place to hide in the daytime. The wind was blowing, so his tracks would soon be wiped out and would not betray his direction. Danny had felt himself begin to harden since the last ordeal with Amee, and now he really didn't care much if he lived or died. He neither trusted anyone nor cared much for anyone except his mother and Jake. He was simply doing his job.

Just as daylight began to break, he saw a farm compound that had a house and a small outbuilding. There were also several animals and a large stack of straw. Danny decided his best chance was to burrow in on the backside of the straw and try to sleep for a while.

He was awakened by something poking at him and instinctively jumped up with his pistol drawn. Had he been in safer circumstances, he would have laughed out loud at himself. He had successfully gotten the drop on a kid goat. Before he could fully enjoy the situation, he had a real problem. A young lady came around the stack of straw, obviously looking for the kid. When she saw Danny with his gun drawn, she froze and, much to Danny's delight, was speechless. She had on the hijab, but it didn't hide her beautiful face any more than her clothing hid her lovely figure. Danny was amazed at how much she looked like Amee. He quickly holstered his pistol, smiled at her, and she lowered her eyes as a good Muslim girl is supposed to do but faintly returned the smile. She didn't seem to be intimidated at all.

Danny had learned a few words of Farsi from Amee, so he attempted to say hello. She giggled and answered, not in Farsi, but in Arabic. It would have been hilarious to anyone listening because Danny then spoke to her in English. He had one more surprise coming; the young lady responded in perfect English. Danny began to think she must be related to Amee because of her mischievous sense of humor.

"You are the American whose plane crashed."

There was no need for a blonde-haired, blue-eyed man dressed in U.S. flight gear to deny it, so he simply said, "Yes. I'm trying to get back to Iraq. I mean you no harm."

The girl responded, "I live here in Iran with my mother and father, but we are Iraqis by birth. We do not take sides in this war; we just want to see the fighting end."

"I can certainly agree with you on that; I'm simply obeying orders. My name is Danny," he said without offering his hand.

"I am Naadirah Mahmood, and I will assist you if I can."

"Do you know if there are any Iranian soldiers in the area?"

"We have not seen any in several days; most of the fighting is to the north, but I would advise you to be careful. Not all the residents in this area are as friendly to your cause as my family, and they have been searching for you."

Naadirah took him to meet her mother, father, and younger brother. They received him well, fed him, and allowed him to rest in their home until nightfall. At dusk, Nazir Mahmood awakened him, and his wife, Azeena, prepared him another meal as well as some food to take with him.

As Danny finished eating, Nazir said, "My daughter will go with you and show you the best and safest route to the border. I would take you myself, but I was kicked by an ox and have an injured leg. I assure you that she is quite capable of this task and can move as far and as fast in a day as any man."

Mr. Mahmood gave him a robe and turban typically worn by rural men in order to make him less obvious. He took a moment to put some black camouflage grease on the edges of his blond hair and face. He thanked the Lord that he was deeply tanned.

"It is only about forty kilometers to the border, so you should have no problem making it in six hours. May Allah bless you," Nazir said.

"I don't know how to thank you for all your kindness. You may very well have saved my life," Danny said as he shook Mr. Mahmood's hand and nodded to Mrs. Mahmood.

It was uncanny how much Naadirah reminded him of Amee, and for a moment he wondered where Amee was and if she had any idea what was happening to him. A full moon was just rising when they started out, and the shadows on the sand dunes camouflaged the desert.

Nadi, as Danny had already dubbed her, laughed at him as he kept referring to his compass. She had nothing with her except the clothes she was wearing, a small pouch of food, and a bottle of water, yet she just kept moving on ahead about as fast as Danny cared to go. She knew the stars so well that it would have been impossible to lose her. If this was a typical rescue, crashing wasn't really so bad. It wasn't long before it was his turn to laugh at Nadi. She was running up a large sand dune and started to slide backward. As she was about to fall head over heals, Danny caught her and went down on his knees with her leaning across them in his arms. For a moment, as their eyes met, he had the impulse to kiss her. He wasn't sure whether he saw Nadi or Amee. She reached up and held him tightly around the neck as he stood and lifted her up. One thing was certain; it made him miss Amee all the more. As he placed her on her feet, she kissed him tenderly on the cheek and said, "Thank you."

"Does Naadirah have a meaning?" Danny asked.

"Yes, it means *rare.*"

Her name was certainly appropriate in respect to his plight. She was indeed a rare find in this dangerous land.

Suddenly, without any warning, two Iranian soldiers on patrol confronted them. Danny made sure his turban had all his blond hair covered and just stood stoop-shouldered with his head down.

"What are you two doing here?" one of the men asked as they both kept their rifles trained on them.

Nadi answered in Farsi. "My brother and I are on an errand for our father, and I think we are lost."

"What is your name?" the other soldier asked as he poked Danny with his rifle. "Why do you not answer me?"

Just as he drew his arm back to hit him, Nadi said, "Please, sir, my brother is not able to hear or speak. Allah has deemed it wise to make him thus."

The men shared sinister glances and smiled. They then approached Nadi as one of them yanked her hijab off and said, "Let's have a look at you."

"Please don't sin against Allah so," Nadi pleaded.

"It is Allah who provides for all the needs of his servants, and he has miraculously provided for ours."

"Sir, I beg you; this violates the Great Prophet's teachings."

"A soldier is given many indulgences because we fight for Allah, and I believe this is one of them."

So far, Danny had stood motionless with his head toward the ground. The men weren't paying any attention to him. They were more interested in the pleasure that awaited them.

Nadi was crying and pleading with them to stop when Danny shuffled up to them with his head still down, grunting as he came. One of the men saw him and turned to hit him. As quickly as a desert viper strikes, Danny grabbed his arm, using his own momentum to pull him on through. As he did, he spun and hit him on the end of the nose with the heel of his hand, driving the bones into his brain. He never moved as he hit the ground. When the other one who was holding Nadi realized what was happening, he reached for his pistol. Danny was quicker and buried his knife in his throat. He fell without making a sound.

Nadi was lying on the ground in disbelief, not realizing her blouse was still partially unbuttoned. Danny came over and knelt beside her. He gently picked her up, buttoned her blouse, and held her for a few minutes until she stopped crying and trembling.

"Sit down and rest for a bit while I take care of these men," Danny gently suggested.

"What are you going to do?" she asked.

"I must bury them and remove all signs of the struggle because there might be others in the area."

"I will help you."

"It won't take me long; you need to rest."

Danny started to dig in the sand with one of the helmets, and without saying a word, Nadi fell on her knees beside him and began to dig with the other one. They soon had a grave deep enough to cover the men, along with their weapons.

"Why do we not take the guns in case we encounter other soldiers?" Nadi asked.

"They would only make it more dangerous for you," Danny said. "Besides, what I can't do with my pistol and knife would not do us any good anyway."

"I understand," she said quietly.

"Nadi, I'm very sorry you had to see what I did to those men."

She laid her index finger on his lips and said, "No, no, not another word. If it had not been for you, my life would have been ruined forever."

She removed her finger and all in the same motion kissed him lightly and tenderly on the lips. Then she turned and said, "It is time we were moving along."

As they continued to plod onward, Danny began to reflect upon the work he was doing for the government with respect to Muslims, as well as his own personal experience with them. So far, he hadn't met a Muslim who wasn't kind to him, with the exception of Abb and the two soldiers. He was also trying to figure out if he was naturally drawn to Arab girls or if Amee had just conditioned him. Whatever the case, he definitely liked Nadi, and it would be easy to fall for her. He could tell without a doubt that the feeling was mutual. After a while, she slowed down and walked beside him, and they began to talk as naturally as he and Amee had in the beginning. She was totally uninhibited but not in a sensual way. She would touch his forearm as she looked at him to make a point, and if she stumbled in the loose sand, she would grab his arm with both of her hands. She was totally at ease with Danny.

She was interested in everything about him and freely answered any question he asked her.

"What caused your family to move to Iran?"

"My father was an official in Saddam Hussein's government and witnessed the escalation of abuses to a point that he could no longer tolerate. He couldn't stand to see any more men tortured, women raped, or whole villages slaughtered. He sent all of us to Iran, and then one day he just disappeared and joined us. There are many Iraqi families like ours in the area."

Nadi had been to school in America for three years, and it was there that she had learned English. She was able to teach her family some conversational English.

"Our dream is to immigrate to the United States someday. I don't know if we will ever see it come true, but I surely am tired of living in isolation."

Danny didn't know if he would ever be in a position to help them, but he would never forget what they did for him.

"The border is just beyond that row of trees," Nadi said as they approached a line of date palms. In the nearly dark night sky, the trees looked like sentinels on guard, rigid, waiting for a signal to spur them to action. Danny had enjoyed talking with Nadi so much the trip actually seemed short.

"This stretch of the border is not strategically located, so there usually aren't any guards around, but we should stay alert just in case," Nadi said.

They moved cautiously up to the tree line and knelt to scrutinize the terrain. There was no barrier at this section of the border, and no one was in sight.

"I guess this is where we must part," Nadi said wistfully. "I wish we had more time together because I have really enjoyed being with you. I am virtually marooned out there, and sometimes it gets unbearable."

"I'm very sorry, Nadi. I have enjoyed being with you also, and I will never forget what you and your family have done for me. If I ever have an opportunity to help you, I will gladly do so."

He took the gold chain from around his neck and placed it upon hers. "I want you to have this as a reminder of me and as a token of my gratitude. It has a gold cross on it, and if that offends you or your family, you can sell it."

"I will never sell it, and I will treasure it forever," Nadi said as the tears rolled down her cheeks.

She took his hand and held onto it as she said, "I will pray for your safety." Then she hugged him, and as she did, she whispered in his ear, "God bless you, Danny," and kissed him on the cheek. He didn't have time to respond to her, which was probably a very good thing. At that moment, they heard a vehicle approaching. They moved back behind the tree line and waited. Soon a camouflaged Humvee appeared, moving slowly along the border. Light was just beginning to break across the eastern horizon behind them, giving Danny and Nadi the advantage. The lights were out on the hummer, but the windows were down, and Danny couldn't believe what he saw. In the front seat, an Arab man was scanning the tree line with binoculars, but in the second seat he saw an American Special Forces uniform.

He explained quickly to Nadi, and just to be sure, she yelled in Farsi, "Please identify yourself. Are you American?"

Ahmed answered in Farsi. "This is an American noncombat search and rescue mission."

Nadi responded, "Answer in English something that only an American would know."

"This year's World Series is set to be a California Classic between the Los Angeles Dodgers and the Oakland Athletics," came the reply in perfect American English.

Danny whispered to Nadi, and she spoke again in English, "Are you ready to show yourself?"

"You show me yours and I'll show you mine; uniform, that is."

With that, Lieutenant Davis stepped out the door on the opposite side and started around the back of the hummer. Danny was ready to make a move, so he yelled from the shadows, "Does anyone there know a Lieutenant Daniel Brannigan?"

"Yes, sir, we have come to rescue him."

Danny walked out into the breaking light and said, "You're too late. I've already been captured by this young lady, and I'm not sure I want to be rescued."

"We'll be on our way then," Lieutenant Davis said. "Glad to see you're okay."

All the rescue team gave a cheer and stepped out of vehicle to greet him.

As he and Nadi walked up to the hummer, Ahmed yelled, "We really need to go as quickly as possible."

Danny hugged Nadi and said, "Thank you, and please convey my gratitude to your parents."

She gave him one final kiss and whispered something in his ear. He nodded and grinned, and suddenly she was gone.

From inside the hummer he heard, "I should have known better than to worry about you. Drop you down in the middle of the desert behind enemy lines and you find a beautiful girl to rescue you. What is it with you and Arab women? Do all of them fall in love with you because you have some strange power over them, or is it your blond hair and blue eyes?"

"Could you blame her? How could she resist all this?" he said as he swept his hand toward his body. "She didn't fall in love with me, though; she had just been very lonely living with her parents in an isolated place."

"Well, you should have told *her* she didn't fall for you."

"I guess it is just my boyish charm."

"By the way," the voice asked, "what did she say to you just now?"

"Oh, that's a secret, and I'm a gentleman, so I would never kiss and tell."

"You're trying to convince the wrong person. What did she say?"

"She just said she was going home to give her little goat a reward."

"A reward for what?"

"For finding her a handsome American man. It was the goat that discovered me in her haystack."

Danny leaned into the hummer and came face to face with Mr. Adams. "Just why are you involved in this, sir?"

"Let's just say I love you."

"Yes, sir. You're a warm and fuzzy fellow."

"The truth is we need you, or we would have just let the Iranians have you."

"Now, that I can believe."

"By the way, a vehicle is approaching behind us. It's time we leave," Danny said.

"It is time to leave, but those are friendly. That's our very own A-team," Mr. Adams replied.

As they began the drive back to Kuwait City, Mr. Adams and Mr. Slocum started the debriefing process on Danny. The air force would deal with the mission and the crash of his plane, but they wanted to know every detail about his encounter with the Iraqi family.

"What questions did they ask and what was their attitude toward the United States?" Slocum inquired.

Danny explained their background and told about their desire to go to America. Mr. Slocum promised to try to help when the war was over. They were quite excited about the prospect of American sympathizers in Iran.

"Are there other incidents worthy of note?" Mr. Adams asked.

"We did have an encounter with two Iranian soldiers," Danny said matter-of-factly.

"What was the nature and outcome of that?"

"I was disguised well enough and sufficiently passed off by Nadi as her deaf mute brother, so that they were no threat to me. It was when they decided to take advantage of her that I had to take them out."

"Just like that, you took them out?" Lieutenant Davis asked with some amazement.

"Would you mind telling us how this went down?" Mr. Adams asked.

"I couldn't be sure whether there were other soldiers in the area, so it was necessary to do it quietly. I eliminated one with my hands and the other with my knife. Then we buried them along with their weapons. I left their identification for their families' sake, so if someone finds them, they will know who they are."

Adams said, "No wonder Nadi looked at you the way she did. You were her knight in shining armor."

Danny blushed, and they all laughed at him.

Suddenly three vehicles came over the hill from the opposite direction. They were not friendly. Immediately there was fire from machine guns and grenade launchers. The Special Forces unit headed straight for them, and the three vehicles split in three different directions. Two special ops soldiers rolled out of the truck, one on each side, and ran in opposite directions. They took positions to return fire while the others moved straight ahead in their Bradley.

"Get out and get down," Ahmed yelled. "Take cover."

Danny knew the Humvee would be a target, so he grabbed a loose M-16 assault rifle as he exited the truck, and as soon as they were in a safe position behind the tree line, he opened fire. Mr.

Adams had jumped behind a bank a few yards away. Danny eliminated two of the enemy who were headed in their direction.

The noise from the other guns ceased, and all was quiet for a while. Lieutenant Davis gave the all clear and everyone stood. As they started for their vehicle, which had been miraculously spared, Danny turned suddenly and aimed his weapon directly at Mr. Adams and fired. Everyone froze, and Mr. Adams just stood there in a state of complete shock. He turned just in time to see an Iranian soldier fall behind him. Danny had saved his life.

It was a short drive back to Kuwait City, and they had one night before making the flight home. They checked into the International Hotel, and as tired as he was, Danny took time for an American hamburger and a Coke. Once he was back at Langley, he would still have to be debriefed by the air force, and he had no idea how long that would take. He didn't want to take a chance on missing his opportunity to satisfy his craving.

Chapter 19

The tires of the plane screeched as they made contact with the runway, and the blue smoke rose momentarily. Danny was aroused from sleep by the jolt. As he deplaned, the unmistakable, fresh smell of the ocean that he had come to love filled his nostrils.

I can't imagine coming back to a better place after several days in the desert, Danny thought. *What a contrast!*

The strangest and most difficult thing about his return was that he didn't know where he stood with Amee. Should he call her or not? The last thing she said was that she wanted time to think things through. He was certain his ordeal was no secret, so he concluded that he should just wait and let her make the first move.

He still had to go through debriefing with the air force and get the mandatory physical. It was hard for him to concentrate on all the questions about the bombing of the target, the dogfight, exactly why he had to eject, what condition the plane was in after the crash, and a thousand other things. His mind kept wandering away to Amee, Arabs, and his involvement with Mr. Adams and Dr. Rubenstein. Meeting just one family living in the middle of a war zone had put it all in perspective for him. They were people with the same needs, aspirations, and fears of families everywhere. These were good people who were willing to place themselves in harm's way to help another human being whom they did not even know. He was well aware of the zealous and sadistic Muslims who would do anything to accomplish their objectives but also of the many others who wanted to coexist and raise their families in peace. Now, Danny could keep it all balanced. He simply needed to remember what he had always known; there are good and bad people in all skin colors, beneath all kinds of dress, and under every religious banner.

Finally, his interrogators were satisfied that they had milked every ounce of information from him they could get. They were greatly impressed with Danny's ability to handle himself in dangerous circumstances. His physical examination revealed that he was still in perfect health. The only change was a slight weight loss, which he could soon take care of with a few pizzas and burgers.

In fact, on that thought he decided to pick up a pizza and take it home with him, eat the whole thing, take a long hot shower, and sleep for two days.

Just as he walked through the door, his phone rang. Amee was crying as she said, "Danny, I've been so worried. I didn't know what happened to you, and all I could think about was the manner in which I sent you away. I need to see you and talk to you. Will you meet me?"

"No, I won't meet you," Danny replied. "But I will pick you up, and we can go out and talk."

Danny had a one-week pass, so he asked if he could get a good night's sleep and meet her tomorrow. He would pick her up after work, and they could spend the evening together. As tired as he was, he couldn't sleep for a while just thinking about his and Amee's relationship. He found himself in a strange situation. He did care for Amee but had become tougher toward life and no longer felt like his happiness depended upon any one thing or person. He had also been surprised by his feelings toward Nadi. He could not deny that he was sincerely attracted to her. Did that mean his love for Amee wasn't as pure as he thought it was? What would he do if it turned out that any of her family was involved in terrorism toward America? Could he stand to have that conflict in his life? Was there even a possibility that Amee faked her conversion? Even to have a passing thought of such a thing added more pain to his tortured soul. The more he pondered, the more confused he became until he finally drifted off to sleep from sheer exhaustion.

When Danny picked Amee up the next afternoon, it was the first time he could ever remember that he had felt awkward around her. He didn't even have that problem the first time he met her. She was experiencing the same difficulty. They just embraced, and he kissed her on the cheek. They discussed where they would eat and then sat in silence for several minutes. She finally broke the silence by telling him how worried she had been and asking him about his experience. They both relaxed a bit when he started to tell his story. It still scared Amee at how close he came to dying.

After dinner they drove out and parked by the beach. It was still warm enough for them to take a walk in the moonlight. They walked hand in hand for a while, and finally Amee spoke.

"Danny, I know I really love you, but I don't know what to do about all the complications in our lives. If we could clear them all away, I know we would be happy."

"I love you too, but I don't have the answers for the things that keep coming between us."

"Do you think we can just cool our jets for a while to see if some of these things can be cleared up?" Amee asked. "We could go on seeing each other but just not force things."

Danny was desperately trying to come up with the right answer. "It's too late for me to turn back. If I can't have you totally, I don't know if I can stand it. You know I love you, but I really don't know what's best for us anymore."

"I think we should give it a try," Danny said. "I don't want to give up without a fight."

"Don't you think this is important enough that we ought to pray about it together?" Amee asked.

Danny felt himself tense up and was sure she must feel it. He was set back on his heels, not knowing what to say. He had not been confronted this boldly about practical Christianity for a long time. It was perfectly obvious to Amee that he was hesitating.

"Well, if I can ask God for something as important as eternal life, can't we ask for his help in this?" she asked.

There was absolutely nothing but sheer honesty that would do for this.

"Amee, there is something I've never shared with you because I didn't think you were ready to deal with it. I believe everything I have ever told you, but the Lord and I have been on the outs for quite a while now. I'm not sure he wants to hear from me."

"Danny, that doesn't make any sense. If he is our heavenly Father, then he loves us even when we are bad. He is perfect because he is God and can't ever be wrong, so the fault has to be yours. You just need to confess and allow him to forgive you, and everything will be all right."

What Amee said stung and tickled him at the same time.

"Wow! It didn't take long for you to become an obnoxious Christian, did it? You might as well get ordained and start preaching."

He laughed. Any one of the best preachers in America could

have preached to Danny for an hour and not accomplished what Amee did in thirty seconds. She was right, and Danny knew it, so the only thing left was to decide whether he was going to do anything about it.

"I'll make you a deal. If you'll let me off the hook tonight and allow me to deal with this alone, I will get things straightened out with the Lord."

"All right, you get one pass and that's all. No matter what happens to us, you must get yourself straightened out with the Lord. With all the things you get into, you'll never make it any other way. You'll wear your guardian angels out."

They both had a good laugh over that, and the tension was finally lifted. When Danny kissed her goodnight, he felt things were as good as they could expect for the time being. When he got back to his room, he was so tired that he intended to go straight to sleep. He just fell into bed, but when he reached to turn the light off, his Bible was lying on his nightstand. Suddenly he was wide-awake, so he started to read. It was as though an unseen hand guided him to every Scripture he needed to consider.

He read that God showed us his love by allowing Christ to die for us while we were *yet* sinners and that if we confess our sins; he is faithful and just to forgive and cleanse us. He read again that nothing can separate us from the love of God and that every good and perfect gift comes down from above. He was reminded that if the Lord gave us his son, he will also freely give us all things to enjoy and that he will withhold no good thing. He was admonished that he must commit his way unto the Lord. By the time he was done, he was ready to get on his knees beside his bed and confess all his wrong feelings as well as his sin. He first confessed his stubbornness and selfishness and ended with his pride. All the pressure of his sinful emotions and willfulness that had been building up behind the dam of his stubbornness suddenly broke loose with full force. He committed himself totally to the will of God that night.

"Captain Brannigan, you have a phone call from the state department," the operator said.

"Captain Brannigan speaking."

"Hello, Danny. This is Richard Slocum. How are you?"

"I'm fine, sir, and how are you?"

"Wonderful. I wanted to let you know that the war is over between Iran and Iraq as of 20 August, and we might have a small window of opportunity to help the family who came to your aid in Iran."

"That's really great news, sir. What do we need to do?"

"I need to get their exact names so I can check them out. Then we must make sure they really want to come to America, and if they do, we need to find some way to get them to the border of Iraq, as close to Kuwait as possible. I will have them airlifted to Kuwait and flown to the United States. I will personally make sure their citizenship is processed in the fast lane."

"Sir, may I ask why you are doing this?"

"Because it's right, and we also want to show that we are interested in people and not just causes. I will also admit that I am interested in helping you because I was impressed with your dedication to your country."

Danny gave him the names of the four of them, and Mr. Slocum promised to call him as soon as he had a firm answer.

The very next day, Danny received the call, amazed at how fast the process had worked. "The answer is affirmative, and the mission is go," Slocum said.

"How do we proceed?" Danny asked.

"We must make contact; do you have any idea of the best way to go about it?"

"The only sure way I know is to go in and get them."

"But we don't have anyone who knows them or how to find them."

"Yes we do. I know them, and I know how to find them."

"You would be putting your life on the line for them. Why would you do that?"

"Because they put their lives on the line for me."

"There is one other matter. I don't think Adams will take too kindly to your going," Slocum said.

"We don't really need to bother him with all this. He is a very busy man, and you can get my base commander, General Burton Travis, to assign me to the state department for a few days."

"I'm not sure about leaving Adams out of the loop. It could start a feud," Slocum said.

"Let me explain my position. I am just like any other air force pilot until he contacts me. It won't be leaving him out of the loop."

"All right. I'll make the call right now if you will promise to explain all this to Adams if he makes an issue out of it."

"You have my word on it," Danny replied.

In a few hours, everything was arranged, and now all Danny had to do was break the news to Amee.

"Are you out of your mind?" Amee exclaimed. "I have just barely gotten you back from the first mission to Iran."

"Can you imagine how that poor family feels? They're isolated with no friends and no future," Danny protested.

"I know, darling. I'm just venting my frustration. Of course you will go, but if you get hurt or don't make it back, I will never forgive you. The first thing I will do when I see you in heaven is punch you. And there's one more thing, old man. If I hear you've been playing kissy-face with Nadi, you will wish you had died over there. The Iranians will be much easier on you than I will."

"Shucks, I was just going to suggest that we take her into our home. She's Muslim, and it's normal for her that a man has more than one wife."

"One thing you forgot in your plan is that I am an Arab but no longer a Muslim, for which you have yourself to thank. Besides, the Bible says the blood of Jesus cleanses from all sin, so murder must be included. Therefore, I will just kill you and be done with it."

Amee threw a pillow at him and said, "No, I won't do that, but consider it this way; if you try anything, you won't have a need for even *one* wife. Understand?"

"I think I get your drift, but you sure know how to take all the fun out of a man's life."

"I'll take care of the fun department," Amee retorted.

Danny drove to Washington later that night, and the next morning he and Richard Slocum left for Kuwait. They spent one night at the Kuwait International Hotel, and early the next morning a Black Hawk helicopter flying low under the radar dropped Danny and one army ranger off at the point where he had met the team before. The Mahmood family had a telephone, but they dared not call them about their plans for fear the phone could be bugged.

Southwestern Iran, September 1988

The plan was that Danny and Sergeant Seth Jones would be back at the rendezvous point the next morning at 0600 with or without the family. Radio silence would be maintained unless they got into serious trouble. Seth Jones was short and stocky. He had dark hair and complexion and eyes as black as coal. He could have passed for an Iranian. He was quick and agile and never tired. Danny and Sergeant Jones agreed that they would cover the first part of the trip as quickly as possible in order to have more time on the return. Danny calculated if they traveled double time and due east for four hours, they would be close to their destination. The rule was that either man could call time, but neither of them was willing to be the first to do so. The reason Danny had kept checking his compass when Nadi led him out was to keep his bearings in case he had to travel without her for some reason. It was paying off now. Since Danny was the ranking officer, he suggested that they dispense with protocol and use each other's first names as long as they were alone. The one advantage Seth had over Danny was that he had been through desert training. On his last trek, Danny had traveled at night and had no idea how hot the desert could get in the daytime. However, he was no stranger to heat, having worked in the field and played baseball in Georgia in July and August. During many baseball games the temperature reached 120 degrees or more on the field, and a pitcher could lose as much as twenty pounds of water weight during a game. He was pretty sure the temperature was rivaling that even at this early hour of the day. It was a miracle that one or both of them didn't die because of their competitive spirit. Neither one of them would give in.

When they had traveled four hours, they did not find the farm. Danny suggested they try a plan they used in the deep woods to find a point of which they knew the approximate location. They would use the compass and start due east, west, north, or south. If they traveled the same amount of time in each of the four directions, they would make a square and return to the exact point they departed from. Today they would start straight ahead and make three left turns; then, if necessary, the next time, they would go to the right. Danny and Seth measured by time and estimated a one-quarter mile square first. When that one didn't pay off, they went the other way. On the third leg of the second try, they saw the smoke from a fire, and just over the first rise was the Mahmood farm. Before they even got to the house, Nadi bounded out the door yelling, "Danny! Danny!"

She literally jumped into Danny's arms and hugged him. She would have kissed him except that her parents were watching. "I can't believe this. I thought I would never see you again."

"I wasn't sure myself, but I am so glad to be here. How did you know it was me? We are in native dress."

"How could I miss that awkward gait of yours?"

"This is U.S. Army Ranger Sergeant Seth Jones. Sergeant, this is the infamous Naadira Mahmood."

"I'm pleased to meet you, ma'am."

"Likewise. Why am I so infamous, Danny, and what are you doing here?"

"You are infamous as a guerilla fighter and smuggler of enemy combatants, and I found you so irresistible that I just couldn't stay away."

"You'll have to come up with a better line than that. I may be an ignorant desert girl, but I've got your number."

"Don't be too quick to brush me off; you could be wrong, you know," Danny said. "Now to the business at hand. Did you not tell me your family wanted to go to the United States?"

"Yes." She held on to the *s* as she looked at him quizzically.

"I have come to take you to America, if you want to go."

She froze in place with her mouth open and her eyes wide. "Surely you must be joking. Just like that?"

"Yes, just like that. Now that the war is over between Iran and Iraq, we have a very narrow window of opportunity to get you out before things tighten up so that we can't get into Iran. In order to have a better chance of success, we must go tonight. This might be our only hope."

She squealed and jumped onto Danny with legs and arms wrapped around him. Danny was fast learning that religion and Muslim customs weren't extremely important to her.

When she finally settled down, they went to talk to her parents and explain the situation to them. Danny told them how Mr. Slocum had called him and offered to help get them out. They also had located sponsors who would help them get resettled. Nazir could not believe what he was hearing.

"Why would an official of the United States do this for someone he has never even met?"

"Because I am such a powerful person in my country," Danny said laughingly. "No, it is one of those rare opportunities to do something unselfish for someone who has put his life in jeopardy for others. Honesty compels me to tell you that there will be some danger involved until we get to Kuwait. Once we are inside our embassy, you will be under the protection of the United States government," Danny assured them.

Nazir, Azeema, Nadi, and even fourteen-year-old Tajim talked for a few minutes and then agreed. The decision was unanimous that it was worth any risk to be truly free.

Danny explained again that they would need to leave as soon as it was dark, and he and Seth offered to help them prepare for the trip in any way they could. The Mahmoods were afraid to talk with any of their neighbors about what they were doing unless they knew beyond a doubt that they would not be betrayed. Tajim ran to the next farm to bring their most trusted neighbor. They were going to leave their farm to him, along with the animals. If asked, he could simply say they had abandoned it.

In a short time, Tajim was back with Dhia, whose wife had prepared food for their journey. Each person was allowed to take only what he could carry at a fast pace. They had packed family treasures into a trunk and asked Dhia to please keep it in case they could ever retrieve it. They all tried to get a little sleep, but only Danny and Seth succeeded. At sundown they had their last meal together, and they departed at dusk. Again, Danny and Seth put on robes and turbans and camouflaged their faces as best they could. Seth certainly looked the part of an Iranian more than Daniel did. As they topped the first hill, the family took one last look at the little farm and then stoically turned and walked away. Danny walked point with Seth as the rear guard and the family in between. Knowing they could not win a large battle anyway, the soldiers each had only brought a handgun and a knife. These were well concealed in their clothing but quickly accessible. For the next couple of hours, Nadi walked beside Danny, talking incessantly. She had endless questions about America and what her family could expect. Danny enjoyed answering all her questions. He had needed someone to talk to for a long time, but the one he'd always talked to before was the one he now needed to talk about. Other than Amee, he had never been able to talk to anyone as openly as he did Nadi. He told her about

Amee and talked about everything he was at liberty to share with her. She was a good listener, and he was trying hard to suppress feelings he could no longer deny were there. He realized, however, that it would be unfair to Nadi to involve her in his life until he could solve some of his problems.

Suddenly, Danny motioned to Nadi and turned to tell the rest of them to be quiet. He listened intently for a moment and said, "That's the sound of engines I hear." They only had time to sit down in a typical Bedouin circle until the convoy passed. As the sound of the armored vehicles died out, Danny said, "I think we dodged that bullet; let's move on." Just as they stood to leave, five Iranian soldiers appeared with their rifles at the ready. They said something in Farsi, and Nadi whispered, "They want to know where our animals are."

Mr. Mahmood answered, "We are just poor farmers who have been to visit our neighbors. It is Allah's will that we walk, because we have no camels or donkeys."

Danny and Seth remained quiet with their heads down, but one of the soldiers came directly to Danny and asked him a question. When he did not receive an answer, he put his rifle butt under Danny's chin and lifted his head. He shouted something to the others, and Danny knew they had been found out. He grabbed the rifle, flipped it, stabbed the man with the bayonet, and shot another one. Seth had drawn his knife and placed it in his sleeve when he first saw the soldiers, so he quickly disposed of another one of them. Mr. Mahmood and Tajim together overpowered a fourth one, and Mr. Mahmood stabbed him.

The fifth one shot Danny, and he fell to the ground. Almost instantly another shot rang out, and before Danny lost consciousness, he saw the soldier fall and Nadi standing rigid with a pistol in her hand. The Iranian had been watching the men so intently that Nadi was able to take a sidearm from one of the fallen soldiers and shoot him. She dropped the gun and fell crying at Danny's side. Mr. Mahmood pulled her away to comfort her so Seth could assess the injuries. The bullet had entered the left side just below the rib cage. Danny was already losing a lot of blood and about to go into shock. They had to move fast, before someone came to check on the soldiers, so Seth grabbed the medical kit and quickly did what he could to stop the bleeding. They had come to a place where there was some small growth and were able to find a couple of trees big enough to make a litter, which Seth and Mr. Mahmood took turns pulling. Fortunately, they weren't far from their rendezvous point.

They walked quietly the rest of the way and made it just after midnight. By this time, Danny was groaning in pain, so Seth gave him some morphine from the medical kit. He went to sleep while Nadi sat and held his hand. She refused to move from his side. After a while he awoke and squeezed her hand. When she looked at him, he winked at her and gave her a faint smile.

"Oh, Danny, you've got to be okay. If not, I couldn't stand it. I would rather have stayed in Iran forever than for you to get hurt."

"Don't worry, you're not gonna get rid of me that easy," he said.

Nadi was trembling as she said, "I know you don't need to hear my problems right now, but I have never taken another person's life, and I don't know how to deal with it. Please tell me how you handle it."

"I hope I never stop being bothered by it," Danny said. "I'm comforted somewhat by the fact that I did what I had to do. I would never choose to kill anyone. Just keep in mind that if you hadn't killed him, we would all probably be dead by now."

Danny hoped he had helped her. At least she drifted off to sleep for a while, and so did he.

They had a breakfast of bread and cheese at 0500, and at 0600, the Black Hawk landed right on time. As the chopper lifted off, the Mahmood family said good-bye to Iran and Iraq forever. When the helicopter landed inside the American embassy in Kuwait City, they were officially under the protection of the United States Government.

An emergency medical team met them and took Danny to the

hospital. The doctor removed the bullet, and he slept for several hours. When the surgeon came to see him, he said, "Well, Lieutenant, you're a lucky man. About one inch higher and you would've taken your last flight. You lost a lot of blood, but you should be able to go home in about a week."

Nadi had refused to leave until she knew he was out of danger, so they let her come in to see him for a few minutes.

She kissed him gently on the forehead and said, "Thank you for everything; I will always love you for what you have done for us."

"Nor will I forget what you and your family did for me."

"I wish you the very best and hope everything works out for you and Amee."

"I really don't know if we have a future together," Danny said.

"If I believed that, I would never let you out of my sight until you spoke of me as I hear you speak of her. I just wish I'd gotten to you first."

Danny couldn't help thinking that meeting her first wouldn't have been all that bad. Nadi kissed him on the cheek and hugged him. It was hard for her to let go, but finally she walked slowly away.

She looked back and said, "I regret I couldn't bring my little goat with me. Maybe he could find you again."

Five days later Danny persuaded the doctor to let him go home on the promise that he would do nothing for two weeks and then take it easy for a while. Mr. Slocum let Danny know that the Mahmoods were settled into the small town of Sandusky, which was located in northern Ohio near Lake Erie. It was rumored that a young army ranger made frequent visits to see them.

Chapter 20

When Danny came off the plane, Amee was there to meet him. She grabbed him and fell on his shoulder, weeping. Finally she said, "That's the last time for you, mister. You will never do such a thing again."

"You won't get much of an argument from me. I think I'm done with rescue missions."

It was too early for Danny to travel at Thanksgiving, and Amee refused to leave him. She prepared a meal for them, and they watched the football game together. Danny noticed that Amee had a faraway look.

"All right, what's going on behind those beautiful eyes?"

"Oh, I'm sorry," Amee responded as she snapped out of her trance. "I was just feeling a little insecure about the future. I wish we had more assurance in our lives. I know I am supposed to trust the Lord, but it would be nice to know things are settled."

Danny really felt the same way but was trying to be manly by not saying it. Now was one of those transparent moments when the guard is down, so he shared his feelings with her.

"Danny, would you consider coming to our home after Christmas for a few days?"

"I'm not sure that's a good idea in light of what my work is all about?"

"I think it is a very good idea. I am mature enough to deal with it, and I think it would be good for you to spend more time with my family in case there are questions that arise later."

Danny still wasn't convinced. It had the potential of putting him in a more compromising position than he was already in, and right now it wasn't an experience he was looking forward to. He didn't mind Amee knowing that he had to give some serious thought to the matter. Finally he reached a reluctant conclusion.

"If you think you can handle it, and you fully realize the position I'm in, I will come."

"Well, folks, looks like we made it just in time," the captain announced as they were descending into Logan International Airport. "The National Weather Service says we are in for a blizzard. The ground temperature is ten degrees below zero and falling. I'm sorry, but it's going to be a nasty night. I hope you don't have far to go and have a very safe and enjoyable evening. Thanks for flying with us today. We'll have you at the gate shortly."

The airport was a madhouse because of the holidays, and the captain was right; Boston was colder than Danny thought any place south of the North Pole could be. Everything was already covered in several inches of snow, and more was on the way. They had arranged with the Salims to pick them up just outside the baggage claim area so no one would have to trudge through the snow and slush. They were right on time, for which Danny and Amee were grateful.

Traffic was extremely light, allowing them to make good time on the way home. Just as they pulled into the driveway, it started to snow again, and in a few minutes, they were experiencing a full-blown blizzard. Mo met them at the door and helped carry the luggage in, but Abb didn't come out of his room. They decided not to push it and just give him some time. The blizzard would keep him at home for a couple of days, and maybe God would give an opportunity to talk to him. Danny had decided to try to help change his attitude. Safa made coffee, and they all spent the next several hours talking about Danny's experience in his two trips to Iran, the Mahmood family, and Amee's work with computers. Both Mo and Dr. Salim were awed at all computers were capable of.

"Danny, I think it is a marvelous thing that both the American government and you did for the Mahmoods. It is one of the kindest things I have ever heard of, and I know you put yourself in danger for an Iraqi family you barely knew," Safa said.

"Oh, I think he knew one of them better than the others," Amee interjected.

"You can't blame me because girls can't resist my charm," Danny said with a smug look.

Because of sheer boredom, Abb eventually wandered out of his room. He came down just in time to hear what was said about the rescue of the Mahmoods. Without anyone noticing, he had stopped to listen. He had to pass through the den to get to the kitchen, so he grunted out a hello as he kept walking. Danny went into the kitchen under the guise of getting a refill on coffee and said, "Hey, Abb. What's up, man?"

"Nothing much," he mumbled.

"Abb, can you and I talk man to man a little bit?"

As Abb stopped and looked at him, his eyes narrowed and his jaws tightened.

"Why do you want to talk?"

"I know there is some kind of problem, but I don't know what. If it is because of me and I can do anything about it, I will. I love your family, and I don't want to be a problem. May I just talk to you in your room for a few minutes?"

Abb turned his back as he said, "I guess so, if that's what you want."

"Abb and I are going to talk for a bit in his room," Danny announced as they walked back through the den.

Amee was shocked and thrilled all at the same time and quietly offered up a prayer for God to bless their discussion.

Danny plopped down on a beanbag as casually as possible while Abb sat on the bed twirling a soccer ball.

"I like your pad, man."

"Yeah, it's okay."

"Abb, let's be straight up and let it all hang out.

"All right, if that's the way you want it."

"We used to be friends, and I just want to know why you resent me now and why you are so opposed to the relationship between Amee and me."

"I was a kid back in Georgia and didn't know what was really going on in the world. Now you've changed my sister to the point that she is in Satan's army."

"Wait a minute; Amee made her own decision."

"Yeah, after she met you."

"May I ask why you hate our country so much?"

Abb snarled his reply. "The imperialism of America and what it is doing to the Middle East."

"What is America doing to the Middle East that is so bad?"

"Desecrating our sacred land and robbing it of its resources and, worst of all, your country defends and supports Israel."

Danny responded very thoughtfully. "Let's try to reason this out. The industrialized countries of the world are the only ones who need the amounts of oil necessary to keep the Arab countries exporting large quantities. The huge revenue from that is what has allowed those countries to develop as they have. It is pure and simple free market enterprise, and OPEC even sets the price. As to the desecration of your land, if you truly believe that a non-Muslim desecrates Muslim soil by even setting foot on it, there is no argument for that. Think it through, Abb. What you end up with is isolationism. You have lived in America for several years, and you are allowed to worship freely. What if the United States had the same policy with respect to Christianity that you are advocating for Islam? No one but Christians would be allowed to come here. Before long, there would be arguments about what kind of Christianity was to dominate, and there would never be peace."

As Danny was talking, Abb just stared at his soccer ball. His jaw was set, and Danny wasn't even sure he was listening.

"With respect to Israel," Danny continued. "I doubt we would ever fully agree, but nations cannot agree on everything. I respect and defend the sovereign rights for all Arab countries the same way I do Israel's. I could give you a great argument for defending their right to be in that land, but you would reject it all out of hand because of the teachings of Islam about the Bible. There is one thing you can't deny even from history, though, and that is the fact that Israel inhabited that area for hundreds of years in the past. You will have to agree that God promised it to Abraham's descendents and that Jews are also his descendents. You are evidently under the influence of those who want to establish Islamic states such as the one in Iran today. If that is your conviction, I would not try to argue you out of it, but I am simply imploring you to think all this through carefully. I will never bring these things up again, but I want to put this on a personal level. I recently had occasion to be in a certain country in the Middle East. My mission there was to help another Arab country. When I got into some serious difficulties and my life was in danger, a Muslim family helped me. They put their own lives at risk in order to save mine and went to great lengths to get me to safety. Their daughter and I became good friends as she guided me to the border where I could be rescued. When I asked what I could ever do to return the favor, she said the only thing she wanted was to live in America someday so she could be free from oppression and fear. With the help of the right people in our government, I have already returned to their home and brought them to the United States. To do so, I had to put my life on the line again, along with another young soldier. I wasn't required to become a Muslim, and they weren't required to become Christians, and we didn't plot the overthrow of anyone's government. It was simply two people helping each other. My point is that in spite of all the cultural and religious differences that family and I connected on the personal level.

"Your sister and I really love each other. I don't know where that relationship will lead because there are many complications, but I hope we'll be friends forever. Your parents and I differ in religion and probably many other things, but we love one another, and Mo has evidently accepted me. I sincerely want you to allow me to be a friend of your family, and I hope that includes you. I'm not even going to ask you for an answer now because I know you will have to weigh all this carefully. I just want you to know one thing. I love you, and that will never change no matter what you do." Danny got up and slapped Abb on the knee and headed for the door.

Abb stopped him and said, "I do love my family, including my sister, and as long as you are a guest here, I will try not to make it more difficult on them. Perhaps in time she will realize this is not good for her. Just don't read into this that I have accepted all you have said and everything is just fine now. I will try to make the best of it."

"I can understand that, and I'm sorry for the bad situation this creates for you. I will pray that we can solve our differences someday."

Danny went back downstairs, and it wasn't long before Abb joined the family. There was an obvious change in his attitude, and Amee looked at Danny and smiled. He was thankful that at least she felt better about the situation.

Everyone agreed that it was nice to be snowed in for a couple of days. It became a wonderful family time as they played games and roasted marshmallows in the fireplace. When things cleared up and they were able to get out, Amee attempted to teach Danny how to ice skate. She found it hilarious as her mighty athlete wobbled around like a newborn calf and fell several times. "No sitting down on the job," she would say or, "The ice really doesn't require that much cleaning." She accused him of not being able to function in shoes that didn't have cleats on them. After it was over he said, "That's the most hard landing I have made since I first started to fly."

Abb was as good as his word. He was civil toward Danny and even tossed the football a little with him. Danny was aware that it was an act, but Amee was thrilled about it. At least he had accomplished something. The visit was over, and Danny and Amee were on their way back to Langley to see what life held for them now. It had been five and a half years since they met, and they had been through enough experiences to qualify them as seasoned adults, but they were still only twenty-three and twenty-two years old, respectively.

Chapter 21

Mr. Adams called their first night at home to tell Danny there would be a meeting the next day. When he arrived, there were several people present. Adams didn't introduce them but explained that they were experts in various fields.

"Evidently we have stirred the wrath of certain people in the Middle East who are determined to make us pay for our interference in Arab affairs there. There is stepped-up chatter about terrorist strikes against us. We aren't sure yet who all is involved, except the Palestine Liberation Organization, Nidal's group, and people working out of Iran and Lebanon."

Dr. Rubenstein spoke up. "Our best guess is that they will try to target either a United States installation outside the country, hit a strategic building in the United States, or cause a major transportation disaster. Our responsibility here is to come up with various scenarios and plan the best ways to prevent them. This is going to be priority number one for us for some time to come. At times we will be required to meet long hours here, and you will all have special assignments occasionally. Speaking of which, Danny, would you wait behind for a few minutes?"

After the others had gone, Mr. Adams said, "Lieutenant Brannigan, I want you to meet General Mort Kelly of Strategic Air Command. General Kelly, this is Lieutenant Daniel Brannigan."

"I'm happy to meet you, Lieutenant. Adams has told me about your recent experience in Iran, and I want to congratulate you on a job well done."

"Thank you, sir."

Mr. Adams continued, "Danny, we believe this project is of the utmost importance. If we don't stop what is in the works, it could be devastating for us. Are you familiar with the SR-71A Blackbird?"

"All I know is what I have read about it."

"We have to do some critical surveillance that we don't even want the Israelis to know about yet, and we need you to fly the Blackbird."

Danny could hardly believe what he was hearing. Other than the space shuttle or one of the prototypes that weren't even supposed to exist, to fly the Blackbird was the biggest dream of every pilot in the air force. It could fly 2,200 plus miles per hour, climb 11,810 feet per minute, and reach a ceiling of 85,000 feet. If a surface-to-air missile were launched, the first defensive measure was to accelerate.

"Sir, it would be a great privilege to fly the sled, but why me?"

"Two reasons: we don't want anyone outside our group to be involved in this mission, and we believe you are capable."

"It is an opportunity I would never turn down."

"That's great; General Kelly will be flying with you."

When they met for dinner that evening, Danny was almost too nervous to eat. He could hardly wait to tell Amee about his good fortune. She always knew when he had something on his mind, and as soon as dinner was over, she said, "All right, you might as well go ahead and spill the beans."

He could not hold back the broad grin on his face as he said, "I have the opportunity every pilot would give his right arm for. I get to fly the most awesome plane the air force has—the SR-71A Blackbird."

He explained to her all about the plane, and although she didn't want to see him go, she was excited for him to have this unique experience.

"I have heard about American men running off with fast women but mine runs off with a fast plane."

"I have some more news," Danny said. "My intelligence work is going to occupy all of my time for a while, and I don't know exactly what to expect. I will always tell you what I am allowed to, but there will be some things I can't tell anyone. Please understand that there is nothing in the world I would keep from you if it were my decision. I will keep you informed the very best I can."

"I understand, and as long as I know you're safe, that's all that matters."

Two days later, Danny was deployed to Beale Air Force Base in California where the Habu (a venomous snake), as it was called, was located. After being checked out on it thoroughly, they required him to take her up for a test run to become familiar with everything. General Kelly was aboard to answer any questions that might arise. It all went smoothly, so the actual mission was scheduled for the next day. It was a beautiful, crisp northern California morning, and on the flat terrain, the sun looked like a giant yellow golf ball lying on a green fairway. There was not a cloud in the sky as they taxied out on the runway. The thrust of the Blackbird was like nothing Danny had ever experienced. When they reached full throttle, he felt like he was permanently laminated to his seat. He was sure his face was wrapped around his head, and he couldn't even move his eyelids. Once they were airborne, it took less than five minutes to reach the cruising altitude of fifty thousand feet. Danny's orders were to cover a grid from Syria to Yemen and from Egypt to Afghanistan. General Kelly was in charge of surveillance equipment. Danny was called upon to fly several other similar missions, which were never fully explained, but he guessed it was an attempt to locate terrorist bases. Up to now, it was the most exhilarating experience he had ever had in a plane.

Terrorism escalated at an alarming rate in the eighties, primarily at the instigation of the Palestine Liberation Organization and Iran, with a few maverick groups thrown in for good measure. The PLO encouraged the killing of five Westerners for every Palestinian who died. It had begun in 1979 in Iran when the Shah was overthrown and left the country, paving the way for the exiled Ayatollah Khomeini to return and establish an Islamic fundamentalist government. On November 4, 1979, a group of militant university students took over the American diplomatic mission in Tehran and held sixty-six hostages for 444 days until January 20, 1981. Just minutes after Ronald Reagan was inaugurated, the hostages were freed.

The Ayatollah Ruhollah Khomeini called upon all Muslims to kill infidels who were corrupters of the faith. He told them if they didn't, they would suffer in their death, but if they killed the infidels and prevented them from propagating their corruption of Islam, their death would be blessed. Even in his last will and testament, Khomeini advocated worldwide terrorism.

On January 18, 1984, Malcolm Kerr, president of American University in Lebanon, was assassinated by gunmen linked to the Hezbollah (Allah's Party) in Iran, and on January 20, Iran was officially declared to be a terrorist nation. On May 21, 1987, an Iraqi Mirage fighter jet attacked a U.S. navy vessel, the USS *Stark,* in the

Persian Gulf, hitting the ship with two Exocet missiles and killing thirty-seven crewmembers. The U.S. increased its presence in the Gulf and began escorting Kuwaiti oil tankers.

The eight-year war between Iran and Iraq ended August 20, 1988, without any of the original grievances being resolved. The economies of both countries were left in shambles after the war, and there were over one million casualties. Iran spent 350 billion dollars, and Iraq was seriously in debt to its Arab backers. Iraq owed Kuwait fourteen billion dollars and arguments about that was one of the primary problems leading up to the invasion of Kuwait by Iraq. On August 2, 1990, Iraqi forces invaded Kuwait, and President Saddam Hussein declared it to be the nineteenth province of Iraq.

Presidents Carter, Reagan, and George H.W. Bush had issued statements that the United States would protect the Saudi kingdom, even to the extent of using military force against any who attacked her. Saddam Hussein began to use the rhetoric of the newly formed Al-Qaeda and other Islamic fundamentalists against Saudi Arabia, charging that the Saudi government was an illegitimate guardian of the holy cities of Mecca and Medina. On August 7, 1990, U.S. troops moved into Saudi Arabia under "Operation Desert Shield," and soon after, two naval battle groups were deployed. On August 8, forty-eight United States Air Force F-15 fighter planes from the First Fighter group at Langley Air Force Base in Virginia landed in Saudi Arabia and immediately began around-the-clock air patrols of the Iraq, Kuwait, and Saudi Arabia borders in order to prevent any further advance by the Iraqi forces. Danny was one of those forty-eight pilots, and he flew an F-15 E Strike Eagle, which is an all-weather strike fighter designed for long-range interdiction of the enemy. The strike fighter is a fighter that is also capable of attacking surface targets. United States military buildup continued until it reached five hundred thousand troops.

On January 17, 1991, a massive air campaign was launched called "Operation Desert Storm," during which more than a thousand sorties a day were flown. Thirty-eight Iraqi MiGs were shot down, five of which Danny was credited with. Between 115 and 140 other Iraqi planes escaped into Iran. The coalition forces expected them to go to Jordan, a country that was friendly to Iraq, and could not react quickly enough to stop the exodus to Iran. Iran never returned the planes, and the crews were kept for several years. Iraq launched missile attacks on coalition bases and on Israel, hoping to draw Israel into the war and separate some Arab countries from it. The strategy proved ineffective. Coalition forces moved to within 150 miles of Baghdad before stopping. One hundred hours after the ground campaign started, President Bush declared a ceasefire, and on February 27 announced that Kuwait had been liberated. Sanctions were placed upon Iraq and two no-fly zones were established, one in the north to protect humanitarian efforts on behalf of the Kurds and one in the south to protect the Shiite Muslims. Danny pulled one tour of patrol duty flying out of Kuwait. On one occasion, an F-16 shot down a MiG that had locked onto it, and another time, Iraqi surface-to-air missiles and radar sites were taken out. Individual credit was not given, but it was unofficially acknowledged that Danny was involved in the downing of the MiG.

Chapter 22

Saudi Arabia, July 1991

"American Soldiers Accused of Molesting Saudi Woman" was a worldwide headline on July 16, 1991. Staff Sergeant Seth Jones was stationed in Saudi Arabia during Operation Desert Storm and remained there for a few months afterward on special duty. Danny had gone to visit his old friend for a few days before going back to Langley. On a rare trip into Riyadh, they gave a ride to a young woman, Nyla Hussein, who later accused them of molesting her. They were not accused of rape; Muslims define molestation quite differently in some instances than others would. For a man who is not her husband to uncover any part of a woman that is covered would constitute molestation. She accused them of removing her hijab and attempting to kiss and fondle her.

The Americans' version was quite different. They said the young woman was friendly and spoke very good English, so they chatted with her as they drove. They were in an open vehicle and reported that she removed her veil in order to take full advantage of the wind. When they stopped at an intersection in Riyadh, she unexpectedly encountered a relative who was sure to discover her without her hijab on. Before he had a chance to see her, she began to cry and scream and jumped out of the vehicle. The two Americans didn't have a clue as to what was happening, but they stopped to see what was wrong. Their passenger began to explain to her uncle in Arabic that they had forced her into their vehicle, ripped off her hijab, and attempted to have their way with her. In mere moments the uncle had summoned a crowd, and the two feared for their lives. Just before the violence started, two Saudi soldiers came by and rescued them, in a manner of speaking. They took them to the local jail, where they were held until they were turned over to American authorities.

When Danny got phone privileges, the first person he called was his mother, to reassure her that he was all right, and the second one went to Amee.

She was already crying when she answered the phone. "Oh, Danny, are you okay?"

He assured her that he was fine and that the whole thing was so ridiculous that surely they could get it resolved soon.

"Please don't underestimate what can happen in that culture," Amee pleaded. "Remember, those are my people; I know them, and I'm afraid. If I have to beg, bribe, or threaten my way, I'm coming over there."

"I would want that more than anything if I could see you, but I can't. Don't try to come. It will be too hard on you."

"They'll have to put me in the brig to keep me here," she said.

Amee was afraid that Danny didn't understand the danger he

was in, and his defense team might not be fully aware of it either. She knew how vicious Muslims could be about such offences and it wouldn't be the first time the U.S. government had made someone a sacrificial lamb to appease another country.

He might not have understood completely about Muslims, but he was painfully aware of what his government was capable of. For the first time in a long time, he felt some old, dark feelings coming back. After everything else he had lost, was he now to lose his freedom also. Was this going to happen after he had committed himself to live for God?

The Saudi government agreed to a court martial by the United States Army if a Saudi minister of justice was allowed to collaborate with the prosecutor.

Danny asked for and was granted an audience with the base commander. He dared not pull any strings because of his special connections but wanted to know what his best chances were.

"The only thing that can really help now is to have a very good lawyer. It has been determined that the defense advocate should be a woman so she can go after the alleged victim more aggressively if need be. We don't have one appointed yet."

"Does it matter what branch of the service she comes from?" Danny asked.

"Since the two of you are from different branches yourselves, I don't think it will matter," the general answered.

"Could I possibly make a suggestion, sir?" Danny inquired.

"It certainly won't do any harm to try if you know a woman you think would be a good choice." The general called JAG headquarters and put in the request for the person Danny suggested.

The next day, Captain Sarah Lassiter arrived from Edwards Air Force Base in California to serve as defense attorney. Shortly after she got there, Amee arrived on a military hop. Danny never did know exactly whom she had to kill to get there. They wouldn't let her see him yet, but she made contact with Sarah.

Amee was of great assistance to Sarah by helping her understand

Muslim women's attire and the laws that governed them. Sarah was surprised to learn that they were not required to wear oppressive clothing according to Sharia law. There were only three basic requirements: (1) The best garment is the garment of righteousness; (2) cover your bosoms; (3) lengthen your garments. Everything else came out of that.

"That's sort of like some Christians have expanded God's requirements," Sarah commented.

Amee also told her that most Muslim women wear these clothes by choice and consider it protection for their virtue. Others believe that when they dress in accepted Islamic fashion, men see them for themselves and not as sexual objects. Some, however, believe the men are using this to shirk their own responsibility to control their lusts. Some husbands and fathers are kind about it and some are abusive.

"I believe a thorough understanding of this will be important to Danny and Seth's case," Amee said.

After her first meeting with Danny and Seth, Sarah was able to get Amee in to see Danny. They even had some privacy of sorts. There was a guard stationed just outside the door. When they embraced, Amee whispered in his ear, "I don't ever want to let you go."

"The feeling is mutual, I assure you," Danny replied. Nothing had made him feel that secure for a long time.

"I really think I can be of some assistance behind the scenes," Amee said. "There might be some things I will understand and some places I can go that others couldn't. I don't want you to misunderstand, Danny, but I'm going to dress in acceptable Muslim fashion. I will only have to wear the hijab, not the whole thing. It certainly won't do me any good to run around in my uniform."

Amee didn't want to say too much to Danny and cause him to worry, but she was planning to do some detective work to see if she could find out what really happened. She was already working on a couple of theories.

The United States Government was going out of their way to

demonstrate that they weren't trying to cover this up or give someone a slap on the wrist. Lieutenant Colonel William Miller was assigned as prosecutor. He had the reputation of being tough and thorough and had lost very few cases.

Amee was able to get a driver assigned to her so that she could make a visit to see Nyla Hussein. Mr. Hussein was in the yard when she arrived, and she introduced herself by only giving her name and explained she was there to get accurate information on the story. She didn't reveal what the purpose for the information was and he didn't ask. He asked her to forgive him for not offering the customary hospitality, explaining that his daughter was not ready for visitors in the house.

"I am sorry for what your family has gone through. I have only a few questions and I won't bother you again. First, may I ask the age of your daughter?"

"She is eighteen."

"Where had she been when the Americans gave her a ride?"

"She was on an errand for me. She goes nowhere without my permission."

"Does she always wear traditional clothing?"

"Without fail. I would allow no exceptions."

"What would happen if she voluntarily took off her hijab?"

"She would be punished severely. That is why I know she did not take off her covering of her own free will."

"May I ask what kind of punishment would be administered?"

"Those are private matters of concern only to my family."

"I understand that, sir. I was only trying to understand all the facts."

He looked at the ground as he replied, "If you must know, she would receive a whipping."

"Mr. Hussein, thank you very much for answering my questions. Would it be possible to speak briefly with your wife?"

He replied quickly and angrily, "No, I will not allow that. I speak for her."

"I did not mean to be offensive. Again, you and you family have my deepest sympathy."

Amee had a wry smile when she returned to the car.

"You must have learned something interesting," the driver said.

"If my suspicions are correct, it will be most interesting," Amee replied.

She couldn't wait to share her findings with Sarah. She was convinced, as was Amee, that Nyla had done just what Danny and Seth said she did. She had taken an opportunity to break away briefly from the oppressive restrictions placed upon her, but when she was about to be exposed, she was so afraid that she accused them of molesting her. They were both sorry for Nyla but had to find some way to clear Danny and Seth.

Amee wasn't done yet. Her instincts told her there was more to be learned about Nyla. She found out she had made several trips to the emergency room of a nearby hospital, and was able to talk with the doctor who had treated her. He agreed to testify to what he ethically could.

The dreaded day arrived, and the court martial began at 0900.

"This court martial is now convened," announced presiding judge Colonel Preston Mitchell.

"Lieutenant Daniel Brannigan and Staff Sergeant Seth Jones, you are charged with criminal sexual assault upon a civilian. How do you plead?"

"Captain Sarah Lassiter for the defense. My clients plead not guilty."

The prosecution presented its case by calling Nyla, her father, her uncle, and several witnesses from among the crowd on the street the day the incident happened. Nyla testified to the fact that both the defendants did pull off her hijab and try to fondle and kiss her. Her uncle testified to her screams and terror as she ran to him, and the men that they did not see the defendants take off her hijab but saw her putting it back on. Sarah offered no argument to the claims of these witnesses. Finally, Mr. Hussein testified to his daughter's fidelity to the Muslim dress and her state when she returned home.

Sarah approached him cautiously, both because she was a woman and because she didn't want to kindle the sympathy of men on the jury whom she knew had daughters.

"Mr. Hussein we are all very sorry for the trauma your family has been through, but I know you are as anxious as the rest of us are to see justice done. I assure you that if these men have done this despicable deed, they will be punished to the fullest extent of the law. To do that, we need your cooperation to prove their guilt beyond a shadow of a doubt. Without that, we cannot punish them; no matter how much we might want to.

"Here is my first question. Do you, as a father and husband, require the women in your home to wear traditional Muslim dress, including both the burka and hijab?"

"Yes, I do, but they have never objected."

"To your knowledge, have any of them ever been seen in public without these articles of clothing?"

"No, they wouldn't do that."

"If you found that your daughter had gone out without them, what would your response be?"

"I would be very disappointed."

"Would you punish her?"

"Yes."

"How would you punish her?"

"That is a matter of no consequence to anyone except to me and my family."

"Yes, sir, I agree that it is not the business of a foreign court to judge your religion, your culture, or your family. Just one more question. If your daughter or your wife came to you and said they wanted to dress differently, what would your response be?"

"I would not allow it under any circumstances."

"What if they insisted?"

"They would never do that, but assuming they did, there are measures one can take."

"Thank you, Mr. Hussein. I know this has not been easy for you."

"The court will be in recess until 0900 tomorrow," the judge announced.

Amee had another mission in mind for that evening. She wanted to see what the young people in Riyadh were doing. She was Arab and looked so young that she didn't have much difficulty blending in to find out what she wanted to know. Before the night was over, she had found three witnesses who were willing to testify for the defense. She informed Sarah, who got them on the witness list early the next morning.

When court was back in session, the prosecution objected to the new witnesses, and the judge overruled.

"You may proceed, Captain Lassiter," the judge said.

"I call Tahani Hassani to the stand."

Tahani moved slowly toward the witness chair, looking straight ahead so as not to catch anyone's eye. He immediately started to fidget as he sat down and kept his head lowered. Sarah wondered if she had made a mistake by putting him on the stand.

"Tahani, I have only one question. Have you ever seen Nyla Hussein in public without her hijab on?"

His answer was virtually inaudible, and Sarah now really feared she had done the wrong thing.

"I must ask you to speak louder," the judge said.

He raised his head this time, and Sara could see the strain on his face, but his eyes told a different story. Sarah was encouraged. He answered clearly and firmly.

"Yes."

"Where was she when you observed this?"

"She was at a party where other young people were gathered."

"Thank you very much."

The other two young people testified to the same thing, and Colonel Miller wanted to get off that point as soon as possible, so he didn't ask any questions. He reserved the right to recall them in case he found a way too impugn their testimony.

Sarah called Dr. Dhia Hadassah to testify.

"Dr. Hadassah, what is your profession?"

"I am an emergency room medical doctor."

"Have you ever treated Nyla Hussein?"

"Yes, on three occasions."

"What was the nature of her medical needs?"

"Your Honor, I object to this line of questioning because it is irrelevant to the case," Captain Miller interjected.

"Objection overruled. Doctor, you may answer the question."

"She had severe welts on her body, some of which had bled and others were festered."

"Did you make any determination about the cause of these injuries?"

"Yes, they were most definitely the result of a severe whipping."

"Do you know who inflicted the wounds?"

"No, she begged me to let it go and said she deserved it."

"Thank you, Doctor."

Colonel Miller asked, "Dr. Hadassah, have you treated other girls who had similar injuries?"

"Yes."

"How many would you say you have treated?"

"I do not know the exact number, but there have been several."

"So this is by no means an isolated incident."

"No, it is not."

"Just to be clear, Doctor. Nyla never divulged who whipped her?"

"No, she did not."

"Redirect, Your Honor," Captain Lassiter requested.

"Proceed."

"Dr. Hadassah, what would you say was the emotional state of Nyla Hussein when you asked who had beaten her?"

"Objection. Dr. Hadassah is a medical doctor, not a psychiatrist or psychologist," Captain Miller protested.

"Overruled. I believe his medical training qualifies him to make this judgment. Please answer the question, Doctor," Colonel Westerly stated.

"She was in a state of extreme fear."

"Thank you, Doctor. No further questions."

The prosecution had disclosed their intent to call two other emergency room medical doctors to show that there were many such cases of Muslim girls being beaten. This they did, and Sarah declined to cross-examine.

"At this time, I would like to recall Mr. Hussein to the stand," Captain Lassiter said.

"Will Mr. Hussein please take the stand?"

"Mr. Hussein, did you whip your daughter so severely that she needed medical attention?"

"Captain Lassiter, that is none of your business."

"Sir, you are right in that it is none of my business as a foreigner and a non-Muslim, but as an officer of this court, it is most definitely my business in the interest of justice. I ask you once again, did you whip your daughter so severely that she needed medical attention?"

"I refuse to answer that for an infidel. You have no right to interfere into my family's private matters."

"No sir, but I have an obligation to prevent an injustice, no matter whom it involves. I am going to assume you have answered my question. For my last witness, I recall Nyla Hussein to the stand."

Mr. Hussein stood and shouted, "I will not allow my daughter to take the stand again in this mockery of a trial."

The judge rapped his gavel and said, "We will have order in the court. Mr. Hussein, if you do not allow your daughter to testify, we cannot proceed, because she has already appeared as a witness for the prosecution."

"Then we will not proceed. My family is through with this entire matter."

At that point, Mrs. Hussein stood weeping and shouted, "Please leave my husband and daughter alone; it was I who whipped my daughter for the flagrant violation of our teachings. She brought disgrace upon her father every time she did it."

Mr. Hussein turned and looked sadly at his wife and then walked over and put his arm around her. He walked back to his daughter and took her in his arms and said, "I'm sorry." He turned to Lieutenant Brannigan and Sergeant Jones and said, "I apologize for what my family has put you through." Then he addressed the court and said, "These young men are not guilty of molesting my daughter."

"Lieutenant Daniel Brannigan and Sergeant Seth Jones, the charges against you are dismissed, and you are free to go with the apologies of this court." With that, Colonel Westerly rapped his gavel, and the court martial was over.

As Mr. Hussein was escorting his wife and daughter out of the courtroom, Nyla turned to the men she had accused and whispered through her tears, "I'm sorry. I didn't mean to get you into trouble. I was just so afraid; I didn't know what else to do. Please forgive me."

That evening Danny, Amee, Sarah, and Seth got together for a victory dinner. In the course of the conversation, Seth told them he and Nadi had been writing and he had visited her and her family. Danny felt a twinge of jealousy, but he would be happy for them both if it became a permanent relationship. He realized now that one Arab romance was enough for him. Sarah had to leave early to prepare for her flight home, and Seth had the good sense to excuse himself also.

"Oh, Danny, I have never been so frightened in my life. I don't think you realized how much danger you were in."

"But you rescued me, my little Arabian princess. As long as you are around, I will always be safe."

"I believe you would joke before a firing squad, but I'm glad you can laugh. However, I will always be around."

It would still take Danny a couple of days to wrap things up, because he had been abruptly snatched away from packing to leave Iraq. Amee had to go on ahead, because she was already testing the patience of her superiors.

Chapter 23

When Danny returned to Langley, he went directly to Amee's apartment, but when he got there, no one answered the door. There was a note with his name on it taped to the outside of the mail drop. It simply said:

> Danny,
>
> I'm sorry I can't be here to greet you. I will love you forever, but I have learned some things that make my situation here unsustainable. I did not expect this and cannot control it. I don't know how it will come out or if we can ever be

together again. I will contact you if ever I can. If you love me, don't try to find me.

Please don't judge me too harshly."

Love,

Amee

Danny was totally dumbfounded and could not even guess what might be going on. He immediately called Mr. Adams, who denied that he had anything at all to do with the matter. His next contact was General Burton Travis, who said he could not discuss anything that had to do with the air force but knew nothing personally. Danny didn't have the heart to call Amee's parents. His body and brain were both numb, and he just plopped down in his chair in a stupor. He thought when Amee became a Christian that it was only a matter of time until they could work out the other things that stood in the way of their being married. Now he was sure that, for whatever reason, God had decided to take away everything he loved. He felt like he ought to wear a sign like a leper, saying, "Danger! Stay away from Daniel Brannigan."

He was startled out of his trance by the ringing of his phone. "Lieutenant Brannigan, General Travis would like to see you in his office ASAP."

When he arrived, the general stuck out his hand and said, "Lieutenant Brannigan, let me be the first to congratulate you on a fine job in the gulf. We are all proud of you. I'm sorry for the bit of trouble you had there, and I'm glad it turned out well. I called you here to tell you that your presence has been requested in Washington this Thursday at 0900 for a ceremony in the Rose Garden."

"Sir, you don't mean a ceremony with the … the …"

"Yes, that is exactly what I mean. As of now, you are granted leave until Monday morning at 0900."

"Yes, sir. Thank you, sir."

Danny's head was still spinning over a meeting with the president of the United States and his first impulse was to call Amee, but instantly reality hit him. He felt like his heart would burst inside his body if he couldn't find out what happened to her.

Washington, DC, March 1991

Accommodations had been made for Danny at the Watergate Hotel. It sort of made him feel weird to be staying there in light of its history. His reservations were made for one of the most luxurious suites, along with arrangements for him to order whatever he wanted to eat or drink and charge it to his room. Jake and Katie were invited to join him, but Katie came alone. She explained that Jake was called away on business, but Danny wondered why he couldn't change whatever he had to in order to be there. On Thursday morning at eight o'clock, a limousine was waiting to drive them to the White House. A member of President George H.W. Bush's personal staff was along to guide him through the day. It was about that time that Danny realized there was something more involved in this than his mere presence.

There were a few other military personnel present, along with the Secretary of Defense, Richard Cheney, and other assorted guests. Mrs. Bush accompanied the president when he arrived. He went straight to the lectern and started his speech, which was carried live worldwide. He recounted recent events in the Middle East and then praised the United States Armed Forces for the magnificent job they did, stating that the people of Kuwait owed them a great debt of gratitude. In order to demonstrate the sacrifice the soldiers made, he presented several who had been severely wounded, some of whom had lost limbs. He introduced the wife of a soldier who had given his life for his country and told his story. Then he announced that he had some awards to make. He was obviously working alphabetically, so Danny was number two on the list.

"May I introduce to you Lieutenant Daniel Brannigan? Lieutenant Brannigan has been in harm's way many times and has always served valiantly. He has downed at least eight enemy planes and put his own life at risk to rescue an Iraqi family from exile in the desert of Iran so that they could be given political asylum in the United States. That family had helped him when his own plane went down in Iran after successfully completing his mission.

"Lieutenant Brannigan, on behalf of a grateful nation, and for service above and beyond the call of duty, I am happy to present you the Congressional Medal of Honor, a prize only awarded to the bravest of the brave."

The president placed the medal around Danny's neck and continued, "As Commander in Chief of the United States Armed Forces, I have asked for the privilege to make one other presentation. You are hereby promoted to the rank of captain." With that, President Bush removed Danny's insignia and replaced it with his captain's bars. He then saluted him. At that moment, all Danny could think was, *I might have been a baseball pitcher, and the closest I would ever have come to the president of the United States would have been if he threw an opening day pitch to me.*

After the ceremony was over, there was a brunch and reception, at which he actually got to talk to the president and Mrs. Bush. Danny had never been so excited or so ill at ease at the same time. By the time he returned to Langley, phone calls were coming in from everywhere, and in a few days, letters of congratulations followed. He was world famous for two or three days.

Danny had some rest and recreation time coming after his duty in the Middle East, so he decided to take a trip to try to get some relief for his troubled mind. During Desert Storm, he had become good friends with a fellow pilot from Oklahoma City who owned a Cessna 172 Sky Hawk. He insisted that Danny take his plane on a trip somewhere, so he arranged to borrow it for a few days.

He flew to Oklahoma City and drove a rental car to the small private airport where his friend kept his plane.

It wasn't a small two-seater like the one he flew from Texas to Colorado, but it was a beautiful, four-seat, high wing Cessna. He checked the plane out, filed his flight plan, and was off into the wild blue yonder. It was a beautiful, clear day, and just the sheer joy of flying was a pleasure in itself.

About two hours later, he saw his destination.

As he set the plane down softly on the grass runway and headed for the hangar at the other end, he saw the old couple waving like crazy, and as soon as he was out of the plane, they were right there waiting for him.

Danny hugged Mama and Papa Johannsen, as they had instructed him to call them.

"Ve are happy to see you, Danny, but ve vere hoping to meet yore pretty girl also."

They immediately wanted him to come to the house to eat. Danny had called and set the visit up with them, and Mama Johannsen cooked enough food for ten farmhands. She was insistent that he eat all of it.

They would have it no other way than for Danny to spend the night. There was no way to reject the offer, so he got his bags out of the plane and settled into one of the most rustically beautiful rooms he had ever seen. He fell in love with everything Western on that trip. After they rested for a while, Papa Johannsen took him for a horseback ride. He rode a sorrel and gave Danny a large buckskin with a long blond mane, stocking feet, and a blaze face named Mustard. He was gentle and responsive and knew exactly what Danny wanted him to do before he moved the reigns. Danny was a natural on a horse.

When they returned, Papa Johannsen showed Danny his cattle, which he was extremely proud of. He had mixed Texas longhorns with Herefords, which produced a hardy and fast-growing breed that had a good temperament and was well suited to the conditions in the Texas panhandle. Mama was equally proud of her orchard, where she had every type of fruit tree and vine known to man. Every year she pickled, canned, and preserved hundreds of jars of fruit products. She gave Danny all he could carry to take home with him.

In the evening, Papa did a real Texas barbecue under a huge cottonwood tree. Afterward, they sat on the long porch in rocking chairs and talked. Well, technically, Danny listened. Although he thoroughly enjoyed it, he was sort of glad the old couple went to bed early, so his ears could get a little rest. In the morning, it took quite awhile to do justice to the big cowboy breakfast Mama Johannsen prepared, so there was time for more talk.

"Papa J, you have done me a great disservice," Danny said.

"Oh, I'm so sorry. How did I ever do dat?"

"After riding the horses and seeing all your animals, I would like to live on a ranch like this someday."

"Vel, I don't blame you. It is a vonderful life. You can yust retire and come here."

"Seriously, I would like to have a ranch or farm someday and use it to take care of war orphans who have no other place to turn. I believe we could make a difference in many lives," Danny said sorrowfully.

"I am sure da good Lord vil provide, if dat iss his will," Mama Johannsen said.

She insisted on preparing some food for the trip back to Oklahoma City, which Danny estimated to be enough to see him across the desert in a wagon train. He took off and circled to give them a wing waggle, and as long as he could see them, they were waving.

Chapter 24

Cuba, Iran, Iraq, Libya, and Syria were all named as state sponsors of terrorism in 1992. Forty percent of the 361 terrorist incidents that year were against the United States. On February 26, 1993, the World Trade Center was bombed, killing six, wounding one thousand, and leaving a one-hundred-by-one-hundred-foot crater in the parking deck. Already the same year, plots to blow up the United Nations building and the Holland and Lincoln Tunnels had been thwarted. Iran had planned to assassinate President George Bush when he visited Kuwait in April.

In the fall of 1993, the CIA began to intercept chatter that indicated something big was being planned. One of the U.S. deep cover agents who had penetrated a terrorist cell confirmed that a major plan was in the works, but so far details were limited to upper-level cell leaders. In the meantime, others were working on counterterrorism measures. The one clear thing was that the incident was not to be a simple hijacking or assassination. The desire was to deliver a blow that America would never forget. To accomplish that, the target itself would have to be of great importance or the amount of damage and loss of life tremendous or preferably both. That information would at least help narrow the list of possible targets.

Targets that would meet the requirements of the terrorists were national landmarks; strategic buildings such as the Pentagon, Capitol, and White House; aircraft; and large gatherings of people, such as ball games, concerts, and amusement parks. The next task was to come up with a plan of prevention. How could such a thing be detected with limited resources and without causing a general panic? The idea was to get ahead of the curve until more specific information was available. Operatives were also picking up certain code words that could possibly specify intended targets, such as "Golden Goose" "Globe Trotter," "Operation Angel," and "Cinderella." In round table discussions, an attempt was made to determine what these could refer to. Some of them could refer to flight, but what specifically? Several suggestions were made, such as Air Force One, the *Concorde,* and even the space shuttle. Cinderella's Castle was probably the first visual symbol that came to mind when Disney World was mentioned. This kind of brainstorming at least had the potential of shrinking the playing field but gave them nothing concrete.

This kept Danny very busy, but not busy enough so that he didn't miss Amee every minute and wonder where she was. The pain he felt did not ease, and the longer it went, the more confused he became about what God was doing to him.

C ✝ ★

When Danny answered the phone, he heard a familiar voice.

"Hello, Danny. This is your real true love. You're just too stubborn to admit it."

"Hi, Nadi. I will fully confess that you're my real true love. Are you ready to run away with me?"

"You have finally blown it, and I'm going to marry someone who knows how to truly appreciate me."

"I guess that would be the unsuspecting Sergeant Seth Jones."

"The same; he has finally asked me to be his wife."

"That's wonderful. How is your family?"

"We are settled in quite well here in Sandusky, and my dad has found a good job. As soon as the paperwork clears, we will officially be citizens of the United States. My dad hopes that someday he can work for the government in some capacity to help with U.S.-Arab relations. But that is not the reason I called."

"And just why did you call?" Danny asked.

"I called to invite you to the wedding. We hope you and Amee can both come."

Danny's silence made her realize she had said something wrong. "What's going on, Danny?"

"I might as well just tell you straight out. Amee is gone, and I don't know where she is. I have no idea what could have happened."

"I am so sorry, Danny, but I'm sure it will all be cleared up in time. I'm sorry to talk to you about our wedding at a time like this."

"Oh no," Danny protested. "I am very happy for you. Please congratulate Seth for me."

"We have set the date for the Saturday before Thanksgiving, and both of us really want you to come. I considered asking you to be my maid of honor, but I just couldn't get past the thought of those hairy legs."

"I would be glad to shave them for you."

"That doesn't seem much better."

Danny agreed to be there for the wedding, and when he hung up the phone, he couldn't help but think briefly what might have been if circumstances had developed a bit sooner.

Sandusky, Ohio, November 1993

Danny arranged a flight to Cleveland and drove the final hour from there to Sandusky, arriving just before rehearsal time on Friday. He had heard nothing from Amee, but the more he thought about it, the more things didn't add up. He called and asked if he might have a few days leave for some personal business. He had been praying about it and resolved that he would not let it hinder his enjoyment of Nadi's wedding, but then he was going to go to Boston.

Religion was not the problem for Seth and Nadi that it had been for Danny and Amee. He was a nominal Christian, and she was a Muslim in name only. Danny knew he should have already witnessed to them and was resolved to do so as soon as possible. The wedding was held at the Mahmood home and performed by a justice of the peace but with the normal trappings of a Christian wedding. Seth's brother was his best man, and Danny and Tajib were attendants.

Seth had finished his tour of duty with Uncle Sam and secured a job with the Ohio State Patrol. He was planning to start his own security business on the side. Nadi was attending Sandusky Community College, pursuing her lifelong dream of becoming a teacher. She was able to get plenty of work as an interpreter in Cleveland since she knew both Arabic and Farsi. It was obvious that they were deeply in love, and each of them at separate times thanked Danny for making their relationship possible. He really didn't feel he had done anything on purpose, but he was glad they felt that way. It was very easy to think of Nadi as the sister he never had, and he even began calling her little sister.

Since Danny had no responsibilities on Saturday until the wedding, he had an opportunity to hang out for a while with Mr. Mahmood and Tajib. Nazir was delighted to see his little family so happy after those days of near isolation in Iran, and he was extremely grateful to be living in America. He had witnessed so many atrocities while he was serving in Saddam Hussein's government that living in a free country meant more to him than it did to most people. He really wanted to give something back if he could. Danny always had a special way with young people, so he and Tajib quickly formed a friendship. He asked about his plans for the future and teased him about girls. Nazir assured Danny that he would always be welcome in their home and hoped he would come to see them from time to time. Danny extended him an invitation to visit them on the farm in Georgia.

It was a beautiful autumn day for an outdoor ceremony. Nadi's favorite color was yellow, so her décor was done in white and yellow. Nadi dressed in pure white accented by a bouquet of yellow roses with one yellow rose in her hair. The arch was covered with white and yellow roses. Seth wore a white tux with a pastel yellow shirt. Danny dressed in uniform, which Amee would have said was just because he wanted to show off his captain's bars. When Nadi walked down the aisle, she looked so much like Amee that Danny thought his heart would stop. He knew at that moment that whatever the outcome, he had to find her.

When all the festivities were over and the bride and groom were gone, Danny bid everyone farewell and started his drive to Dayton to visit Wright-Patterson Air Force Base. He had always wanted to see the Air Force Museum and the Aviation Hall of Fame, and there would never be a better opportunity. On the way back to Cleveland, he drove through Amish country. The curious manner in which the Amish dressed and lived, as well as the beautiful farms and horses, intrigued him. Danny thought that this was another example of the freedom that Americans enjoy. They can be different, live differently, and worship differently than anyone else in society and still be accepted as good Americans. All they have to do is fulfill some general obligations that are required of everyone.

Thank God for the United States, even with all her imperfections, he thought.

Danny drove back to Cleveland and caught a flight to Boston. He knew he would have to be very careful if he were going to snoop around. He couldn't even entertain the thought of the embarrassment if any of the Salim family recognized him. The only thing worse was the uncertainty he was going through by not knowing what was happening to Amee.

Somewhere in Russia, December 1993

"Come in, comrade. We are glad you have decided to join us."

Several men dressed in typical Arab attire were seated around the table, but the man they were addressing was wearing Russian military attire. He had his back to the door, and the only thing that identified his rank or position was the partially visible insignia on his sleeve, which revealed that he was a pilot in the Russian Air Force. Even from the back it was obvious he was muscular. He stood straight and rigid, and so far the only sound he had made was a slight cough.

The same man spoke again. "I'm sure this is a difficult decision for you, but I assure you that you are doing the right thing. You have an opportunity to help us deal with a common enemy, as well as to benefit your family greatly. As much as we encourage you to do this, so far, it is your decision, but I must warn you that once the decision is made, there is no backing out. If you agree, your family will be rewarded greatly, but if you give us your word and then fail in your mission, they will be dealt with severely. Do you understand?"

The Russian simply nodded that he understood and then spoke in a very low voice. "I do have one requirement of my own. I must be assured that there has been a transfer of the money before I leave on the mission."

"You will have verification that the money is in a Swiss bank account, and your wife will have the number. Now, I must have your answer. Will you do this?"

Again the man nodded, but this time that was not good enough for the delegation.

"I must have a verbal answer. I need you to swear on the death of your eldest child."

"I swear on the death of my eldest son that I will carry out the mission I have been assigned."

"We will be in touch very soon."

With that, the men left the room, and the Russian simply sat down with his head in his hands for a long time. Then he got up and stoically walked from the room.

Danny concluded that the best place to start his search for Amee was to catch the bus at a remote destination and ride by the Salim house and the mosque just to see what he might observe. His plan backfired when he arrived at a stop a few blocks from the Salim home. He thought his heart would burst in his body as he saw Amee waiting for the bus. He was seated near the rear, so he slouched in the seat and pulled the hood of his sweater up over his head. Much to his relief, she sat near the front. He couldn't believe what he was seeing as she got off at her parents' home. As the bus pulled away, he watched her walk into the house. What was he to do now? He went back to his room and called General Travis's office.

"General Travis, this is Captain Brannigan. How are you?"

"Fine, Danny, and how are you?"

"I'm well, but seriously confused. I'm in Boston, partly on personal leave and partly on company business, and I have just received the shock of my life. I saw Lieutenant Ameenah Salim go into her family's house. Even with all the interconnections of my primary job and my close relationship with Amee, I won't ask you to reveal anything you shouldn't, but I do have one question that I hope you can answer."

"Ask, and if I can, I'll give you an answer."

"Is Amee AWOL?"

"No, she definitely is not."

"Thank you, sir. I appreciate the info. Is there anything that might be pertinent to our intelligence group's effort that I should know?"

"Nothing that I am at liberty to discuss. I would suggest that if you have any other questions you call Adams."

That pretty much told Danny all he needed to know.

He called Mr. Adams.

"Hey, Dan. How are you?" Adams cheerfully asked.

"As frustrated as a termite on petrified wood," Danny replied.

"Can I do anything to help clear up the frustration?"

"I surely hope so. Have you had any personal contact with Amee?"

"Why do you ask?"

"Let's not dance," Danny responded. "I don't hear any music."

"All right," Adams replied. "I don't know how much I should say because her privacy is also involved."

"I think I have earned the right to call in one favor. Besides, I think all this might be tied up in what we are all doing."

"You are correct, Dan," Adams said. "You know we have had her family under surveillance, as well as other Middle Easterners. A few weeks ago, she asked General Travis for a family hardship leave. He granted the leave, but since he was aware of what our group is doing, he called me. I have kept up with her whereabouts since then. I have also known where you were at all times, because I didn't want you to get into something that would hurt your career. I pretty much determined that you didn't know what was going on. I suspect now that things might not be good with her family, but I haven't learned anything specific. Since you are there, be careful, but see what you can find out. I can help you a bit with that. We have become aware of an Arab Benevolence League that might have something to do with this. Check them out and see what you can learn. I'll wait to hear from you."

Danny got the phone number and address for the Arab Benevolence League. He called and asked if he might speak to Dr. Salim.

"I'm sorry, but there is no one here by that name. There are other groups such as ours, so you might try one of them."

"I'll do that; he's just an old friend from college."

He placed his handkerchief over the phone, called back again, and changed his voice. He reached a different person anyway. This time it was a young lady.

"Hello. Abrahim Salim said I could reach him at this number. Is he in, please?

She obviously hesitated and then stammered out, "I ... I'm sorry, sir, but there is no one here by that name."

Danny thanked her and hung up, satisfied he had accomplished his objective. Obviously, they knew Abb on some level.

He decided to take a real risk and went to Boston College. He felt certain that Mo would help him if he could, and he was the one Salim he had no doubts about.

"What are you doing sneaking around here?" Mo had come up from behind, and Danny didn't see him.

"I was spying on you." Danny had been taught that sometimes truth was the ultimate subterfuge. "I wanted to see if you were hiding a girlfriend somewhere."

The quizzical look on Mo's face said that he was completely surprised to see Danny.

"Man, I'm glad to see you, but why're you here? Was Amee expecting you?"

"No, and I really don't want her to know I'm here because I don't want to embarrass her. I didn't know for sure she was here until today. She just left without explanation, and I suspected it had something to do with me. I couldn't go on without knowing if she was all right. You're the one I felt I could trust to be completely objective, so please don't rat me out."

"I certainly won't do that, and I hope you and Amee don't have differences you can't work out," Mo replied.

"So do I. Anyway, I am satisfied for now, so I'll go home tomorrow, but please let me know if she is ever in any danger. I do love her, and I want her to be happy, with or without me."

Danny really meant what he had just said. Now he could completely trust the Lord to have his way in everything.

"How're all the other members of the family?"

"They're all fine," Mo responded. "Dad's working too hard; Mom's busy doing her usual things, and Abb mostly hangs out with his friends from the mosque."

Danny shook his hand and said, "I hope to see you again soon, but if I don't, I wish you all the very best."

"You too, man," Mo said as they parted.

Danny's purpose in going to see Mo was to try to read him and learn anything he could, but he completely struck out. Mo was either sincere in everything he said or a very good liar.

He decided to go by the Arab Benevolence League and check it out. He found the location and hailed a cab, but he purposely gave the driver an address down the block. He got out and just strolled down the sidewalk, stopping here and there to look into a window, and even bought the obligatory newspaper that spies must have in order to be authentic. At that point, he laughed at himself. The league had a suite in a large building, so Danny went in to look around. He hung around the lobby for a while reading his paper. Before long, two men got off the elevator, and as they walked by Danny, what he heard nearly caused him to fall out of his seat.

"They want to talk to you further about Globe Trotter. If we are to act, we must set the plan in motion now."

Danny was sure that no one but God could have put him in that very spot at that precise moment. He didn't know what was being planned, but he knew which code name they must concentrate on, and he knew the time was near. He went back to the phone booth and placed a call to Mr. Adams.

"Sir, you're not going to believe what I picked up by chance. I overheard two men at the Arab Benevolence League talking, and they mentioned 'Globe Trotter,' saying that if they were to act, it must be soon."

"That's tremendous work, Danny. Many groups such as the Arab Benevolence League are front organizations to finance terrorism. We can begin to monitor their phone calls and even keep up with the transfer of funds. It opens up many doors, but we have learned by experience that they probably won't discuss actual terrorism plans either in their offices or on landlines. We must try to find some way to track individuals to see if we can possibly get a number for their mobile phones."

"I'll do my best while I am here to get further information on individuals operating from these offices," Danny said, "but I'll be a bit limited because several people in the Muslim community here have seen me."

"Stay in touch," Mr. Adams said.

Danny decided to hang around the vicinity and see what he could pick up. There were two things that made him a natural for this job. He had keen powers of observation and an instinct about people that was seldom wrong. He was also very good at reading body language. He positioned himself across the street where there was a large plate glass window. The light was just right for him to use it as a mirror to observe the building that housed the league, so he squatted down against a lamppost with his back toward the league building. His vigil soon paid off. The same two men he had overheard before drove up in a car. One of the men went into the building, and as the other one drove away, Danny saw him pick up his car phone. The only possible way to get the mobile phone number was to establish who the owner of the car was. He wrote down the license number and called it in to Mr. Adams. Danny was able to get photographs of the two men he saw in the lobby but nothing else. He was never able to learn exactly what it was that alarmed Amee about her family.

Brannigan Farm, Christmas 1993

Danny drove to Georgia for Christmas, arriving late Saturday afternoon. Jake and Katie were watching for him and were out the door before he was completely stopped. There was so much to catch up on that they sat up late into the night. Finally, Jake called time because they had to be up early for church.

The next morning, Captain Brannigan came down in his dress uniform, complete with gold bars and Medal of Honor. Mom thought he was the most handsome officer in the air force and would be so proud to show him off at church. The pastor asked Danny to give a testimony that morning of God's protection and blessings upon him. It was the last thing in the world he wanted to do. How could he tell others things he wasn't sure of himself? Maybe God did protect him, but it was hard to feel that he had blessed him. He sucked it up and decided to say what they wanted to hear. As he gave his testimony, someone else was speaking to him. His intention was to say all the things that would satisfy the pastor and congregation, but he realized he truly believed what he was saying. He felt like a tremendous burden had been lifted, and for the first time in a long time he didn't feel defeated. After church there was a question and answer time, and members of the congregation had endless questions for Danny. He answered them for about half an hour and then begged off because it was lunchtime. As usual, Katie had lunch practically ready when she got home from church. She would always make a dessert on Saturday and put something in the Crock-Pot before they left for church on Sunday. Then she would pop some rolls in the oven and make a salad while they were baking. Lunch was always ready within thirty minutes after they got home. No one was better at such things than her.

They enjoyed a leisurely lunch, and after a while Jake asked, "Who's going to be a saint this afternoon?"

"What do you mean saint?" Danny asked.

"S-A-I-N-T. Sunday Afternoon Is Nap Time."

Danny snorted. "I thought I was going to learn something."

"You did," Jake said as he started up the stairs. "This is *practical* theology."

Chapter 25

General Travis had called Danny into his office to speak with him privately.

"Captain Brannigan, I have an offer for you that you may choose to accept or reject. The decision is yours."

"This is a rare opportunity, but it will require a great deal of time and effort. I have spoken to Adams, and he believes he can spare you for a month to give you this once-in-a-lifetime experience. NASA is sending the space shuttle to the *Mir* Space Station for an unscheduled trip, and because of some unforeseen circumstances, their pilot will be unable to go. After scanning the records of every pilot in the air force who meets the general requirements, they like your qualifications and experience best of all. Many factors are considered, including health, strength, intelligence, and other variables. You meet the basic requirements of one thousand hours in jet aircraft and a degree in engineering. You have also demonstrated qualities of leadership and ability to perform under pressure. You would still have to meet some specific requirements and undergo extensive training in order to receive final approval. I know you might want some time to consider everything, but we have to move quickly."

Danny had been sitting there trying not to show such emotion that he came off like a schoolboy. This would be like winning the seventh game in the World Series with a no hitter. Even now it was hard not to jump up and shout, but he managed to keep his composure, except for probably looking like the cat that swallowed the canary.

"Sir, this is something I dreamed about when I was a boy but never dared to hope that I would ever have the opportunity to do. There is no question but that I want to do it. What is the next step?"

"You will have to leave as soon as possible in order to get your training in. What astronauts normally do in several months, you will have to accomplish in one month. You'll need to be ready to leave for Kennedy Space Center Monday morning at 0800. We will have one of the men fly you down in a Raptor."

It was at times like this that Danny missed Amee most. There was no one else he wanted to share the special moments of his life with, other than his parents. When he thought of her, his heart ached. He wondered what she was really involved in and if she were safe. Perhaps if he didn't go on this mission, he could find some of the answers he so desperately needed. Another thing that gnawed at him was that Mr. Adams had so readily agreed for him to go. Was he trying to get him out of the way for some reason? He wondered if there was something going on with Amee that Adams didn't want him involved in.

Captain Jack Turpin, a good friend, flew him down. The F-22 Raptor made the flight time from Langley to Kennedy Space Center very short. It was a beautiful spring day, and they flew the coastline all the way. The sun was just coming up as they left, and as it broke the horizon over the Atlantic, it appeared to shine *up* through the clouds that were lazily floating by. There was an explosion of color more dazzling than any fireworks show Danny had ever seen. As they reached their flying altitude, they could see the curvature of the horizon, and the ocean looked like a shimmering crystal ball. He thought about how the earth must look from space and how few people were fortunate enough to see it.

Before he had time to think much about what lay ahead of him, they were landing. He bid a quick farewell to Jack and was whisked off to learn what he was facing for the next month. There is normally a rigorous one-year training course, so Danny was really putting the big bag in the little one to be ready by lift off. Simulator training is done at the Johnson Space Center in Houston, which meant another trip in a fighter jet. He flew this one himself because it was a round trip. At six feet four, Danny was at the very limit of the height restriction, but he met and exceeded all the other physical requirements, such as blood pressure and eyesight.

Two weeks before liftoff, there is a dress rehearsal called the terminal countdown demonstration. Astronauts practice emergency evacuation from the launch site and go through the countdown right up to the liftoff. Pilot astronauts are commanders of missions, much like the captain of a ship. The biggest surprise to Danny was learning that the second pilot serves as assistant to the commander and is second in command. His primary duty is controlling and operating the shuttle. Commander John Stedman was all business but very kind, and Danny was grateful that he could fly with someone from whom he could learn so much.

The other astronauts were friendly and helpful. There was a female member of the team, who was very pretty. He thought how funny it would be to tell Amee about Diana Payton, who was the mission specialist on the crew. He would tell her about Diana's silky blonde hair that shimmered every time she moved her head, which was often because she was very animated when she talked. He certainly wouldn't leave out her big blue eyes that sparkled when she was excited or her gorgeous figure that not even her flight suit could fully hide. However, he *would* leave out the fact that she was thirty-five years old and married.

Mission Specialist Todd Amstutz had grown up on a ranch in Wyoming and never quite gotten the cowboy out of him. He had a degree in chemistry and considered space the final frontier for experiments in his field. Communications specialist Louis Fonteneau rounded out the team. He was quite possibly the most naturally funny man Danny had ever met, and he made full use of his Cajun descent for the sake of humor. He never ran out of Cajun stories, which he loved to tell Danny.

"Danny Boy, did you hear about the Cajun who got tired of the bayou and moved to Florida? He went into the employment office and filled out an application. When the officer saw that he had no formal training, he asked, 'Can you pick lemons?' The Cajun answered, 'Whew boy! Can I ever pick dem lemon. I garontee; I done been marry five time.'"

Flying the simulator was no big challenge to Danny, but learning all the technical data in such a short time was. The first time he sat at the console of the actual shuttle, he was overwhelmed. The orbiter had five on-board computers that handled data processing and controlled critical flight systems. The computers monitored equipment and talked to each other. They even voted to settle arguments, and they controlled critical adjustments, especially during launch and landing. Pilots essentially fly the computers, which fly the shuttle. To make this easier, the shuttles have a Multifunctional Electronic Display Subsystem (MEDS), which is a full color, flat, eleven-panel display system. The MEDS, also known as the "glass cockpit," provides graphic portrayals of key light indicators (attitude, altitude, speed). The MEDS panels are easy to read and make it easier for shuttle pilots to interact with the orbiter. Danny wasn't going to the moon as he had told his mother, but it was the next best thing—he was going into space.

The Russian backup pilot at the *Mir* space station had developed some physical problems, and they were taking medicine for him. Since his fitness to fly was uncertain, a possible replacement, Antov Pavlovski, was going with them aboard the orbiter. Without this key crewmember, the Russians reentry into the earth's atmosphere could be in serious jeopardy. It was a great opportunity to further improve relations between the two countries. Antov and Danny had a great deal in common because they were both pilots with combat experience. They talked every time they had the opportunity, attempting to outdo each other telling war stories.

The month passed faster than any Danny could ever remember one passing.

Family members were invited to be present for the launch, so Jake and Katie drove down. They were allowed to talk with Danny by phone shortly before liftoff. Jake had started calling him Lieutenant, and now that he had his bars, he called him Captain.

"How you doing, Captain?"

"Just fine, sir. How 'bout you?"

"I'm great, but your mother is going bonkers."

"I can only imagine; she would nearly have a heart attack when I played football."

Katie broke in and said, "You two have talked about me long enough. I may very well be the only one in this family who is sane, so I must ask you one more time, are you sure you really want to do this?"

"Mom, there is nothing I have ever wanted more. I have fantasized about it since I was a kid but never entertained the thought that I would actually get to do it. I love you very much, and I don't want you to worry. My mission will be safer than your trip back home, and I'll be back before you know it."

"I love you as much as a mother can love a son, Danny. Please be careful and come back to us safe."

Jake asked if he might talk with Danny for a few minutes alone, so Katie said good-bye and went off to have her cry.

"Danny, I'm sure I'm about to shock you, and I'm sorry it has to be like this rather than face to face. There is just no time to do it any other way."

Several things raced through Danny's mind at that moment, and none of them were good.

Jake continued, "We have a mutual friend named Adams. I don't work directly with him but we work in the same field. There is nothing wrong with him, but he can't contact you right now without it being too obvious. In order to put your mind at ease about me, he gave me permission to tell you that for the moment you may consider me 'Guardian Angel.' When your baseball career ended, it was I who suggested that Mr. Adams contact you about working with him. I know you must have a thousand questions, but we don't have time to deal with them now."

Danny was shocked speechless, and he felt like his head was spinning. It was difficult for him to sort out his emotions. On the one hand he was awed at Jake's revelation, but he also felt resentment toward him for not telling him what was going on. Did he really know Jake at all, and were there other surprises? Could not Jake have told him when they were having the conversations about terrorism? He felt like other people had been controlling his life without his permission. He finally managed to get out a sentence. "There is one question that I must have an answer to before we can go on."

"All right, we surely have time for that. What is your question?"

"Are you really who you told my mother and me you are, or have we been living with an imposter all these years?"

"I am exactly who and what I told you I was, except that there is another dimension to my life that I couldn't share with you. I am a deeply embedded operative with Mossad and have been for many years. As such, I have been an advisor and a liaison between Israel and the United States intelligence community. I was a natural for this because I have dual citizenship. The only connection I have with your group is that we collaborate from time to time on issues that are of vital interest to us all. We have always believed that someday there would be a terrorist plot so large all the others would pale beside it. We believe that time might have come.

"Neither Adams nor I had anything to do with you being on this mission, except to highly recommend you. However, we have recently learned that something big is in the works. Our details are sketchy at best, but we decided we had to bring you into it as a precaution. You know that for some time certain code words have been picked up in wiretaps and radio transmissions, and we have been trying to figure out what they mean. Some of them might even be decoys, but we believe Globe Trotter is authentic and is to be initiated soon. It may be that one or more Russians are involved because we have heard the word *comrade* used several times. This individual seems to be essential to the success of the plot. It is only a stab in the dark, but one of the possibilities is that Globe Trotter could refer to the space station or the space shuttle. It is at least worth consideration since this mission is to the *Mir* space station, where there are several Russians involved. We have no idea what they could even do to either the shuttle or the station, but you need to keep your eyes open for anything suspicious."

"Wow! You certainly have blown my mind with all this. I will have to chew on it while I'm gone, but as to the possible terrorism, I will be wary and watch everything the best I can. Please don't let mom know there is even the possibility of danger."

"Unless something actually happens, I won't tell her anything. I'm very sorry to have to send you off in this manner."

"That's okay. This is my job, and as with everything else, I will trust the Lord. Please do one thing for me. If something should happen to me, tell Amee I love her."

"I promise you I will do that. We will be praying for you, Son. I love you."

"I love you too, Dad."

Jake walked away with a tear in his eye and his heart swelling. He was so proud of his son.

The shuttle was sitting on Pad 39B. The countdown had started from T minus forty-three hours, but with built-in hold times, it would take seventy-two hours. The crew reported to Kennedy Space Center at about 2:00 p.m. with a long checklist of things that must be done in the last three days. One of the things pilots did was to fly several takeoffs and landings in the T-38 Talon training jet. This was the only part of the process that Danny felt comfortable with. The countdown was now at T minus three, and the crew was in the white room making final preparation for boarding. It was at that point that a gremlin began to tie knots in his guts. Reality was setting in. He busied himself going over his notes, thinking about Amee, and anything else that would occupy his mind.

Now everyone was in his place, strapped and ready for launch. Finally, the last sequence began. "T minus ten, T minus nine, T minus eight, T minus seven, T minus six, T minus five, T minus four, T minus three, T minus two, T minus one, liftoff; we have liftoff!" Danny thought he was prepared for it, but there is no way to comprehend the kind of thrust it takes to lift the 4.5 million pound shuttle off the ground and take it into orbit. Each booster is 149 feet long and twelve feet in diameter and is capable of producing 3,300,000 pounds of thrust. After about two minutes, the boosters are spent and are detached from the external tank. They fall into a predetermined point in the ocean and are retrieved for reuse. The external fuel tank is then separated from the orbiter and follows a ballistic trajectory to a remote spot in the ocean. It is not recovered.

Danny was still trying to absorb the fact that 4.5 million pounds could be placed into orbit in ten minutes when he felt the Reaction Control System engines fire.

The thing that intrigued Danny about the orbiter in the first place was that it landed essentially as a glider. To think about an aircraft the size of a DC-9 making a dead stick landing was truly amazing to him. What was a little unnerving was that it didn't have power for a second try because, as a safety precaution, the fuel for all the engines was purposely used or dumped prior to landing. There was only one chance to get it right. That made Danny thankful that he was the backup pilot and not the commander. As he went back through all the procedures, he realized how many things had to be executed perfectly for the landing to occur properly.

Once orbit was achieved, everyone had a job to do. Danny was responsible for inspection of several of the systems, as well as the backup operator of the robotic arm that would be used to transfer the payload they were delivering. He was also essentially the housekeeper, making sure everything was in its place. Any spare time he had must be given to familiarizing himself with piloting the shuttle. He found that astronauts have a good sense of humor, even to the point of practical jokes, especially on rookies. One of the things that they retold to every new astronaut was about Wally Shirra. During training, one nurse was especially annoying about specimens of body fluids. One day, he filled a five-gallon bucket with warm water, detergent, and iodine and left it on her desk. Such things as that were probably what kept everyone sane during the stressful duty, but none of the levity was ever allowed to affect the fulfillment of his or her responsibilities.

Danny had time to talk with Antov more during the flight and found they had much in common. He had flown a MiG 29 in Afghanistan and Danny the F-15 E Strike Eagle in Iraq. Of course, each man was sure he had the superior plane, but the one thing they agreed on was that the key to the plane's performance was the pilot. They talked about their families and Antov's two little girls, and of course, he showed Danny their photographs. Danny felt a strong kinship with him, and in another time and place they could have become good friends, but right now Danny had to be skeptical about everyone. If there was a terrorist plot, any Russian could be the perpetrator. In a short time, Danny needed to spend as much time as possible with the commander, learning everything he could. He hoped he would not need to use his newly gained knowledge, but he wanted to be prepared for all eventualities.

Chapter 26

Mir Space Station, April 1994

The docking went smoothly with the space station, but they found that the sick cosmonaut, Peter Andropov, had taken a turn for the worse. He had been having severe stomach cramps, vomiting, and a low-grade fever. His condition could not be effectively diagnosed and treated at the space station, but at least his pain could be controlled. The Russian commander determined that it would be best for Peter to return to Earth on the special shuttle and that Antov would take his place. In view of the circumstances, the mission would not last for the full seven days. They would leave as soon as it was feasible. Danny especially enjoyed learning how to operate the robotic arm that transferred the payload from the orbiter to *Mir.* He also got the ten-cent tour of the space station, a privilege very few would ever have. He had already decided that he would welcome the opportunity to make the trip again under better circumstances.

Tylenol controlled Peter's fever, and the painkiller they brought relieved him greatly and caused him to sleep. It was the best thing for him and didn't really interrupt operations because Antov was prepared to take over his duties immediately. When Danny had a bit of free time, he went back to check on Peter to see if he could be of any help to him. He was still in a deep sleep, so he took the opportunity to look around. Because Danny was interested in every aspect of life on the space station, he was opening and closing doors and drawers without even giving it a thought.

"May I ask what you are looking for?"

It was Mikhail Krusenchey, a former KGB agent who was now a security analyst for the Russian space program.

Danny was startled and said, "Oh, I came to check on Peter, and since he was asleep, I was just looking around. This is my first time aboard the space station and will probably be my last."

"I understand, but you know these are our private quarters."

"Yes, and I'm very sorry to have intruded," Danny said as he moved toward the door. "Please forgive me for invading your privacy."

"No problem. I'm glad you were concerned about our comrade."

There was a mirror by the door, and on his way out, Danny could see Mikhail go straight to his locker and begin checking it out.

Danny moved slowly in order to observe everything he could, although he had no idea what he was observing. Evidently Mikhail was satisfied. He walked over and laid his hand on Peter's head, like he was checking for fever, then started for the door. Danny moved out quickly in order not to reveal the fact that he was spying.

"Have you had this kind of stomach problem before or just since you arrived at the space station?" Danny asked Peter as he sat with him in the galley.

"I've never had any problem with my stomach," Peter replied. "I have eaten borscht and beef stroganoff and drunk vodka late into the night without so much as a gas pain. I don't understand it, unless I was exposed to a virus or something before we blasted off."

"I'm so very sorry, and if there's anything I can do, please let me know."

"There is one thing you can do, if you don't mind," Peter said.

"Of course, anything."

"Would you walk with me back to my bed? I'm a little wobbly."

Danny walked with him back to his quarters, and Peter lay down as soon as he got to his bunk, immediately drifting off to sleep. Danny couldn't get Mikhail's response to him out of his mind. He knew he was busy and wouldn't be back for a while, so he couldn't resist taking a quick look into the locker that had concerned him so much.

He hurriedly looked through the contents of the locker and found the normal items one would expect. However, far in the back, there was something inside a sock, so he shook it out. It was a medicine bottle with capsules inside. Danny knew better than to remove one because Mikhail impressed him as a man who would know exactly how many were in the bottle. He opened one of them and carefully poured out a little of the contents into a tissue. The capsule was filled with a grayish-white powder that was completely odorless, but at this point, he was afraid to taste it. If he still felt it was necessary, he could have it analyzed when he got back to Earth. However, Danny had such a curious nature and analytical mind that he did a little medical research on the computer. First, he looked up all the symptoms he could find on stomach ailments that involved cramps and fever. Next, he searched for all the possible causes, among which were certain poisons. That led him to study all the poisons and their characteristics, and one of them perfectly matched the powder he found in the capsules: arsenic.

He learned that arsenic is a chemical element with a tin white to gray color and no smell until it is smashed or burned. Then it has a smell very similar to garlic. It is lethal if ingested in large enough quantities, causing multiple organ failure, but if caught in time, the victim can be saved. As soon as he could arrange it, Danny took his sample into the lab and put the most miniscule amount possible into a metal container and burned it. The garlic odor was unmistakable, leaving no doubt as to what it was. What was he to do now? Neither the space station nor the shuttle came equipped with a sheriff or a jail, and besides, it would only be his word against Mikhail's. He took time to think about his options and to pray for wisdom.

He decided that the first thing to do was to protect Peter until they could take him back with them. Whatever the reason, he was the only one who was being poisoned. None of the other Americans or Russians had manifested even one symptom of stomach trouble. If there were indeed a terrorist plot, one of the factors had to be either getting Peter off *Mir* or getting Antov on or possibly both. Suddenly, it dawned on Danny that Antov had access to the space shuttle. However, there was little opportunity for him to sabotage it because of the security at Kennedy Space Center and the constant presence of the other crewmembers. At this point, nothing could be left to chance, so when he had time, he asked the commander if he could go aboard the orbiter and spend a little more time getting familiar with everything. Permission was granted, and Danny checked everything he could possibly think of. He was reasonably convinced that there was nothing wrong aboard the shuttle.

If there was a confrontation in space, there was no telling what Mikhail would do, and Danny didn't know if any of the other Russians were involved. He determined it would be better to wait until he had more answers or at least a better forum for dealing with Mikhail. His present problem was how to keep Peter from ingesting more of the arsenic. He didn't even know how it was being administered. All he could do at the moment was to be very observant and see if he could pick up any clues.

Danny went to check on Peter and found him violently ill. He had been vomiting, and when he urinated, he grimaced in pain. It was obvious that the poison was already affecting his kidneys. When Peter settled down a bit, Danny asked him what he had eaten or drunk.

"Nothing at all in a long while. I haven't had anything in my mouth except a piece of gum Mikhail gave me. He said it might help settle my stomach since it was peppermint."

Danny gave Peter a pain pill, and when he went to sleep, he looked through the trash and found the gum wrapper on which there was indeed residue of the arsenic, confirming that it had been sprinkled on the gum. The space shuttle was scheduled to leave the next day, so Danny had to keep Peter from getting any more poison into his system until they left.

When he was awake again, Danny said, "I've done a little research, and I don't think you ought to chew gum. It stirs up the acids in your stomach and will tend to make you sicker." Peter agreed to that, but oddly enough, Mikhail didn't offer him gum or anything else again.

The next morning, as they prepared to separate from the space station, Peter was feeling better. Danny assumed it was because he wasn't given any more arsenic and hoped he hadn't ingested enough to cause any permanent damage. He was feeling so much stronger that when Danny picked up his bag to place it on the orbiter for him, he insisted on carrying it himself.

"You must be feeling better if you can carry that." Danny laughed. "It would challenge a well man. What do you have in there, your rock collection?

Peter even laughed a little and said, "No, it is filled with books."

"Then you must have brought your entire library. Try not to get a hernia."

Peter asked if he might watch the MEDS as they detached from *Mir*. The commander gave him permission to do so.

Danny still had no explanation for the poisoning unless it was either a personal grudge or Mikhail wanted him off the MIR for some reason. He didn't see any benefit in involving anyone else in the situation until he had more evidence to go on. Proper protocol onboard the shuttle would have called for him to report his findings to the commander, but because of the clandestine nature of his work with Mr. Adams, he was justified in keeping it to himself for now. Besides, up to this point, they weren't actually on the shuttle. If there were any further developments or the possibility of danger to the crew, he would immediately divulge what he had learned.

For the first time since the launch, Danny recalled what Jake said to him and thought about how many times he had heard the word *comrade* on *Mir.* But now that they had left the space station, what could anyone possibly do to harm the shuttle? No Russian had even been near it except Antov. Danny decided that since he couldn't come up with any answers, he shouldn't bear the total responsibility. He called Commander Stedman aside to inform him in case there was some attempt to harm the orbiter.

"Sir, I had hoped this conversation would not be necessary, but I believe now it is. I am a fighter pilot for the air force, but I also have another role that I am not at liberty to fully divulge to anyone. I can tell you that it has to do with the security of the United States. My being chosen for this mission originally had nothing to do with my work in intelligence, but that has changed. I still don't know that there is any cause for alarm, but I feel that I must inform you about what I do know."

Colonel Stedman's brow was furrowed, and his jaw muscles were working in a clear sign of tension or anger. For a moment, Danny thought he might be making a mistake, but the commander is the law in space, just as the captain of a ship is at sea.

"Go on. Just what is it you know?"

Danny continued, "We have intelligence to indicate some kind of terror plot is in the works involving the code word *Globe Trotter.* We haven't been able to identify what Globe Trotter is yet, but most of our people believe it is something that travels around the earth. Some speculated targets are Air Force One and the Concorde, but the space shuttle has also been mentioned as a possibility. While listening in on the chatter, the word *comrade* was used many times, leading some to believe the Russians might be involved, or at least one Russian. I would never have mentioned any of this except for what I discovered at the space station."

Now Commander Stedman's face had become stern and his jaw set. "Just what did you learn at the space station?"

"At one point, I went to check on Peter, and he was asleep, so I decided to wait for a few minutes. I was just looking around out of curiosity, and Mikhail came in. He was upset because I was there and told me so. I apologized and started to leave, but in a mirror next to the door I saw Mikhail instantly go to his locker and check it out. The next day, Peter asked me to walk with him from the galley to his bunk. As soon as he was there, he went to sleep, and I was compelled to try to find out what Mikhail was so concerned about in his locker. In a sock I found a medicine bottle with capsules inside, so I opened one and took a bit of the contents with me. To make a long story short, I found that it was arsenic, and further investigation revealed that he was giving it to Peter on chewing gum."

"Why did you not feel it your duty to report this to me?" the commander asked.

"It was hard to know what to do, and I only discovered this yesterday. I got Peter to agree not to chew any more gum by telling him it wasn't good for his condition, but oddly enough, Mikhail never offered him anything else. I didn't have any hard evidence of anything and didn't want to have a dangerous confrontation in a setting where we had no control. If this had been on the shuttle, of course I would have told you, but it was on *Mir* where we have no authority. Actually, I'm torn sometimes between my two roles, but I am telling you now because the shuttle *is* your responsibility."

"What do you think anyone could do to harm the orbiter?" the commander asked.

"That's part of the dilemma also; I can't imagine anything they could do because none of the Russians even came close to the shuttle except for Antov. We have very tight security at Kennedy, and I have checked everything I know how to check since he left the shuttle, so I really don't think he could have done anything. Besides, the shuttle doesn't seem to be a large enough target to meet the criteria for what we have been hearing."

"There is one Russian on board, you know," Commander Stedman said.

"Yes, but he is obviously the victim, and someone wants him off the space station."

"I can appreciate how complicated your life must be at times," Commander Stedman said. "But I am glad you came to me with this. At least we can both keep our eyes and ears open. I think it best that we don't say anything to the rest of the crew or to Peter at this time."

Danny agreed and felt relieved that he wasn't bearing the load alone.

He went over and over everything that had happened since he was in Boston, trying to connect the dots. Once again he came face to face with the painful truth that someone in Amee's family could very well be involved. Her mysterious disappearance did not make things any easier. Any way Danny sliced it, there was sufficient reason to suspect Globe Trotter might refer to the mission they were now on. That possibility could not be ignored. He shared all of this with Commander Stedman, except for mentioning the Salim family, and the commander agreed with his conclusion. About the only hope they had left was that the plan had been scrapped. There is always communication between the orbiter and mission control in Houston, except for a short time at reentry into the earth's atmosphere. Danny asked Commander Stedman if there was any way to get a secure line to mission control and if they could patch it through to Kennedy Space Center and Langley Air Force Base.

"Yes, that's available for such times as these when neither the entire crew nor everyone at mission control needs to know what is being said.

"Could you please ask mission control to contact General Burton Travis, the base commander at Langley, and request that he have Guardian Angel call Thunderbird? They will take it from there."

The commander grinned. "Could I maybe get you a trench coat or something? You guys are really cloak and dagger, aren't you? I'll get on it right away."

"I forgot to tell you; when this is over, I have to kill you," Danny said.

"Well, you might have to stand in line because it seems like someone else is also intent on doing it."

In about five minutes, a call came through for Danny.

"Danny, this is Adams. What's happening?"

"Have you talked to my father?"

"Yes, he called as soon as you lifted off."

"Did he tell you what he said to me?"

"Yes."

"Well, it seems like he might be right. I think something peculiar has been going on with this mission."

"Give me the skinny."

Danny quickly gave him the bare-bones facts and asked if he could shed any light on the matter.

"I certainly don't know as many particulars as you do, but we will set up a war room and see what we can come up with."

"The one thing that would be most helpful right now is if we could get a handle on how the space shuttle could possibly be sabotaged or used," Danny said.

"I'll talk to the good doctor and get back to you as soon as possible," Mr. Adams replied.

"Just remember that we have less than two hours," Danny reminded him.

In moments, Mr. Adams called again to let Danny know that mission control was going to request they make one more orbit in order to give them a little more time. They would have one and one half hour more. As far as anyone else knew, except Commander

Stedman, the idea originated with mission control. Not an eyebrow was raised when the request came through. While Danny had a few minutes, he went to check on Peter. He picked up his bag to move it over and noticed it was much lighter than it had been when they left. Evidently he had taken his books out. He was sound asleep, so Danny didn't try to rouse him.

Perryville, Georgia, Two Hours and Fifty-three Minutes Until Touchdown

Jake found it necessary to take some risks he had not taken before because of the gravity of the circumstances. He never used the house phone for anything pertaining to his intelligence work, but the matter was urgent. He had left Katie outside and quickly made a call to Mr. Adams.

"I believe the shuttle is the target they have been planning for, and the matter is critical," Adams told him.

"Yes, I have as much confidence in Danny as anyone I know. He is intelligent and can handle himself in most any situation, but we must get him all the information to work with that we possibly can. Please call me as soon as you know anything," Jake said.

As he hung up the phone and turned around, he was nose to nose with Katie. The fire in her eyes was so brilliant that it turned her green eyes yellow.

"What's going on?" she demanded. "To whom were you talking, and what does it have to do with Danny?"

"Please come sit down, and I will explain," Jake said quietly.

Katie sat down on the sofa, peering at him so intently that it felt as if her eyes were drilling holes in him. Jake sat on the coffee table with his knees pressed up against hers, her hands in his.

"I'll try to explain the best I can. Danny knows everything I'm about to tell you, but he didn't know it until just before liftoff. That's what I was talking to him about, and he didn't want you to worry."

As simply and quietly as Jake could, he explained what they thought might be going on and what his part in it was. He also told her that Danny's life had another dimension to it that he wasn't able to tell anyone about.

"What is it with the men in my life? Do war and terrorism have to have them all? Can't I at least have one who isn't tied up in such things?" Katie asked through her tears. "And why does the government of a Christian nation try to destroy the biblical relationship between a husband and wife? Why couldn't you and Danny just tell me what you were doing? Am I such a big security risk?"

"No, my darling Katie. It's *your* safety and security we are all concerned about. We want to protect this country from madmen and you personally from ever having to answer any questions about us. I assure you that this is the only thing in my life you didn't know about. Everything I ever told you is true, and I told you everything but this."

Katie fell into Jake's arms and sobbed. "Oh, I just had to vent. I don't doubt you whatsoever, and I'm so very proud of you both. You might fool my head, Jacob Reese, but you will never be able to fool my heart. I guess that explains all those business trips you had to make that I always wondered about. Now, get ready. We're going to Florida, and on the way, you can tell me exactly what's going on with Danny."

When Jake came out with his luggage, he also had a bag phone and a sheepish grin. "I might as well take this with us now that you know everything. Adams will probably want to get in touch with me."

Katie just shook her head and sucked her teeth at him.

They had a seven-hour trip ahead of them, and Katie knew everything would be over when they arrived, but she intended to get there as quickly as possible.

"You realize there's a possibility that they might land at Edwards, so we need to check along the way," Jake said.

"The weather looks good, and I haven't heard reports of any storms, so I think they will land at Kennedy," Katie said, as if she had some inside information. Truthfully, Jake wasn't sure she didn't.

As they drove, she asked Jake one question after another about Danny's situation and then about his own life. She just couldn't believe he was an agent for the Mossad.

"I'm a liaison between Israel and the United States. This is possible because I am also a citizen of Israel. The only times I've ever been away from you was on Mossad business. My cover was designed to be so deep that even other agents would not know about it. I guess in a crazy sort of way I'm a mole in my own country."

"Why did you come to Georgia?"

"They wanted me to be more centrally located and have easy access to a major airport. I saw your ad for a foreman in the farm bureau journal and felt it would be natural for me. I never imagined we would fall in love; that was just the Lord's added blessing."

The reason Amee gave for family hardship leave was that one of her brothers was in serious trouble and her family needed her. She had received a frantic call from her mother and father, and learned when she arrived that her brother was involved in some kind of terrorist plot and had disappeared. She had been trying to help her father put all the pieces together. When they had all the facts, they decided Mr. Salim would try to contact someone in the government, and Amee would work through her channels. It was about four hours before the shuttle was scheduled to land.

She called Langley to try to get in touch with Danny, so he could get the information to someone who could help. The duty officer told her that Danny would not be back for a few days, because he was on the Space Shuttle mission. She felt like someone had drained all the life out of her and she could hardly stand. Frantically she called General Travis and told him everything. She asked if he could possibly get her in touch with someone who could help. "I will have someone call you shortly," he said.

She had barely hung up the phone when Mr. Adams called. He identified himself and asked what she needed.

Amee said, "I have some urgent news!"

"What kind of news?"

"There is a terrorist plot to crash the space shuttle into either Miami or Los Angeles."

"How could you know that, and how could it possibly be done?"

"Sir, please don't play twenty questions with me. Many lives hang in the balance. We will fill in the details later."

"Okay, Lieutenant Salim, what do you know?"

"There has been some kind of collusion between a radical Muslim group and the Russians. One of the Russians has smuggled explosives on board and is supposed to alter the landing trajectory. Please get on it, and let's deal with the rest of it later."

He could hear her start to cry.

"I know how you must feel, but don't go soft on me now. Danny needs you more than he ever has. We already know about the situation, but I needed to find out how much you knew. Danny and the Captain are aware of everything."

Amee said, "I'm catching the next flight to Daytona Beach and will drive to the cape. Sir, can you possibly get me inside?"

"I will certainly try," Mr. Adams said.

When she arrived at the airport, she had a car waiting, and it took her less than an hour to get to the space center.

Mr. Adams immediately called mission control and requested the secure line to the shuttle.

"That's impossible for a few minutes. Interface with the earth's atmosphere has begun, and there is no way to make contact. We have ionic interference."

"How long will this persist?" Mr. Adams asked.

"About twelve minutes."

About twenty-five minutes earlier, mission control had given the command for the shuttle to come home. When that happened, they were flying upside down and nose first. They fired the RCS engines to spin the orbiter around 180 degrees so it would be flying tail first. They then fired the OMS engines to slow it down and allow it of fall back to earth. Next, the RCS thrusters were fired again to flip it over so that they were finally flying nose first with the bottom facing the atmosphere, which would allow the heat shield to experience most of the friction from reentry. As a safety precaution, the remaining fuel in the forward RCS thrusters was burned. The orbiter had been traveling 17,500 miles per hour in orbit, which is literally faster than a speeding bullet, and must be slowed down. Because of its speed, heat on the surface of the shuttle builds up to 3,000 degrees Fahrenheit. It is during this time that there is an ionic interruption of communication.

"Hello, Houston. This is Commander John Stedman. We're back in the neighborhood."

The most critical point had been passed, and the mission control room erupted in applause. The applause rang extremely hollow in the ears of Major Brannigan and Commander Stedman.

Chapter 27

"Commander Stedman, this is the flight director. I know there isn't much time, but it is imperative that we speak to you and Major Brannigan on the secure line."

Adams advised them of Amee's information at just over an hour from touchdown. He had arranged for Amee to be allowed to come into the space center. The computers were flying the shuttle, and would soon begin the series of *S* curves to slow it down for landing. Everyone was seated and strapped in, so Danny and the commander decided they must communicate with Peter to see if he could possibly help them determine who placed the explosives on board and where they put them. This meant all the crew would know what was happening, but it was time for that anyway.

"This is Commander Stedman to all crewmembers. I'm sorry that what I'm about to say has to come in this manner, but we have a situation that must be addressed. Time is of the essence. We believe the orbiter has been sabotaged by at least one of the Russians, who placed explosives on board and possibly altered the landing trajectory so that we will land in the middle of Miami if we don't correct. We know Peter's illness has been used to help implement this plot. He was poisoned with arsenic so that he would be sick enough to need medicine, and they would need a replacement pilot. Peter, we urgently need your help. What can you tell us to help us discover where the explosives are? Peter? Peter?"

The commander paused for a reply, but there was only silence.

"Mr. Andropov, have you nothing at all to say?"

"Commander Stedman, this is Fonteneau. I don't think you are going to get an answer. I believe Andropov is dead. His chin is on his chest, and his arms are hanging by his side."

Something just didn't add up, so Danny began to analyze every detail of the situation. Surely Antov could not have brought explosives on board, and no other Russian ever went near the shuttle. Peter showed no symptoms of arsenic poisoning when he came on board, so how could he now be dead? Suddenly it hit him! He had completely missed this one. Even now it was hard for him to believe it, but Peter must have poisoned himself. He had evidently decided to implicate Mikhail after he saw his reaction when Danny was looking around his quarters. Now it made perfect sense that Peter's bag was much lighter when Danny moved it in the shuttle. The only explosive that would pack the kind of wallop needed to accomplish the terrorist's purpose and was stable enough to transport was C4. They were running out of time and had no fuel for altering their descent. Danny was rapidly going over the facts, trying to come up with something that might give them any kind of hope.

He checked the flight program and found that their trajectory was indeed off by several degrees. A quick calibration showed that they were headed straight for the middle of Miami. He logged onto the computers to change back to the original flight plan, but the program would not allow him to do it. The commander tried and failed, and time was getting critically short. Mission control could offer no help. Danny recalled the advanced computer training Amee was doing at Langley and wondered if there was anyone present with that kind of ability. He quickly explained what he was thinking to mission control and was astounded when they replied, "Are you referring to Lieutenant Ameenah Salim?"

"That's exactly who I am referring to," Danny replied.

When they advised him that she was present at Kennedy, he couldn't believe it.

There was no time for any other conversation at present, so both Danny and Amee had to be professional. However, if anyone were monitoring the blood pressure of either of them, they would probably have disqualified them from service.

"This is Lieutenant Salim. What can I do to help?"

Amee had been studying the exact computer program the space shuttle was using.

"Peter has managed to code the flight program so he would be the only one who could alter it. I desperately need to get in."

Try as she might, Amee wasn't able to get through to change it.

"Captain Brannigan, with the time we have left, there is only one thing I can do, and I don't know if it will help. I can make the computer abort the entire program and give you manual control much earlier."

Commander Stedman, who was listening to the conversation, responded, "There would be so many factors involved, I don't know if I can fly it in. The computer can do all those things at once, but I don't know if a human can."

"Commander, this is Adams at Langley. I certainly don't want to get into the middle of NASA business, but I have a suggestion to make. I know Captain Brannigan has never flown the shuttle before, but I also know what he can do with jets. He has studied gliding since he was a boy, espousing super heavy, swept-wing gliders even before many aeronautical engineers did. I have total confidence that he could fly it in."

The commander looked at Danny and raised his eyebrows. Danny simply nodded and mouthed, "I'll do my best."

"Okay, that seems to be our only option at this point. I'm certainly willing for Captain Brannigan to try to land it."

"All right, Amee. Break her chains and set her free," Danny said, "and let us know the second it is accomplished."

"I think you will know when it happens," Amee responded.

She had been working all during the conversation, and all she needed to do was to press enter.

"Are we go?" Amee asked.

"Go," answered mission control.

"Go," confirmed Commander Stedman.

Danny repeated, "Go."

Amee hit the key; there was a serious shudder and surge, and Danny was flying the space shuttle.

The emergency crew was alerted, and everything and everyone else was evacuated from the landing strip.

They still didn't know where the explosives were and how they were to be detonated. If any kind of detonator other than impact was used, there was going to be a very big boom. The small comfort they had was that there wouldn't be any other loss of life.

"Commander, we are coming in on a greatly exaggerated trajectory, and if we change our degree of approach, we will increase our speed more than the chutes can accommodate. I don't believe we have time to make more *S* curves. Can we possibly make two cylindrical turns?" Danny inquired.

"That has never been attempted or even calculated, so I honestly don't know," Commander Stedman replied.

Danny responded, "I have done in-depth studies of gliders since I was a child and have figured every possible aspect of them. Our elevation is sufficient, but our weight is too great, and our distance to touch down is too short. We can compensate to some degree by wing tilt, but as heavy as the orbiter is, that would be difficult to calculate. The only possibility is for the pilot to do it by feel, and I want to be honest with you; I could only be confident about this if I had flown the shuttle several times before."

"Do you know of any other way?"

"No sir, I don't."

"Are you willing to try it?"

"If you say so, I will do my very best."

"All right," replied Commander Stedman. "I don't see that we have any other choice. Let's go."

All communication was now open to every station.

"Lieutenant Salim, are you there?" Danny asked.

"Yes, I'm here."

"Is there any possibility that you could quickly calculate from the computer program exactly where the *S* curves would begin?"

"I will get on it right now."

"Mission control, this is Captain Brannigan. If I don't get an answer from Lieutenant Salim in time, I will have to make the best estimation I can. I will rely on Commander Stedman's experience."

Danny asked the commander to tell him when they reached the critical point, and now it was just a matter of whether he or Amee spoke first. The commander watched the monitors intently, and just as he turned to tell Danny it was time, Amee spoke.

"Captain Brannigan, I have the exact information. You should wait a few seconds. I will give you a countdown from ten."

There was silence for what seemed like an eternity, and finally Amee spoke again.

"Ten, nine, eight, seven, six, five, four, three, two, one. Mark. Sweetheart ... uh ... I mean Captain Brannigan, do you need assistance with the width of the *S* curves?" Amee said. As tense as the situation was, everyone in the whole system got a good laugh.

"Only if you can give it right now."

"I have a split screen showing your flight on one side and previous ones on the other. I can tell you when to begin your turns and let you know how your angle is."

"I knew one day I would find a good reason for putting up with you. Tell me when."

Amee told him when to start his turn. One critical thing would be the wing tilt because the angle of the turn could be vital. She guided him through the process without a bobble. Now he was on his own because there was no computer program for the cylindrical turns. The objective here was to line up with the runway, and two turns would complicate that, but Danny's plan was to make a spiral descent down an imaginary cylinder in order to get them back to a safe altitude. In his mind he pictured a huge silo and one of those old crop dusters flying around it.

He didn't have time to pray, although his heart was always toward the Lord now, but he knew there were at least three people who were praying for him. What he was attempting would be as much by instinct as it was by technical know-how. If he tilted too much, it could deteriorate the glide ability, and a sharp correction could take them completely off course. Too wide a circle would make it impossible to line up with the runway. Again, Commander Stedman watched the gauges, or more correctly, the screen, so he could tell Danny if anything was critically off. They made the first spiral perfectly, and Danny got a visual on the runway before he made the second one.

On the second turn, the commander said, "We're still going to come in too high. I don't think you can land at this angle. The ship won't stand the strain."

Without even replying to the commander, Danny tipped the wing to a critical level, and they sped up and descended rapidly. There was a collective gasp by the entire crew, as well as those on the ground.

"I don't think she's going to be able to come out of this," Commander Stedman said.

At that very moment, Danny turned the shuttle sharply the other way, and it continued to descend rapidly but left the circular pattern. It made a wide crescent sweep in the opposite direction, which in effect gave them a reverse cylindrical turn with a much greater circumference. As he came around, he was perfectly lined up for the runway and at a much better altitude and angle of descent.

"I've never seen anything like that," the commander said. "How did you know it would work?"

"I didn't know for sure," Danny responded. "I just couldn't think of anything else to try. The maneuver was one of my theories about gliders, but I never had an opportunity to test it. I made a mental calculation that we could line up with the runway."

"I suggest everyone make whatever preparations you need to make," Commander Stedman announced. "In a few moments, we will either be safely back on Earth or we will be at the nerve center of some major fireworks."

At that moment the wheels touched the runway, and the parachute was deployed. It was fairly certain that there were deeply embedded fingerprints left at each station. They couldn't be sure they were safe until they were out of the shuttle, and the emergency crew accomplished that as quickly as possible. The bomb squad was standing by and went in the moment the crew was out. It wasn't difficult for them to locate the C4. Obviously he had intended for it to explode on impact, for which everyone was thankful. If they had crashed where he planned, the explosion would have been tremendous and the loss of life great. They took Peter's body away to do an autopsy.

When Danny walked through the doorway, Amee literally flew into his arms and kissed him through her tears.

"Don't you ever scare me like this again as long as you live," she said.

"I assure you that it's not on my agenda," Danny responded.

Katie and Jake were still a few hours away, so Danny called to let them know all was well. When they finally arrived, Katie held his face in her hands and just looked at him. She kissed him and said, "Do you have any idea how many years of my life you have scared me out of? I love you so much and couldn't believe the Lord would take another of my men from me, but that doesn't mean I wasn't worried stiff."

The autopsy revealed that Peter had died from cyanide poisoning. Evidently the arsenic had been used to produce the symptoms that would get him off the space station, but he wanted to die a bit quicker and less painfully. NASA and the State Department had already contacted the Russians and explained the circumstances, which they were in the process of investigating. What had happened was obvious, but why it happened and who else was involved were yet to be determined. It was hard to believe anyone would suffer through what Peter did for any cause. Danny was advised that he would no doubt be called upon to talk to the Russian delegation when they arrived. It was essential to solve the matter for the sake of future safety and cooperation between the two countries. This would fit into Amee's plans to spend a few more days in Florida, although she had not counted on doing it this way.

Danny already hated the fact that he had to go through debriefing. He didn't know how much time it would take, but any delay in finally being able to talk to Amee was too long. Because of his special circumstances, Danny was allowed some latitude in his sessions.

Chapter 28

Jake and Katie felt they must start for home because they had not had time to make sufficient preparation for the care of the farm.

Amee and Danny certainly had some talking to do, so they drove to the nearest motel and got a couple of rooms so they could clean up. She was unusually quiet and somber on the way, and Danny could only guess at what was going through her mind. What was really bothering her was how she could tell Danny that it was a member of her own family that betrayed him and his crew.

"How is it that you were at the space center? Did they call you?"

"No, I actually called them."

"Why?"

Amee started to cry.

"What's the matter, darling? Why are you crying?"

"It's just so hard to have to tell you this."

"Tell me what?"

She started sobbing convulsively but managed to get out. "Oh, Danny. I knew what was going on before anyone else did."

"How did you know?"

She could hardly get the words out now. "Because it was a member of my own family who betrayed us."

Danny was sure now that he should have done something different about Abb. Maybe he could have prevented his participation in this.

"I am so sorry to hear that. I know how you love your family."

"My dad called me," Amee continued, "to tell me that he had learned of the plot from a mutual friend at the Arab Benevolence League."

Danny could hardly believe what he was hearing. Was Dr. Salim also involved in this?

"Sweetheart, tell me what happened when your dad called you."

"He said I must get a message to someone who could help because a member of our very own family was involved. At that point none of us knew you were on the shuttle."

"That actually speaks better of your father because it wasn't just a personal thing, but it shows that he genuinely hates such violence."

"I am glad for that, but it won't make up for the fact that one of us is involved in this awful business.

"I knew there were Muslims who would go to any length to destroy the United States, but I never dreamed any of my family would be involved."

"Amee, I'm sorry; I should have done more to try to stop Abb," Danny said.

"No, Danny, it was Mo! All this time, he was just playing the quiet game while he made plots to kill Americans and pretended not to have any problem with our relationship."

"I would never have suspected Mo. Where is he now?" Danny asked.

"We don't really know. They raided the Arab Benevolence League, but he had already been spirited away somewhere."

Amee was concerned about her family, so she called home immediately. Her mom answered the phone.

"Mom, how're you doing? I love you very much and will see you as soon as I can. I am here with Danny, and he sends his love. May I speak to Dad?"

"Surely you must know he is not here. He is in Virginia."

"Virginia! What is he doing there?"

"He is with some group who has been involved with what Danny is doing."

"I love you, Mom, but I must go for now. I will call you later."

Amee's face was one big question when she turned to Danny, and she could barely speak.

"Danny, my dad is in Virginia, and from what Mom said, I believe he might be with Mr. Adams."

Danny's jaw was set, and Amee could hear the anger in his voice as he spoke. "I can't believe Adams arrested him because of Mo."

"It's time we both pay him a visit."

It was the first time Danny had referred to his boss as anything but Mr. Adams.

The next call was to Langley.

"Adams here."

"Mr. Adams, this is Captain Brannigan."

"Well, Danny Boy, how are you after your ordeal?"

"I'm well, but there is a matter we must deal with immediately."

Mr. Adams had never heard that kind of curtness in Danny's voice and knew something very important must be bothering him.

"All right, you and I have never pulled any punches. What is it?"

"Do you have Dr. Salim there?"

"Dr. Salim is here, but I don't *have* him."

"Then why is he there?"

"Danny, I think you and Amee ought to just come on up and let's all sit down and talk."

"I think that is a good idea. We will be there as soon as possible."

Langley Air Force Base, Virginia, Six Hours Later

Danny and Amee had caught the first flight out to Newport News Williamsburg Airport. They went straight to the meeting room where Mr. Adams, Dr. Salim, and Dr. Rubenstein were. When they walked in, Dr. Salim rose to greet them, and Danny shook his hand. Amee hugged her dad and clung to him.

"Well, I suppose it is time to put all the cards on the table," Mr. Adams said. "I know you kids must have some serious questions about what has been going on with your father."

"You can certainly say that again," Amee said.

Danny's approach was different; he had been trained to listen first and see what he could learn.

"We are just confused about why Dr. Salim is here."

"Do you want to explain or shall I?" Mr. Adams asked as he looked at Dr. Salim.

"I believe it would be more appropriate for me to do it, and then you may add anything you wish or correct me if you feel it is necessary," Dr. Salim responded. "Sometime ago I became aware of some alarming circumstances concerning the Arab Benevolence League. I knew there were some among us who were more radical, but I did not think our leaders would engage in terrorism. For the last few years, voices like that of Osama Bin Laden have drowned out the voices of reason. As it became increasingly clear that we were headed for something terrible, I chose to stay quiet and see if I could do anything to prevent it. I am sorry to report that I failed in that attempt, and when I finally learned what was being planned, I tried to contact the proper person in the United States government to report it. I got nowhere, but in a matter of hours there came a knock on my door, and Mr. Adams was there to see me."

Danny looked at Mr. Adams and said, "You … you … my Christian testimony won't allow me to say what I'm thinking. You tapped Dr. Salim's phone. I want you to know that I deeply resent that."

"I told you that my work didn't allow me to be a warm and fuzzy fellow. Did you think that I wouldn't follow up on every possibility when you told me what you found out in Boston? But right now, you had better be glad I did tap his line because that was the only way we would ever have known about his call to Washington."

Dr. Salim continued, "Since that moment, I have worked closely with these gentlemen to thwart any attempt at terror. We did not put all the pieces together until you were already on the *Mir* space station. I didn't even know you were on the mission until you were already there." I would never have dreamed that one of my own sons was involved. If only I could have rescued him from such insanity."

"What happens from here?" Danny asked Mr. Adams.

"Those connected to the Arab Benevolence League surely will know by now that Dr. Salim is working with us, and that places his family in danger. The only safe thing to do will be to relocate them somewhere that they are not likely to be found.

"I'm just glad we can end this meeting on a happy note. I guess we are all going to be one big, loving family," Mr. Adams said.

"If that is true, you are certainly the black sheep of it," Danny retorted.

"I think I'm rubbing off on you. You might make it yet," Mr. Adams yelled as they walked away.

Once they were outside, Amee said, "I don't think I can take any more intrigue in my life for a long time. Daniel Brannigan, we have to get some things settled quickly or I will be too crazy to care."

Amee hugged and kissed her dad, and Danny hugged him and said, "Doc, thank you for putting your life and future on the line for what is right."

Amee said, "Now that we are being totally honest, Dad, I feel it is time that I tell you something that I have been putting off because I didn't want to hurt you and Mom."

"You mean about becoming a Christian and desiring to marry Danny?"

Amee was aghast. "How did you know?"

"I explained to Danny once that parents aren't as dense as you young folks think. The signs were too obvious, but we knew you were just trying to spare our feelings and that you would tell us when you were ready."

Amee hugged him again and said, "I think you are the best father in the whole world."

"I think I am too," Dr. Salim said. "Your mother and I have talked about this, and you have our blessing on your marriage if that is what you choose to do. By the way, I have been tremendously impressed with both your life and Danny's, and it prompted me to study more about Christianity. When we have some time, I want us all to sit down and talk about it. Right now, you have a wedding to plan."

After they put Dr. Salim on a plane for Boston, they went back to Amee's apartment and talked until the wee hours of the morning.

For a long time, the subject was the recent adventure. Both of them needed to vent. At times they laughed and at times they cried. Finally, the inevitable could be put off no longer; they had to discuss their personal relationship.

Danny began the conversation. "I don't know where to begin; so much has happened to us. I know I love you and always will, but if we are going to be together, everything has to be clear between us. I am so sorry for any pain I have caused you because of my suspicions. Can you ever forgive me and put that behind you?"

"Danny, I admit that I have felt betrayed at times, because I knew my own heart. I couldn't understand then how you could ever have one doubt about me, but because of all that has happened I do understand now. I have loved you since the first day I saw you, and if everyone else had stayed out of it, we would never have had a problem. I can't imagine life without you, and all I ask is that you look me in the eye and tell me you will never doubt me again."

Danny took her into his arms, looked directly into her eyes, and said, "My darling Amee, my Sunday's Child, I love you more than life itself and will never doubt you again."

Then he got down on one knee and said, "Sweetheart, I know I'm supposed to have a ring ready for this occasion, but I will not put it off any longer. Will you please marry me?"

"I don't know. I will have to think about it. You seem to ramble too much."

"What if I promise to amend my rambling ways and agree to go no farther than the moon?"

"Sorry, that won't do."

"Okay, I promise to stay on earth."

"Oh, all right. I'll marry you. If I don't, you'll probably fool some other unsuspecting Arab girl."

They embraced for the kind of passionate kiss they had desired for a long time. When they finally came up for air, Amee said, "Wow! If I'd known you could do that, I would have agreed to marry you sooner. Where did you learn such things?"

"Oh, somewhere in the desert."

"Listen, mister. You're fast ruining a good thing."

"Point taken," Danny said.

"There's just one more thing," Amee said. "I had better check to make sure it wasn't a fluke and you can do it again."

So they checked it again ... and again ... and again.

Before Danny left, he had told her all about his visit to the ranch, and immediately Amee wanted to know if they could have the wedding there.

When Danny picked her up the next day, he asked if she would mind grabbing something to eat at the mall while he did just a bit of shopping. They got a sandwich, and then he took her into the most exclusive jewelry store in the city.

She had already started to protest. "Danny, no, no, no."

"Listen, little lady. This is not your call," he responded in his best John Wayne voice.

Danny pushed her through the door, and they sat down at the sales counter in front of the diamonds. "The lady would like to see some engagement rings," Danny said.

"Oh, congratulations to you both," the lady replied.

"No, I'm not involved," Danny said. "She just wants a ring in case an eligible bachelor comes along."

"I really don't need a ring at all now," Amee said to the lady.

The saleswoman laughed, and as she started to take out some rings, Danny said, "Show her something in a solitaire."

He held up two fingers where Amee could not see him and mouthed, "Two carats."

When Amee saw the tray of stones, she looked sternly at Danny and said emphatically, "No."

He very tenderly replied, "This is my call, and I assure you it is okay."

Reluctantly, Amee started to look at the different stones and settings, and it was obvious when she found just the right one. Danny chose the most brilliant two-carat diamond in the tray and set it on the ring. Amee was breathless but started to shake her head when he kissed her gently on the forehead and said to the lady, "I believe we have found just the perfect one. How soon can you have it ready?"

"It will take about one hour for the jeweler to prepare it."

"Good, we'll be back in one hour."

As they walked out the door, Amee said, "Sweetheart, I'm

thrilled that you wanted me to have that ring, but we can't afford it."

"Oh, yes, we can; we are buying it on time, and if you get a real good second job, you can have it paid off in about five years."

"I don't know why I put up with you at all."

"'Cause I'm the answer to all your hopes and dreams," Danny responded with a haughty look.

"That remains to be seen. But you shouldn't have bought such a ring."

Danny became quite serious and said, "I have saved my money and made some good investments. I don't want you to worry about this anymore."

She kissed him and dropped the subject.

They picked up the ring, and Danny got down on his knees right in the front of the store where all the passersby could see and placed it on her finger. About fifty people had gathered, and they all applauded. For the rest of the day, Danny laughed at her when he caught her just looking at the ring. They also bought their wedding rings.

Mr. Adams called to inform them about the Russian situation. Peter had incurable cancer and had been recruited by a radical Muslim group from his home region to become a suicide bomber.

"They don't believe he ever took any of the arsenic but used it to create a diversion. The symptoms of his cancer would have produced the reaction he was having. The Muslims agreed to pay his family a large sum of money if he would do this for them, but the Russian authorities apprehended all of them, and even now they're cooperating with our State Department to trace the plot to those who are working in the United States. They send their sincere regrets to every American involved and promise greater diligence to make sure nothing similar ever happens again."

When Mr. Adams was ready to sign off, he said, "By the way, it's Arthur."

"What do you mean?" Danny asked.

"My name is Arthur Adams."

"I'm very happy to know you, Art," Danny replied and hung up before Adams had a chance to reply.

A few days later, Danny was surprised to get a package from Russia. When he opened it, there was a note from Mikhail and a bottle of vodka. His note said,

> I'm sorry I spoke to you so rudely on *Mir*. I did not know what you were trying to do, or I would have helped you. I am glad you succeeded in getting home safely, and I hope to see you again someday.
>
> —Mikhail

He and Amee got a good laugh out of the vodka before pouring it down the drain. No one outside the government ever knew that the space shuttle mission was anything but routine.

Chapter 29

Mama and Papa Johannsen were beside themselves at the prospect of a wedding on the ranch, and plans were set in motion on every front. Danny and Amee set the date for Saturday, April 30. Everyone would meet there a week earlier and finalize plans. Danny asked Pastor Leland Evans to come and officiate, all expenses paid. They contacted Sarah to come and serve as Amee's maid of honor. Danny asked Jake to do him the honor of being his best man, and it was one of the few times anyone had seen him actually cry. Seth and Nadi were coming, as were several friends from Langley. Mr. Adams, Dr. Rubenstein, and General Travis were invited, but no one was sure if they would make it.

The next couple of weeks passed quickly, and every minute of every day was used in some kind of shopping. Danny realized this was the point at which he needed to disappear for a while.

Mama and Papa must have had all the ranch hands and every neighbor who didn't run fast enough working at preparing the ranch. The five bedrooms in the ranch house were all cleaned, aired, and ready, as was the bunkhouse. There was room for the entire wedding party. The wedding was going to be on the huge lawn, which was surrounded by Mama's fruit trees and shrubs. To make things perfect, they were all in full bloom with different shades of pink, red, violet, blue, and yellow.

The day that had been so far away suddenly arrived! All Danny had to do was to find some way not to hyperventilate before 2:00 p.m. Jake took him out for a drive to occupy him for a while. Both Sarah and Safa were attending to Amee's needs and having a good time. Dr. Salim's plan for staying out of the way was to read a book. After a light noon luncheon at which neither Danny nor Amee were able to eat, it was time for final touches. Of course, Danny was not allowed to see her before the ceremony anyway.

Finally, they joined Reverend Evans in the den, which was reserved for the groom, and Jake made sure Danny had everything in place. The pastor said, "This is your last chance, Danny. Either you go out the window now and get on Mustard and ride, or in a few minutes you are going to be a married man."

"I don't have the strength to run, and if I did, Amee would probably let me go and thank the Lord, so I'd better see it through."

"In that case, do you have the license?" the pastor asked. "I have to make sure everything is legal."

Danny didn't even remember if he had a license, but they had taken care of that the first day they got to Texas. Jake produced the license, and the pastor filled it out and handed Danny his copy.

"That is to prove you two are really married should you need to do so before it is officially recorded. I will mail it to the county clerk, and in about a month, you can obtain an official copy from that office in the county courthouse. Now, don't get any ideas, because if the wedding isn't finalized as planned, I simply tear the license up."

"Thank you, Pastor. Dad, do you have the ring?"

"Nobody said anything about a ring," Jake replied.

"This isn't the time to say a thing like that. You are joking, aren't you?"

"Of course I'm joking. Here it is, right here," Jake said as he held up his pinky with the ring on it. Then, pretending to tug hard at it, he said, "If I could just get it off."

They had a brief prayer, and it was time to listen for the song that was their cue to exit.

When the pastor, Jake, and Danny walked out to take their positions, Danny saw the fully decorated yard for the first time. Amee had chosen to use red and white roses like the ones she remembered in Jordan and to have Sarah wear a red dress to match the red roses. Tracie, the five-year-old daughter of a church member, served as flower girl and spread red and white rose petals down the aisle. When Sarah came in she was gorgeous, but when Amee started down the aisle, Danny felt weak in the knees. She was always beautiful, but he didn't know just how beautiful until that moment. She had chosen a satin, split back, A-line dress with a beaded cuff, hem, and inset. It had a chapel train, and the inset was the exact shade of red as the roses and Sarah's dress. The veil was a fingertip, two-tier Monique with a scalloped, beaded edge and beaded flower motif. Danny was totally convinced that an angel must surely look a great deal like Amee. He figured he was a sight standing there in his dress uniform with tears falling off his chin.

As Amee started down the aisle on the arm of her father, she was still not sure it wasn't all a dream. She thought, *How did that awkward high school jock I met eleven years ago become this poised and confident air force captain and the most handsome man in the world?* Most incredible of all was that she was a true believer in Christ and marching down the aisle in a Christian wedding with her Muslim parents and brother participating. If nothing else would make a person believe in God, this certainly should. Katie and Safa had already lit the unity candle, and that alone was an amazing thing. One of the most wonderful aspects of the whole thing was that her mom, dad, and brother would hear a clear presentation of the gospel that day.

Her focus was brought back to the ceremony as the pastor asked, "Who gives this woman to be married to this man?"

"Her mother and I," her father answered as he placed her hand in Danny's. Amee kissed him, and he went to join Safa in the second row. When she took Danny's arm and they walked up the steps to the platform, Amee was sure she was the happiest girl in the world. The two of them alternately smiled and cried throughout the ceremony, and had it not been filmed, they would probably not have remembered any of it. Sarah sang "Wind Beneath My Wings" and "The Wedding Prayer." Pastor Evans gave a brief message on the significance of marriage and how it represented the union between Christ and the church. They made it without incident through their vows and exchange of rings.

"I now pronounce you husband and wife. You may kiss the bride!"

It might not have been the most enjoyable kiss they had ever shared, but it surely was the most satisfying. Only one thing was going through Amee's mind: *Danny is finally all mine.*

That fact was underscored as the preacher turned them toward the congregation and said, "I present to you Mr. and Mrs. Daniel Brannigan." Before they had time to savor the moment, the recessional started, and they quickly moved down the aisle. They stopped briefly on the way out to present each mother one long-stemmed rose and give each a kiss. When they got to the last row, there sat Dr. Rubenstein and Mr. Adams. Dr. R was smiling from ear to ear, and Danny could have sworn he saw a tear in the corner of Mr. Adams's eye.

At the reception Mama and Papa J had an amazing surprise

for them. They presented them with the deed to the ranch. As they were about to protest, papa said, "Shush! Ve know dat you vant to someday help poor unfortunate children, and ve haf no vun to leef it to. Ve yust vant a place to stay as long as ve lif. Ven you are ready to come here, ve vill move into da little ranch house." The tears were dripping from both Danny and Amee's chins, and they were speechless. There was nothing more to be said anyway, so they just hugged them.

When the reception was over and they were ready to leave, there was one more surprise for everyone. Papa J had put a sidesaddle on El Dorado, a beautiful palomino, and saddled Danny's horse, Mustard, and had them waiting. After throwing the bouquet and enduring the hail of rice, they mounted the horses and took off at a gallop down the long driveway. They circled back to the barn and jumped in Danny's truck, which had been hidden there and left for good. They had secured a chalet in an undisclosed place in the Rocky Mountains. They flew from Amarillo to Denver and rented a car.

Epilogue

Shortly after Danny and Amee returned from their honeymoon, Mama and Papa J called to tell them they were ready to retire and wanted to move into the ranch house, if they were ready to move to Texas. After a short discussion, they decided it was time. All it would take to make Amee's life perfect was to have her family become Christians. She prayed for that every day, especially for God to get hold of Mo wherever he was and help him understand. She asked God to send someone to him like he had to her.

Danny and Amee persuaded her parents to move to Texas, since he needed to relocate anyway. They were ecstatic when Abb decided to move with them. What had happened with Mo had finally convinced him that he was wrong about his association with the radicals.

When they got settled in, Dr. Salim called the family together so Danny and Amee could explain their Christian faith to them. He confessed that he was tired of a religion of hate and one that offered no real peace. He gave the opportunity for anyone who didn't wish to listen to excuse himself, but no one left. Amee was thrilled that not even Abb showed any resentment. For the next two hours, Danny meticulously explained what the Bible taught about Jesus Christ and salvation. When he finished, Amee gave her very first testimony about how she had been saved and how precious the Lord was to her. She told them what joy she had in her life and finished by saying how much she wanted to see them receive Christ.

Next, Danny told them exactly what he had told Amee that Christmas Eve in front of the fire. Then the Holy Spirit took over, and he asked if any of them wanted to pray. He shouldn't have been shocked that all three were ready to receive Christ as their Savior. One by one, they each called upon the Lord, and when they were finished, Danny gave them scriptural assurance of their salvation. All of them rejoiced together far into the night. After Danny and Amee went to their room, she was so hyper that she couldn't stop talking. She always talked, but Danny had never seen her like this. She chattered away about how good God was and how her family was complete. Then suddenly she stopped as if she had choked on something.

"Danny, I want to be baptized."

He laughed and asked, "Why have you suddenly decided you want to be baptized?"

"Because I want to honor my Savior in every way and obey his commands."

Danny thought that now baptism was settled, he might get a little rest, but she wasn't through.

"Danny, we should talk to everyone like we talked to my folks tonight because there are probably a lot of people who want to be saved if they just knew how."

"I suspect you are right. That's what we call witnessing."

"Well, that's what I want to do."

When she finally did go to sleep, Danny lay awake for some time thinking about his life and how wonderful the Lord was. He couldn't imagine why he had wasted so much time in doubt and misery. He whispered to the Lord how much he loved him and reconfirmed his commitment to serve him the rest of his life.